The Finish'd Rake
or, Gallantry in Perfection
Anonymous

The Secret History of Mama Oello, Princess Royal of Peru
Anonymous

The Masterpiece of Imposture
by
Elizabeth Harding

The Temple Rakes, or Innocence Preserved
Anonymous

with a new introduction
for the Garland Edition by
Josephine Grieder

Garland Publishing, Inc., New York & London

1973

The new introduction for the

Garland *Foundations of the Novel* Edition

is Copyright © 1973, by

Garland Publishing, Inc., New York & London

All Rights Reserved

Library of Congress Cataloging in Publication Data
Main entry under title:

The Finish'd rake.

    (Foundations of the novel)
    Facsimile reprints.
    CONTENTS: The finish'd rake [Printed for A. Dodd, E. Cook, and J. Jolyffe, London, 1733]--The secret history of Mama Oello, Princess Royal of Peru [Printed for J. Dent, London, 1733]--Harding, Elizabeth. The masterpiece of imposture [Printed for the author, London, 1734] [etc.]
    1. English fiction--18th century. I. The Secret history of Mama Oello, Princess Royal of Peru. 1973. II. Harding, Elizabeth. The masterpiece of imposture. 1973. III. The Temple rakes. 1973. IV. Series.
PZ1. F469 1973 [PR1297.F5]   823'.5'08
ISBN 0-8240-0569-4   70-170584

Printed in the United States of America

Introduction

The present volume is a grab-bag of 1730s fiction, interesting in its variety of genre and technique. The Finish'd Rake; or Gallantry in Perfection *(1733) is a personal memoir by an anonymous young nobleman, written with verve and humor and an occasional dash of sex to titillate the reader.* The Secret History of Mama Oella, Princess Royal of Peru *(1733), supposedly taken from Garcilaso de la Vega, owes nothing to that author but its Peruvian vocabulary; a key novel, it is a thinly disguised account of the circumstances surrounding the marriage of Princess Ann, George II's eldest daughter, to the Stadholder of Holland that particular year. Elizabeth Harding's* The Masterpiece of Imposture *(1734) demonstrates the existence of male and female rogues as adept, if not as celebrated, as Moll Flanders. Finally,* The Temple Rakes, or Innocence Preserved *(1735) shows true love's defeat of worldly vice.*

It is not unsuitable to discuss The Finish'd Rake *and* The Temple Rakes *in tandem, for they share certain characteristics. Both are distinguished, for instance, by considerable attention to realistic characterization. The "finished rake," who narrates his own story, spares no pains to detail his roguery and seductions, of which he appears rather proud. His success, as a schoolboy, in forcing the headmaster to grant him unusual freedom, the theft of the butcher's calf which he engineers, and*

INTRODUCTION

particularly the attacks he launches on the virtue of the milliner and his "fair cousin" prove him a man of wit and address, skillful in reading the character of his victims and reasonably compassionate in dealing with them after he has achieved his ends. His counterpart in The Temple Rakes is Townley, a man *"very destitute either of virtuous or generous Principles" (p. 18) who has given "himself up to the most sensual Indulgencies of his Appetites" (p. 10).* Townley does, however, redeem himself and his offensive behavior towards Arabella, though Belmour must duel him to bring about such an improvement. Belmour and Arabella themselves are typical young lovers, but the girl's aunt, Mrs. Villiard, is a more individual figure. Having been irregular in her own marital conduct, she sees the possibility of profit in exploiting Arabella's innocence; and her promotion of the rich Jew Mr. D—z and of Townley is both unscrupulous and adroit, though foiled by her niece's good sense.

Both the settings and the incidents of these two novels maintain the realistic approach established by the characterization. As a scholar at Cambridge, the "finished rake" knows the school's procedures and successfully uses them to bring off the theft of the calf. He also capitalizes on the milliner's social and business situation in playing his game. In a Calais inn he amusingly demonstrates British superiority in the cultivation of French graces. London and its social activities provide the background of Townley and Belmour's adventures: their acquaintance with Arabella begins in a perfectly

INTRODUCTION

plausible way during an evening at Vauxhall, where Mrs. Villiard is exhibiting her, and continues at Ranelagh Gardens; the gentlemen saunter through Green Park and Hyde Park; after the duel, they pass by way of Bloomsbury Square to the Temple. Physical description, though kept to a minimum, always involves the familiar.[1]

Whether either of these two books can be called morally uplifting is doubtful; on the other hand, the charitable and prudent reader may peruse them as illustrations of what a modest young lady ought to avoid. Never trust a man who makes "the last favor" the price of marriage, for he'll never keep his connubial promise, teaches the "finished rake." Beware of lady companions who too freely condone a rendez-vous with the opposite sex and beware particularly of a man alone, demonstrates The Temple Rakes. *But fortunately, the morality passes quite subliminally into the reader's consciousness; the novels' real merit comes from the directness and plausibility of the stories and characterizations.*

Mrs. Elizabeth Harding's The Masterpiece of Imposture *is a curious work, perhaps fiction, perhaps not.*[2] *Resembling a rogue novel, it is told by the victim; and the illiteracy of the style only reinforces the impression of the ease with which two clever scoundrels can take advantage of the ignorant and gullible. Mrs. Harding, a Catholic, is betrayed by her memory of John Gordon's kindness in France into a much too trusting acceptance*

INTRODUCTION

of his profession of indigence. Even with proof in hand that he is a forger and a liar, she cannot resist his persuasion; and though she takes him to court at the end, the only satisfaction she receives is moral, not financial.

Mrs. Harding's chief animosity is reserved, however, for his "sham Countess," and both religious sincerity and moral indignation would seem to motivate her dislike. The Countess, when in France, adroitly profits from her pose of a persecuted English Catholic as she wheedles money from the Cardinal de Fleury, various nobles and Jesuits, and even the papal nuncio; with such assistance she sets up as a fine lady and, appropriating suitable titles and relatives, is accepted as such by Parisian society. Nor, when all else fails, does she hesitate to prostitute herself and give her amiable lover the pox. Foisted by the unscrupulous Gordon on Mrs. Harding, with whom they travel, the Countess cheats the poor woman of spoons, a hat, and a trunk full of clothes. Little wonder that Mrs. Harding continually anathematizes her as "that wicked and base Impostor" (p. 3), "that wicked woman" (p. 18), and "Her counterfeit Ladyship" (p. 20).

As in the previous stories, the moral implications of this work come from its demonstration of the means by which unprincipled scoundrels prey off their victims. As Mrs. Harding says, her view in writing "is to expose a Villain, and do Justice to the Publick, that a Rogue may find his due Discouragement in the World, and honest People be preserved from his Designs, by which, I

INTRODUCTION

myself have been but too great a Sufferer" (p. 5). But its merit lies in the extraordinarily graphic detail which the authoress supplies: the goods she is bilked of, the ruses they cozen her with, the innocent trust with which all and sundry accept these deceptions. One sympathizes with the victims, but one reads with fascination of the methods.

The Secret History of Mama Oello *could hardly have been very secret to those contemporary readers aware of court intrigues during the year 1733, for it is a very thinly disguised and highly accurate account of the state of affairs at the time of the Princess Ann's marriage to the Stadholder of Holland. Mama Oello (Ann) is, of course, in love with another, her dear Loque Yupanki (the second Lord Carmichael, afterward Earl of Hyndford); but politics dictate that her father, Manco Capac (George II), marry her off to Atabalipa (the Stadholder). Earnestly promoting the match is the Curaca Robilda, Manco Capac's chief minister (Sir Robert Walpole). Loque Yupanki is banished to his lands beyond the river Apurimac (Tweed), then recalled. The marriage plans appear to founder, due to Atabalipa's reluctance to come to Peru (Great Britain). The novel terminates abruptly, with nothing resolved — though the unfortunate Ann was in fact unwillingly united to her Dutch betrothed.*

The novel remains of interest not because of its sympathy with the romantic misfortunes of a royal princess, but rather because of the hostile Tory portrait

INTRODUCTION

of Walpole and his political methods. Loque Yupanki tries to persuade the princess to arrange the dismissal of the minister, hated "on Account of his perswading her Royal Grandfather and Father to impose heavy Taxes on their Subjects in time of Peace." He points out to her the parliamentary opposition to Robilda, in spite of the fact that "by his immense Treasures, he had secur'd the Majority of them to his Interest" (p. 8). The princess sees too clearly that the plan is impracticable. She believes Robilda "firmly attached to her, and her Family's Interest, even to the Prejudice of his own Country"; at the same time, she knows his influence over the king and queen, who always follows his counsels "tho' he often abus'd his Trust, and shelter'd himself under the Royal Wing, when he had transacted any Thing base or Offensive" (p. 13). Robilda brings up before the convention of states a scheme (the excise tax on tobacco) but, realizing the likelihood of its failing, withdraws it before a vote can be taken. Credit for the defeat is given to those whom Robilda's party calls malcontents but "the Generality of the People ... distinguish ... by the honourable Appellation of Patriots, being those who stand up for their Country's Good" (p. 20). The populace, delighted at the shelving of the scheme, dance in the streets and burn Robilda in effigy. Toward the end, the staunch Loque Yupanki delivers to the gods his opinion of the political situation: "behold Extortion, Bribery, and Corruption, triumphantly lording it over your Favourite Empire; whilst Virtue, Probity, and true Merit skulk from Place

INTRODUCTION

to Place entirely disregarded" (p. 41).

These four works contribute little, obviously, to the history of the novel; none can be considered the source of any particular development in the form of fiction. Taken together, however, they represent an interesting reflection of the taste of the period, for one may infer that their direct connection to contemporary settings, mores, and events was an element attractive to — and perhaps even desired by — the reading public. Fiction such as this is a long step from idealized romances or adventure novels; perhaps it may be considered preparation for the superior realistic novels that were to follow.

Josephine Grieder

INTRODUCTION

NOTES

[1] *Occasionally a Hogarthian realism even creeps in, as in Mr. D---z's attempted rape of Arabella: "the poor young Lady on the Couch, with her Cap and Handkerchief torn off, her Nose all bloody, her Mouth in a foam, and the yellow-faced Jew, with his Wig off, at top of her, keeping her down by his Weight, and endeavouring to force her own Handkerchief into her Mouth, to prevent her crying out" (p. 49).*

[2] *The title page says it contains "The Reality of an History and the Amusement of a Romance; being an Answer to the late Memoirs of the said* John Gordon of Glencat.*" In fact, in 1733 the* Memoirs of the Life of John Gordon, of Glencat . . . Who was Thirteen Years in the Scotch College at Paris *were published; and certain details (the relations with his uncle; his abjuring of Catholicism) correspond exactly to those in Mrs. Harding's account. The British Museum also gives Mrs. Harding credit for* Innocentia Patefacta, and Malitia Detecta: being The Case of Mr. Charles Dean . . . Who was lately (but Innocently) Executed at Tyburn . . . Written by an Impartial Hand, and Lover of Justice *(no imp., 1711), because her name is signed to the dedication; the style of this work is, however, considerably more literate than that of the former.*

The Finish'd Rake
or, Gallantry in Perfection

Anonymous

Bibliographical note:

*This facsimile has been made from a copy in the
Bodleian Library of Oxford University
(Vet.A.4e1359)*

THE Finish'd Rake;
OR,
Gallantry in Perfection.

BEING THE

Genuine and *Entertaining*

ADVENTURES,

OF A

Young Gentleman of Fortune.

FAITHFULLY

Extracted from Memoirs written with his own Hand, and design'd by him to be publish'd, as is believed, had he not been prevented by Death.

THE WHOLE

Being interspers'd with several Curious, Whimsical, and Uncommon Incidents; particularly his Intrigue with a fine COQUETTE MILLINER, near one of our most Noted Inns of Court, whilst he was a Student.

— Women, born to be controul'd,
Stoop to the Forward and the Bold;
But yet you know they seldom fail,
To make the stoutest Men turn Tail;
And bravely scorn to turn their Backs
Upon the desperat'st Attacks. HUD.

LONDON:
Printed for A. DODD, without *Temple-Bar*; E. COOK, under the *Royal-Exchange*; and J. JOLYFFE, in St. *James's Street.* [Price One Shilling.]

THE
Finish'd Rake;
OR,
Gallantry in Perfection.

IT is customary for Persons, whose Actions have made some Noise in the World, to have their Lives transmitted down to Posterity; and that by those who are wholly unqualified for such an Undertaking, being generally such as have been altogether unacquainted with the People whose Histories they pretend to write, only through common Report, and consequently must take all their Accounts upon Trust. To avoid the like Fate after my Decease, I thought proper, with my own Hand, to throw together the most remarkable Transactions of my Life, tho' no Man living has a greater Aversion to Scribling than myself.

I had besides this another View in so doing, which is, that as my Adventures have been very uncommon, and most of them have carried their own Punishment along with them,

A they

they may serve as a Warning to deter other People from following my Example; left they should meet with the same Misfortunes, and be made sensible, like me, to their Cost, that the best that can be expected from a dissolute Life, is a *broken Constitution*, and an *incumber'd Estate*, not to mention a *lost Character*, and *perpetual Remorse*, if they have the good Fortune to escape *utter Ruin*.

As the Adventures of my Childhood cannot be supposed to have been worthy my Readers Attention, I shall not detain them long therewith, but only premise in General, That I am the only Son of a Gentleman of a considerable Estate, who spared no Expence in my Education; being so old fashioned as to think, that a Man might be at the same Time a good Scholar, and a fine Gentleman, and that all Accomplishments and good Breeding, were not included in a *Tupee*, or a *Solitaire:* In short, he was no great Friend to your mere *Petits Maitres*, whose *whole Merit* consists in their *Dress*; accordingly he took Care I should both be able to *read, write*, and *spell tolerably*, before he sent me to Travel; which is more than many can say, who were of a more *distinguished Rank* and *Fortune* than myself. At School I was remarkable for being very ready at my Book, and as ready at all manner of Mischief; insomuch, that tho' I never had, nor indeed wanted, any Correction for the former I frequently suffer'd in the

Flesh

Flesh for the latter, and I cannot but say that generally I richly deserved it.

Whilst I was under the Discipline of the *Ferula*, I committed one Prank, which for its Singularity deserves to be here mentioned, and which sufficiently shewed, even in my tender Years, that I would bear no Controul, and that I should be a *finish'd Libertine:* It was as follows.

Amongst all the Grievances under which I labour'd at School, none sat so heavy upon me, or went so much against the Grain, as the narrow Bounds to which my Master confined us who boarded with him: He having purchased a small Field for us to play in, to be seen beyond which would have been a *capital* and *unpardonable Crime:* Accordingly the boldest of the Scholars had never dared transgress the aforesaid Limits, it being more dreaded by them, than the passing the *Rubicon* was by the *Roman* Army.

Whilst in the lower Forms, I was forced to submit patiently to this Confinement, like the Rest, tho' I look'd upon it as a *great Invasion of the Liberty of the Subject*, and *murmur'd at it heartily* within myself. But, when I came to be *Monitor* of the School, the Case was alter'd, and I soon form'd a Scheme not only to enlarge my Privileges, but to break through all Bounds whatsoever.

I have already observed that I took my Learning very readily, for which Reason my Master used often to employ me to hear the under Boys their Leſſons, which I could do as well as himſelf. In Time he would intruſt the Care of the whole School to me for an Afternoon, and finding me very capable thereof, and not averſe to it, would at laſt leave it to me for a Day or two, or more; in ſhort I did the Buſineſs of an *Uſher*, and was (if I may uſe that Expreſſion) his *prime Miniſter*.

This was what I wanted; I had ſoon the Senſe to perceive he could not do well without me; wherefore, as I was ſo uſeful to him, I reſolved he ſhould likewiſe conform to my Meaſures, and at leaſt *connive at*, if not *openly conſent to*, the *extraordinary Liberties* I ſhould take; having (as I well knew) but this Alternative; either to give me my Will, or be at the Expence of keeping an *Uſher*, unleſs he would confine himſelf never to be a Moment out of the School, a Fatigue which would have been worſe than Death to him.

Accordingly one Evening, when a Troop of Horſe came into the Town, and I knew my Maſter was there likewiſe, I very fairly walked up into the Market-Place, where they were to be drawn up, before they filed off to their Quarters. My Maſter, when he ſaw me there, could ſcarce believe his Eyes; however he took no notice of me for the Preſent, being fully determined to make me dearly repent my Inſolence when he came Home, but he reckoned without his Hoſt, as he found afterwards.

I had

I had not long been got back to his Habitation, before he followed, and sending for me, asked me, with a stern Look, the Meaning of my Excursion: To this I immediately answered, without being in the least daunted; that being as useful to him as an *Usher*, I expected more Liberty than the rest of the Scholars; that my Father did not send me to him to look after his School; and that, in short, he might chuse which he pleased, either to allow me reasonable Liberties, take an *Usher*, or stay at home always and look after School himself.

Never was Man more surprized than my Master, at such a blunt Speech from a Boy not quite fifteen; he raged and stormed like any *Bedlamite*, gave me several Cuffs on the Ear, and vow'd he would flay me alive next Morning for my Impudence: I told him very calmly, that as to that indeed, he might use his Pleasure, but that the first Time he turned his Back he should find his School in an Uproar; besides which, I would acquaint my Parents with the Cause of my being so used, who would not fail to send me where I should not lose my Time in teaching others.

This last Threat brought my Master to Compliance, tho' he did not think proper to let me know it that Night; but next Morning, sending for me into his Chamber, he began to expostulate with me about the Liberty I had taken so abruptly the Night before; telling me he would not have denied me any thing

thing in Reason, if I had asked his Leave, but that I directly flew in the Face of Authority, and was an actual Rebel; however, he concluded, he was willing to pardon me in Consideration of my having always minded my Studies, and would even wink at my taking the Liberty I desired, provided I never made an ill Use of it, and he heard no Complaint of me; but that to salve Appearances he would seem to be very angry, and I must ask his Pardon before the rest of the Boys. To this I readily agreed; so I got the better of my Master, obtained all the Liberty I desired, and led a very pleasant Life, till my Father thought fit to remove me to the University, which he did in about six Months.

Tho' I was but a Younker when I enter'd at *Cambridge*, I soon distinguished my self there for a Lad of Mettle, being always ready to make one when any unlucky Prank was proposed, and, which was very agreeable to me, I seldom wanted an Opportunity to signalize myself by some new Roguery. Indeed I had little else to do, for as I was perfectly well grounded in the Classicks before I went thither, I could perform most of my Exercises almost off-hand, and my Tutor was such a dull Wretch, that I could learn nothing from him, so that I was entirely my own Master, and had Time enough for all manner of Mischief, as the Town often found to their Cost.

As I was very Young, not being quite sixteen, when I went to the University, and very few are enter'd there so soon, I met with not many Companions of my own Age, but was forced to associate myself with such as, tho' they were of the same Standing with myself, were arrived at Man's Estate: These took a great deal of Pleasure in prompting me to all manner of Debauchery by their own Examples, to which I was naturally but too prone of myself, without any Instigation.

Amongst the Rest, they did not forget to initiate me in the *Mysteries* of *Venus*, in which I soon grew a great Proficient, no *Laundress*, nor *Bed-maker*, if she was tolerable, being able to escape me: Not that I was entirely a Novice before, as far as *Hands* or *Eyes* could *go*, the Maids at School (thank 'em) having been pretty *communicative* of their *most secret Charms*, as far as they thought they durst venture without danger of a *Tell-tale*; which had like to have brought me into an ugly Scrape, had not my Master been one of a Thousand.

The Maids, who used to cut our Suppers, being at other Business, my Mistress one Summer's Evening went into the Pantry to parcel out our Allowances: Whilst she was thus employ'd, in came I from play, and running into the Pantry which was somewhat dark, whipt my Hand up her Coats, taking her for one of the Wenches, and caught her by the SOFT ANVIL, *on which all Mankind were hammer'd*, *hammer'd*, before she was aware of my Intention, having been used to that Sport with those saucy Sluts her Servants. *Very well, Sir*, said she, crying out with Surprize, *You are a mighty pretty Gentleman, I shall take Care to acquaint your Master with your Impudence.*

A Thunder-bolt falling at my Foot could not have surprized or frighten'd me more, than the hearing her Voice; I gave myself over for lost, and expected no less than to be flay'd alive next Morning, not doubting but she would be as good as her Word, because I never had been one of her Favourites. However I never heard any more of it, and imagined she had been so good-humour'd as to conceal it, till a little before I left School; when my Master's Mother assured me she had told him of it with all the aggravating Circumstances imaginable, and before Company; altho' he never had taken any notice thereof to me. It was certainly very well judged of him, and very generous; for a moderate Correction would not have sufficed for such an Affront, and he was unwilling to proceed to Extremes with me, being sensible I did not mean it to his Wife, and that I should not even have ventured to take such Liberties with the Wenches, had not they first given me Encouragement by their Impudence: And indeed I can't help observing hereupon, that I believe more Boys are spoiled by profligate Sluts at a Boarding-School, than by any other

Thing

Thing whatsoever: It were to be wished therefore, that none were hired into such Places, but such as have the best of Characters.

To return from whence I have Digressed, I observed above that I had Time enough at the University for all manner of Mischief; accordingly there was seldom any piece of Roguery committed in College wherein I had not a Hand, if I was not the first Contriver thereof. But of all my Pranks whilst I continued there, none, I think, comes up to the Trick I play'd a Butcher, who was perpetually making Complaints of one or other of our Scholars, and was for that Reason heartily hated by the whole College. One Day above all the rest, when this Fellow had been preferring some fresh Accusation against three or four of us, the Parties aggrieved were wishing heartily for an Opportunity to be revenged of the old Rogue. As I happened to be in their Company, I told them, that if they would follow my Advice, I would put them in a way, not only to be thoroughly revenged of him, but prevent his ever coming to make any Complaints for the Future. Follow your Advice, said they: Aye, with all our Hearts, if you would but be as good as your Word; but which way would you go about it? Oh, very easily, replied I; keep but your own Counsel, and meet me to Night about Ten a Clock at the *Rose*.

They still continued very instant with me, to tell them what I design'd to do. Whereupon

upon taking them to my Chambers, the back Windows of which look'd directly upon the Butcher's House, I shew'd them a fine Calf which he had just kill'd, and hung up in his Yard, with intent to cut up for Sale at Market next Day. Do you see that Calf there, said I; yes, answer'd they, what of that? What of that, you Fools? Why, if you will be ruled by me, we will steal it from him this very Night, and then I think you will be pretty well even with him. Aye, but said they, How is it possible? Oh, let me alone for that, replied I, and only do as I direct you, and all will be well; I will engage he never comes to complain more.

Every thing being thus agreed on, I went to the College Cook, and secured him in our Interest; after which, at the Hour appointed, I went to the Place of Rendezvous, provided with a supernumerary Fellow-Commoner's Gown and Hat, a Rope-Ladder, and a dark Lanthorn. I there found my Companions, whom I acquainted succinctly how I design'd to put our Project in Execution, which they all approved; after which, drinking a couple of Bottles of Wine, and waiting till we thought all the Family were fast asleep, we marched very quietly to the Butcher's Yard.

Having fastened our Rope-Ladder, three of us soon got over the Wall, and in an Instant unhook'd the Calf, which hung under a Shed, and handed it over to our Companions, who were on the other Side to receive it. Then
dressing

dreffing the Calf up in the Fellow-Commoner's Habit, and two of us fupporting it on each fide, whilft one walk'd before with the Lanthorn, we began our March to the College-Gate, which was not above thirty Paces from the Butcher's Houfe.

As I was a Fellow-Commoner and the reft of my Companions but Penfioners, 'twas agreed I fhould knock at the College-Gate, which I accordingly did, and the Porter coming to open it with a Candle and Lanthorn as ufual, (for the Nights were exceeding dark) I made a Stumble as if accidentally, and kick'd the Lanthorn into the middle of the Quadrangle. The Porter had juft had glimpfe enough of my Companions, to perceive they were fupporting fomething in a Gown, whereupon taking it for a Gentleman that ufed very often to come in drunk, and kept late Hours: Very well, Mr. *Such-a-one*, fays he, naming him; you think I don't fee you, but I do, and fhall take Care to acquaint the Mafter therewith to-morrow.

In the mean while my Companions made the beft of their Way, with their Purchafe, to the College Kitchen, where the Cook was waiting for us; whilft I ftaid behind a little to amufe the Porter, and help to look for his Lanthorn, after which I haften'd after them and delivered the Cow's Baby up to the Cook's Difcretion, who foon difpofed of it in fuch a Manner, as it would have puzzled all

all the Fortune-tellers in *England* to have given any Tale or Tidings of it.

It would be impossible to describe the Uproar that was at the Butcher's next Morning, as soon as the Calf was missing: How any Persons cou'd get into his Yard, the Walls being pretty high, and when there, how they could get the Calf over, or when over, how they could carry it off, was a piece of Conjuration that pass'd their Understanding; and as the *Cambridge* and *Oxford* Scholars have long been thought by the Ignorant to deal with the Devil, the Butcher and his Family were now almost tempted to believe it, for 'twas unanimously agreed that it could be done by none but some of our College, who ow'd him a Grudge; and so far indeed they were in the Right.

Hereupon away goes the Butcher openmouth'd to the Master of our College, with a Complaint that some of us had robb'd him of a fine Calf. This Story appeared so improbable, that the Master star'd the Man full in the Face, and thought him crack-brain'd; however, as the Fellow persisted in it, and made a sad Noise, he sent for the Porter, and enquired who was out late the Night before, and whether he saw any of us bring in any large Bundle.

The Porter, as well he might, answer'd in the Negative, litttle thinking the Calf was turn'd *Fellow-Commoner;* to satisfy the the Fellow, who was very importunate, a thorough

thorough Search was made throughout the College, but no Signs nor Tokens were to be found of the Theft; for, although good part of the Calf was at that very Time roasting in the College Kitchen, they were very far from suspecting it to be the Calf in Question, not in the least imagining that the Cook was an Accomplice with us.

Hereupon the Master flew into a violent Passion with the Butcher, and threaten'd to send him to the Castle, if ever he came to trouble him with any more Complaints against us; the poor Fellow, thus shubb'd was forced to pocket up his Loss, nor durst ever after pester us with any Complaints, whatever Cause he had for so doing, tho' he often had sufficient Reason.

Two Years I continued at the University, after which my Father removed me to the *Temple*, where instead of studying the Law, I study'd nothing but *Intriguing*, in which I soon grew a great Proficient, and as I had a very handsome Allowance from my Father, I flew at a higher Game than when at *Cambridge*, so that a Spruce Laundress wou'd hardly go down with me, I was grown so very nice and difficult.

I had not been long at the *Temple*, before I resolved to single out a *Coquette* Milliner, who was the *reigning Toast* of all the *Petits Maitres* in that contentious District, as the *Fair One* to whom I would first make my Addresses: No sooner had I taken this Resolution, but I

put

put it in Execution; and going thither directly under Colour of buying a pair of Gloves, took that Opportunity of complimenting her upon the Number of her Conquests (for her Shop was like a *Prime Minister's Levee*,) and the Superiority of her Charms over those of her Rivals, the Vintners pretty Bar-keepers, the Coffee-House Sparklers, and her Sister Milliners and Sempstresses about the Bar.

She returned my Compliment in such a Manner, as shewed me this was a Language she was pretty much used to, and that she did not think it was a jot more than she deserv'd; at the same Time I could plainly perceive, that like her Sister *Coquetts*, she was not at all displeased at seeing the Number of her Admirers increased, for which Reason (as I imagine) she smiled upon me graciously at parting, that she might not lose her new Conquest, by putting me out of all Hopes.

After this I frequented her Shop very often, making use still of the same Pretence of buying several Trifles, for which I was sure to pay through the Nose; nevertheless I never thought it advisable to dispute with her whatever Price she set upon her Goods, being firmly resolved, if possible, to make her repay it me with Interest, tho' in *another sort of Coin*; which was not however, the easiest Task I had ever undertaken.

The Gipsy was indeed very pretty, and knew it well enough to set a very extraordinary

Value

Value upon her Charms; besides this, she did not want for Wit, or at least had a ready way of Talking, and a competent Assurance, which is too often mistaken for the other; especially in a Woman whom one admires, and who has a tolerable Person to set it off. Then she valued herself upon an uncomatable Virtue, a great Insensibility of Love, and a perfect Indifference for all her Adorers; thro' all which any one might easily perceive, that her Design was to catch at the first *Butter-Fly* who had a tolerable Estate, was *Fool* enough to fall heartily in Love with her, and *Noodle* enough to run Hand-over-Head, and marry her without any farther Consideration.

Having gain'd the Insight into her Ladyship's Temper and Designs, I proceeded accordingly in my Attacks, like a Master of the Art of War, and instead of pretending to take *Love's Citadel* by Storm, changed my Siege into a Blockade, and proceeded by the way of Sapping: In short, from a vigorous brisk Lover, I grew a most obsequious whining Slave, insomuch that Madam, who had a very good Opinion of her own Charms, did not in the least question but I was smitten, and was the *Woodcock* for which she had been long lying in wait.

Accordingly she chang'd her manner of Behaviour with me, treated me more favourably than the rest of her Admirers; and granted me several Liberties which she denied them,

them; such as admitting me to drink Tea with her in her Parlour, and permitting me to treat her and her favourite Acquaintance with a Play, a Favour for which I was not a little envied by all the Gay *Templers* my Rivals, and which made me not a little Vain of the Preference I had gained over them.

I still pretended to be dying for her, continued my Visits every Day, was as ardent as ever in my Courtship, complain'd of my Pains, and talk'd of Flames and Darts as much as ever, but without declaring myself one way or other, or offering to bring Things to a Conclusion, till I found, by thus dallying with her, I had fool'd her into Love in good Earnest, and she began to be very uneasy at not knowing for certain what I was driving at, and what she had to expect from me; for she was not without Hopes that my Designs were honourable, having never as yet offer'd at taking any Liberties that could offend the most rigid Virtue; or which is still more scrupulous, the most *profess'd Prude*.

In order then to bring me to a positive Declaration, she thought it adviseable to quicken me up, and to spur me on, by making me jealous, and giving Encouragement to one Mr. *B—*, a *Templer*, who at that time very much frequented her Shop, was an accomplish'd young Gentleman, and indeed, but that Fancy passes Beauty, every way my Superiour.

This

This was what I wanted; for although I was not actually jealous, and saw through her Design, which I attribute to my not being sincerely in Love with her, for none are so blind as those who are really intoxicated with that Passion, I pretended as much Jealousy as the most passionate Lover that ever whin'd in a Romance: This I had not done, but that it squared very well with my own Ends.

My Jealousy, however, was not so furious to make me quarrel with, and challenge every one that look'd upon my *Dulcinea* besides myself, nor yet every one she vouchsafed to smile upon; for I was still reasonable enough to know that her Interest obliged her to it: Neither did my Jealousy transport me so far, as to make me declare myself her *honourable Slave*, and insist upon her *breaking* with all other *Pretenders to her Favour*; for I well knew that then she might shut up Shop, and I must be obliged in Honour to *keep her*, after I had gained my Ends, which I thought but little better than *Matrimony*.

My Jealousy went no farther, than to sigh most inordinately, when in her Company, (for out of it I was as merry as a Cricket; a sure Sign I was Heart-whole) to look very Melancholy and Pensive, and sit sometimes as mute as a Fish for an Hour or two together. This, however, did my Business as effectually as I could have wish'd; for my Fair-One imagining that my silence proceeded from my great Dread of her Displeasure should I offer to complain, I having always acted the timid and respectful Lover, enquired several times what ailed me, on purpose to give me an Opportunity of breaking the Ice.

Finding however, that this did not answer her Ends, she was forced at last to ask me downright, whether any Company that she kept gave me any Uneasiness; for, said she, I have observ'd you always look particularly cloudy, whenever Mr. *B* — comes in. If that be the Case, continued she, as he professes a great Value for me, and I look upon him as a Gentleman every way qualified to make a Woman happy, and for aught I know his Designs may be honourable, I see no Reason why I should not entertain him, especially since you have never yet explained your self upon that Head, although you have had all the Liberty imaginable.

Madam, answer'd I, with a seeming Reluctancy, since you force me to speak, without which I should never have dared to open my Mouth, I shall make no scruple to own that your late Encouragement of Mr. *B* — has given me no small Uneasiness, but that is not the only, nor yet the greatest Cause of my late Trouble and Melancholy: Some Discourses which I have heard within this little while, and with which I am unwilling to wound your Ears, have created in me an Anguish which I am afraid I shall not soon get over, and which makes it necessary for me to stop where I am, without coming to any farther

ther Explanation, which I should otherwise have done before now.

What Discourses can you have heard of me, said she, with a noble Pride, that should give you any Anxiety, or with which you should be afraid of wounding my Ears? Speak out, I dare the utmost Malice of your detracting Sex; and must tell you, that I thought my Behaviour since you have known me, would have prevented your easily believing any Aspersions which any unworthy Wretch should cast upon me: However let me know them, let the Consequence be what it will.

Madam, replied I, your Commands must always be sacred to me, else would not I offend your Ears by repeating what must give you Pain, as it did me, in the Hearing; and as to what you were pleased to say, about my easily believing any Aspersions that should be cast upon you, I will assure you, I am far from believing them, and shall always do you Justice in my own Opinion; but that does not prevent their giving me infinite Disquiet; so much as I am afraid will make me miserable as long as I live, since I find it impossible, as Things stand, I should ever be happy in your Possession, which was the utmost of my Ambition, my Designs having never been otherwise than honourable.

Sir, said she, interrupting me, be pleas'd to explain your self, you talk in Riddles; I don't understand two Words of all you have said;

said: All that I can underſtand is, that I have been baſely and villanouſly bely'd by ſome unworthy Villains, and that you have been pleaſed to believe them, for all your Pretences, elſe why ſhould their Lies create any Uneaſineſs in you? But come, let us hear the utmoſt their Malice has been able to Invent; I can aſſure you it will not give me ſo much Pain, as you ſay it did you, in the hearing it.

Hereupon I told her, that being in Company with ſome Acquaintance, amongſt other Diſcourſe her Name happen'd to be mention'd, whether deſignedly or not, I could not be certain; that thereupon ſome of them began to banter me upon my approaching her always with ſo much Timidity and Reſpect; adding, that wou'd never do, for ſhe loved a Man of more Mettle and Vigour, or elſe they were very much miſtaken in her; and that Mr. H——, naming a Gentleman who had formerly viſited her, had not been ſo great a Favourite with her if he had behaved himſelf as I did; intimating farther, that ſhe was very much bely'd, if ſhe had not granted him all the Favours it was in her Power to grant him.

This Story was partly true, partly falſe; Mr. H—, who was a vain-glorious Coxcomb, and loved to give himſelf Airs, had viſited her formerly, as I did then, on pretence his Deſigns were honourable; but no ſooner did ſhe find they were otherwiſe, then ſhe deſired him to keep away; upon which, in Revenge

for

for his Disappointment, he, with some others whom she had serv'd in the same Manner, trumpt up this malicious Aspersion which was now out of Date, and never had been believed by any Person of Credit, and Reputation; but it served my purpose for the Present, as well as if it had been true.

Upon my reviving therefore the impudent Slander, one would have thought all the Blood in her Body had come into her Face; however composing herself in a little Time, and finding I was silent; And is this all (said she) this hellish Slander, which is now almost forgotten, and never was believed at first! And do you of all Men give Credit to it! How have I been deceived! But I see plainly you grow weary of my Company, and therefore have trumpt up this for a Pretence to leave me, which you need not have done, for as nothing has pass'd between us, but some fine Speeches, which I always took to be, as now I find them, Words of Course, you was always at Liberty, when you pleas'd, without such a barbarous Contrivance: In what a fine Condition had I been, had I been Fool enough to have believ'd you, and set my Heart upon you.

Far be any such base Thought from my Heart Madam, said I; I have already told you I never did believe it, and I again assure you, I never can credit any Stories to your Disadvantage, but still I am nevertheless wretched; for as long as there is a Possibility ty of my being deceiv'd, I never can be made happy in your Possession; for should I after Marriage find my self mistaken in my good Opinion of your Virtue, my Resentment wou'd transport me to some horrid Extremity, which would prove fatal to us both: And the Dread of what any such shocking Conviction wou'd transport me to, will always keep me from venturing on what otherwise I should most ardently Covet, and what would make me the happiest of Mankind.

O no Compliments, good Sir, cry'd she, interrupting me with a disdainful Air, if I cou'd contribute so much as you pretend to your Happiness, I hardly think you wou'd deny your self that Satisfaction for any foolish Scruples and Doubts that might arise in your Mind, and because there is a Possibility I may have forfeited my Honour; for the same Possibility lies against the whole Sex, and consequently you must resolve never to run the Venture: Besides, should I consent to marry you, after this Declaration, that alone ought to convince you that I am conscious of my own Innocence, for otherwise I must be worse then distracted.

All that you have said is very true, Madam, replyed I, but nevertheless it is possible (not that I suppose it wou'd be the Case) that a Woman who has forfeited her Virtue, may be rash enough to run the Hazard of marrying, in hopes the Man will not be so good a
Judge

judge in such Cases to discover the Loss of her Virgin Treasure.

Sir, answered she, by what I can perceive, you are either very ingenious in tormenting your self with unjust and injurious Suspicions, or else, as I before observed, you make it a Pretence for breaking off your Visits, which you might have done without all this going about the Bush for it, for no Body will pretend to constrain you.

No, Madam, I don't imagine you will, said I, you have not the Value for me, nor is my Company so dear to you, to make you give your self the least Trouble about keeping me; I wish it was, but I am not so happy to have the Loss of me, give you the least Regret.

It is but an imprudent Part in me, reply'd she, after what has now pass'd, to confess my having had any Value for you, but I am such a Friend to Sincerity and plain Dealing, that I will freely own, I would have done as much to have made you easy as any Man whatever; but since your Doubts, and Fears, and Scruples, make that impossible, I see no other Remedy but to sit down each of us contented as we are.

No, not absolutely impossible, Madam, cry'd I, hastily interrupting her, there is still a Way to make us both happy, at least if being for ever united wou'd make you so, but 'tis what I dare not hope for, and therefore dare not propose; you do not love me to that
exalted

exalted Degree, to confent to grant me what alone will remove all Scruples, and make my Condition to be envied by my whole Sex; then fhould the Prieft that Inftant join our Hands, and Doubts, and Fears, and Scruples, be no more.

I fhould be worfe than mad fhould I believe you, faid fhe, fighing, when to convince you I have not loft my Honour with another, (as you pretend to be inform'd) fhall I in earneft yield it up to you, in hopes you will afterwards be juft to marry me! Too well I know the Falfhood of your Sex; too often have I heard your ungenerous Maxim, that fhe who yields to one, will with another; and what Reafon have I to think you would not fay the fame? What Reafon to believe you would be juft, when I had no more to give, or you to ask?

I would, by all that's Sacred, my Charmer, faid I, well pleas'd I had brought her fo much as to hear my Defign mentioned with any Patience; knowing that the Fort that Parleys is not far from Surrendring; and that the only way for a Woman to be fafe in fuch Cafes, efpecially where fhe likes the Perfon, is to fhut her Ears, and avoid him: Refolving therefore not to lofe her for a few Oaths, but to lay clofer Siege to her than ever, not fearing, but in fome tender unguarded Moment or other, her very Eyes would betray her Wifhes, and I fhould gain my Point.

It

It was no little Difficulty, however after this, to obtain my Ends, notwithstanding I had a bosom Friend within, that pleaded in my Behalf very earnestly, and was bribed by Love to betray the Fort. In short, I have since been convinced, that she had more real Virtue than half the Prudes in the Kingdom, tho' I then believed there was no such thing in the World as a modest Woman; a base heretical Tenet, which I now recant.

For a long Time then did I attack my Fair One; diffident of her own Strength, she carefully avoided all Occasions of being alone with me, insomuch that I sometimes began to doubt of my Success, fearing she would at last have Prudence and Resolution enough no longer to admit my Visits; which made me determine not to let slip the very first Opportunity to urge my Suit as warmly as possible, without having Recourse to brutal Force.

One happy Day then (as I then thought it, tho' I have been since of another Mind) going to my Charmer's as usual, and not seeing her in the Shop, I ran directly into the Parlour, a Liberty I had frequently before taken, without being perceived by her Women behind the Counter, who were very busy in serving Customers. Not finding her there neither, I stole softly up into her Bed-Chamber, where I surprized the Fair One in a very melancholy, yet very inviting Posture. She was in a loose Undress, her Head lay pensively reclined upon her Arms;

whilst

whilſt a ſilent Tear trickled down her pretty Cheeks, and drop'd in Pearls upon her ſnowy Boſom, from whence a gentle Sigh would every now and then force its Paſſage unperceived.

By all theſe Symptoms, it was eaſy for me to gueſs, that her Mind was at that Time employed upon me; ſhe was ſo buried in Thought, that I was cloſe by her, before ſhe was ſenſible of my being there; wherefore that I might ſtartle her as little as poſſible, by my ſudden approaching her ſo unawares, I fell upon my Knees beſide her, and ſeizing her by the other Hand, which hung negligently down by her, and preſſing it eagerly to my Lips; why, my lovely Inchantreſs, ſaid I, do I find you in this diſconſolate Poſture, fit only for thoſe who are ſo unhappy as to have incurr'd your Diſpleaſure?

She gave a Shriek, on being ſo unexpectedly ſurprized, and fainted away; but being ſoon recover'd by my Care; why, ſaid ſhe, with a languiſhing Air, and bluſhing, do you thus preſs into my Retirement? And why, O why, do you pry into a Weakneſs, I would feign hide, if poſſible, from myſelf? I caught her in my Arms, preſs'd her to my Breaſt, and printing an ardent Kiſs upon her ruby Lips, which ſhe received with a ſort of unwilling Willingneſs, my Angel, my Charmer, anſwered I, What ſtupid Wretch could ſee thee thus diſſolv'd in Tears, and not uſe his utmoſt Endeavours to give you Eaſe?

And

And can one give you Eafe without knowing your Diftemper? Oh! that I were Phyfician enough to cure it! But, I forget, you would not accept me if I were.

At thefe Words a lively Scarlet overfpread her Face, which was fucceeded by a deadly Pale, and fhe had fwooned away a fecond Time but that I upheld her; at laft, leave me, I conjure you, faid fhe with a Sigh, leave me to myfelf, if you have yet any Value or Refpect for me; fatal to my Peace was the firft Hour we were acquainted, for I muft never expect Quiet more. Forbid it Heaven, Madam, replied I haftily; 'twere better I were dead, than that I fhould caufe you one Moment's Uneafinefs; by all that's Great and Good, there is nothing in my Power which I would not do to ferve you, and make you as happy as your Heart can wifh; but confefs the Truth, my Fair One, Are not you your felf the only Caufe of your own Unhappinefs, as well as mine? Does it not proceed from your Diffidence of my Honour? Or elfe why might not you this Moment put an End to my Pain, by removing all my Scruples, and let to-morrow's Sun fee our Fates united for ever? Come, look Confent, my Faireft, and let us both be happy: By thy bright Eyes I fwear, nought e'er fhall part us, nor fhalt thou ever grieve thy Condefcenfion.

Oh! that I durft believe you, faid fhe fighing; but you are a Man, and all your Sex are falfe; all perjur'd Wretches, born for

Woman's Ruin, and fhe that trufts is fure to be undone: By Heaven, you fhall believe, and truft me too, replied I, drawing her gently towards the Bed, nor fhall you be fuffer'd to be fo much your own Enemy, to defer longer what will make both happy; come, my Treafure, you muft, and fhall; fay, fpeak the Word. I never can, nor never will confent, anfwer'd fhe, faintly ftruggling; for Heaven's Sake let me go, and oblige me not to expofe myfelf, by calling out for help: How can you pretend to love me, and yet attempt my Ruin? Won't you defift, and muft I alarm the Houfe? You would not furely be fo imprudent, refum'd I, but to prevent the Worft, I'll put it out of your Power, by fmothering you with Kiffes, and ftopping your Breath.

By this Time I had got her clofe to the Bed, on which I gently threw her down, fhe all the while ftruggling and trembling between her Virgin Fears, and long conftrained Defire; I fhall draw the Curtain upon what follow'd, which muft be left to the Reader's Imagination, and only fay that I was loft in Raptures, and happy beyond my utmoft Expectation, yet cou'd I not obtain my Wifhes, till I had bound my felf in a Thoufand Oaths to marry her the next Morning.

My firft Tranfports were hardly over, and I was ftill running over all her Charms with eager Eyes, when my pretty Victim, who was drown'd in Tears, ask'd me if I was not

now

now convinced, and whether I wou'd not be so just to keep my Promise and end all her Tears, by making her my Wife. It would have been barbarous and inhuman then to have deny'd her, tho' it was then the farthest from my Thoughts, wherefore I renew'd all my Vows, kiss'd away her Tears, again enjoy'd her, and left her seemingly contented.

But tho' I had gain'd my Ends, on this deluded Virgin, and look'd upon all my Oaths and Protestations as Wind, I had too much Honour to expose her, and glory in her Ruin, as our modern *Petits Maitres* would have done: On the contrary, I bent all my Thoughts on providing her a Husband, who should repair the Injury I had done her, and form'd a Scheme for that purpose, which I had the Satisfaction afterwards of seeing succeed, and she is now alive, and happy, in the Enjoyment of a tender Husband, with a plentiful Estate, and a numerous Offspring; nor are her Joys imbitter'd by any Sorrows, unless 'tis now and then the Remembrance of such a perjur'd Wretch as my self, whom I dare say she heartily Pities, but no longer Values, or Esteems.

I carry'd this Intrigue with my pretty Milliner so long, that she grew at last very near as insipid to me as if she had been my Wife; not but the Gipsy had excellent Things in her, and was well worth the Trouble I had taken to obtain her. I took then almost as much Pains to get rid of her, as ever I had done to
gain

gain her; for, although she was really virtuous at the Bottom, and it wou'd have been impossible to seduce her, without having first made my self Master of her Heart, which I cou'd never have done had I not pretended honourable Courtship, and thereby put her off her Guard, besides swearing a hundred Times solemnly to marry her; yet being once won, like all the rest of her Sex, who still doat on their first Undoer, she still loved me with an unbated Fondness, and it was a very difficult Matter to wean her; tho' she was soon sensible that I never intended to make her my Wife: So hard it is to grow indifferent, where once one has really loved, in spite of all the *Failings,* and even *Vices,* of the Person beloved.

Not but I cou'd easily have obtain'd my End, by repeated Slights; but tho' I no longer loved, I esteemed her: And having a real Value for her, as she well deserved, was willing to part fairly; not yet being *Scoundrel* enough, tho' I was *Rake* enough, to use a Woman ill, only for loving me *too well:* Like a certain Person I have now in my Eye, who could not carry his good Manners so far as to use the Bride well even the first Night, tho' she brought him a vast Fortune, when his own Father had discarded him, and no Body would have trusted him a single Groat.

I took Courage then at last, and broke the Ice to her, after this Manner: One Day when she was representing to me with Tears, that

that our Amour might at laſt be attended with very ill Conſequences, and that ſhe was not altogether ſure how it might be with her even then; my Dear anſwered I, very ſeriouſly, what you obſerve is very true, and has often given me a great deal of Uneaſineſs, tho' I did not know how to tell you as much. Not but that I cou'd eaſily provide for any Expences that might happen, let the worſt that cou'd befal you, nor ſhou'd I value it of a Farthing, but I love you too ſincerely, not to wiſh to ſee you above all Accidents whatſoever; and can't bear the Thoughts of hearing your Character in the leaſt reflected upon; and this in my Opinion can be no way ſo ſafely warded againſt as by a good Husband, and you know it is not in my Power to offer you my ſervice in that Reſpect, whilſt my Father and Uncle are living. I have hitherto behaved my ſelf in ſuch a Manner, that there is not the leaſt Suſpicion of any thing between us, wherefore, if you wou'd be adviſed by me, give me leave to recommend Mr. *D——* to you as a Gentleman with whom you may be entirely happy, and above Scandal. He has a good Eſtate, is intirely independent, of an amicable, ſweet Temper, has ſeen but little of the World; and being a Man of the ſtricteſt Honour, and very virtuous Principles himſelf, is far from harbouring an ill Opinion of another. If, with all theſe good Qualities, you think proper to

accept

accept of him, I will undertake to bring it to bear.

All the Time I was fpeaking, the difconfolate *Fair-One* hearken'd to me very patiently, but finding I. had done, fhe threw her fnowy Arms about my Neck, and burfting into a violent Paffion of Crying; Ungrateful Man, *faid fhe*, do I live to hear fuch a Propofal from you; from you by whom I am undone, and for whom I have given up All! Did ever I think I cou'd live to bear the Reproaches my Confcience daily makes me! As for my firft Frailty, 'twas excufable, violent raging Love, your folemn Oaths, my own Youth and Innocence all plead for me, but to perfift in the fame now when the Mask is pull'd of, and I know you never intend to repair the Injuries you have done me, is a Folly not to be forgiven; yet, blufhing, I muft own it, the Deceiver ftill is dear to me, and I cannot bear the Thoughts of parting with him, even tho' certain Ruin and Infamy fhou'd be my Portion, as, in all Probability, it one Day will.

For that very Reafon, faid I my Angel, I gave you this Advice; nor need we part even then; I. ftill may vifit you, my Charmer, and ftill adore you, only the Confequences may not prove fo fatal. O talk not of it, faid fhe, haftily interrupting me, I cou'd almoft defpife you for the Thoughts; What! Do you Imagine I wou'd turn Proftitute, or that I would fuffer your Embraces, after being

ing marry'd to another! No, I wou'd sooner suffer Death: Mention it therefore unto me no more, unless grown weary of my Arms, you seek another Fair, and wish from me to be releas'd for ever.

You misinterpret much my good Intentions, Madam, reply'd I, because, out of my Zeal for your Welfare, I wou'd wish to see you advantageously marry'd for Fear of Accidents, it not being in my Power, whilst my Father and Uncle are living, to dispose of myself without their Consent: Is that a Sign I am grown weary of your Arms? No, Madam, it is rather a Sign I prefer your Happiness to my own; but whatever your Opinion may be of me, I am still so much your Friend to wish you wou'd consider of it seriously; you may not every Day meet with such an Offer. It is very well, Sir, answer'd she, haughtily, I see your Drift, and perhaps, may take your Counsel; but suppose I shou'd, How are you sure you can bring your Project to bear? Is Mr. *D*—'s Heart altogether at your Disposal? Not altogether, Madam, said I, but if I am not mightily mistaken, he is pretty well inclin'd that way already, for I have heard him speak of you in Terms very much to your Advantage; and, to tell you the Truth, he has even desired me to introduce him, but I wou'd not presume to do it, without first asking your Leave. Well, then said she, you may bring him when you please; I will endeavour to set as little Value upon you, as I

E find

find you do upon me; at least continued she with a deep Sigh, if Mr. *D*—— shou'd be so weak to settle his Affection upon me, I will punish my fond Heart, for having loved one so ungrateful, by taking one, whom, probably, I never can love.

This was what I wanted, wherefore I never stood to vindicate myself, but took my Leave for that Time, and carrying Mr. *D*—— with me, the next Day, to visit her, to pique me, she received him very graciously; this encouraged him so much, that the next Day he ventur'd to go thither by himself, and she still receiving him very civilly, he repeated his Visits every Day 'till the Charms of her Temper, join'd to those of her Person, gain'd an absolute Conquest over him, and he made her a Declaration in Form.

This opened her Eyes, and made her see the Difference between his Passion and mine; in short, beyond my Hopes, she conceived a real Esteem for him, as he well deserved, which by his obliging and tender Behaviour, was soon heighten'd into a sincere Love, and in three Months their Hands were join'd, to their mutual Satisfaction. Some Time afterwards I waited on her to wish her Joy; she received me very courteously, and thank'd me for being the Instrument of her having the best of Husbands, but at the same Time desired me to spare my self the Trouble of ever visiting her for the future, since the Sight of me only brought her Folly to her Remembrance,

brance, and made her abhor both her self and me.

Being thus fairly delivered of my old Miſtreſs to my no ſmall Satisfaction, I was not long idle, but bent all my Thoughts on finding out an Object worthy to ſucceed her, which I did in a very ſhort Time: This was a young Lady of a good Family, exquiſite Beauty, and tolerable Fortune, who having loſt her Mother when very young, was educated under the Care of an Aunt, by the Father's Side, to whom I was likewiſe related. This, together with our being brought up together in our Childhood, gave me the Privilege of viſiting her unſuſpected, almoſt at any Hour, and any Seaſon.

Her Aunt was one, who having been marry'd in the Prime of her Years, for Intereſt, to a Man of threeſcore, had been eaſily tempted to be falſe to his Bed; being conſcious therefore of her own Frailty, and not willing her Niece, for whom ſhe had a great Love, ſhould be guilty of the like, ſhe kept a very watchful Eye over her Conduct, and this it was incited me to render all her Vigilancy vain. I took Care however, to give no Suſpicion of my Deſign, which wou'd have broken all my Meaſures, and pretending an abſolute Indifferency for the whole Sex, would often ſpend an Afternoon, at Back-gammon with the Aunt, with as much ſeeming Satisfaction as if it had been with the fineſt Woman in the Kingdom. This ſoon made me a great

E 2   Favourite

Favourite with the old Lady, who was a great Lover of that Game, and quite lull'd asleep all Mistrust, so that she, who wou'd not have trusted her Niece out of her Sight with another He-Thing, (as she used to call the Men,) wou'd leave me sometimes for Hours together to read a Play or Novel to her; a Service I was always very ready to accept.

These Opportunities I never fail'd improving to my own Advantage, taking all the Pains imaginable to make myself agreeable to my Fair Cousin, (for so I used to call her,) before I attempted to take the least Liberty in the World with her. I had soon the Satisfaction to perceive that my Labour was not all lost, for my Cousin who was in a manner deny'd all Men's Company but mine, and who began to feel within herself a strong Disposition to fulfil the great Command, *Increase and multiply*, cou'd not help discovering by her Eyes, which sparkled with Desire, the secret Wishes of her Soul, and how impatient she was of the Restraint she lay under. I was too well acquainted with the Language of those Tell-tales, to be Ignorant of this favourable Disposition of her Mind; I had nothing then to do but to fix her Desires, which were not settled on any particular Object, on myself, and to conceal my Design from the old Dragon that watch'd the Golden Fruit. The first was very easy, since I had no Rivals to struggle with, and was allow'd Opportunities which were deny'd to every
Thing

Thing in Breeches besides; and the second I accomplish'd without much Difficulty, by affecting not only an indifferent, but even a rude Behaviour to her, when in her Aunt's Company, tho' when alone with her, I was the most complaisant Creature in the Universe.

She did not want Sense enough to take Notice of this Difference in my Carriage, and was for some Time at a Loss how to account for it, I having never given her any Cause to suspect my Design, being resolved to be assur'd of my Prey, before I offer'd to make a stoop at it: Whenever therefore her Aunt and she had any Dispute, I was sure to side with the Former, right or wrong. One Day then, being left to our selves, a little after I had been joining with her Aunt, in blaming her for some Trifle or other, she cou'd not forbear asking me the Reason I always took her Aunt's Part against her? Indeed, Cousin answer'd I, I have a very good Reason for so doing; for shou'd I seem to side with you, I know your Aunt so well, that she wou'd suspect something more than Ordinary between us, and not allow me the Liberty of entertaining you in private as I do at present, a Liberty I wou'd not willingly be deprived of at any Rate. I don't know, said she, but you may be in the right of it, for I believe it is your thwarting me always before her, that makes you so great a Favourite with her; for you are the only Man she ventures to leave alone with me. The more is my Happiness, Madam, reply'd I,
gently

gently preffing her Hand, wherefore if you will give me Leave, I will continue to behave in the fame Manner, that fhe may always allow me the fame Bleffing. O, you flatter me, Coufin, anfwer'd fhe blufhing; however as you are almoft the only Company I have, I fhou'd be forry, to be deprived of that too, fo I wou'd not have you alter your Behaviour to me in the leaft. I am glad, faid I, Madam, I have your Permiffion to diffemble a Rudenefs which does not at all fuit with my Inclination; I wifh you would permit me likewife to declare a Paffion for you which is far from being diffembled, and which my Eyes muft long 'ere this have revealed to you. I am entirely a Stranger, Coufin, reply'd fhe, to the Language of the Eyes, wherefore I can fay nothing to that Article, but I fhou'd be very forry you fhou'd pitch upon me to make your Jefts of; and if you are in earneft, I believe you need not defpair; fince if you declare your felf to my Father, he will hardly refufe you, and it will be a Means both of delivering me from this Reftraint, which is very odious to me, and of faving your felf abundance of needlefs Proteftations and Ceremony.

I was pretty much confounded at this frank, and yet prudent Anfwer, but as I was one not eafily put to a Nonplus, I foon recover'd from my Surprize, and had my Reply ready: I am fo far of your Opinion, Madam, rejoin'd I, that if I fhou'd declare my felf to your Father

Father, he wou'd not difdain to accept of me, and fhou'd long fince have demanded you in Form, but to my Misfortune I have a Father as well as you, on whom I depend, not to mention an Uncle, from whom I have great Expectations. Now to my Sorrow, tho' I look upon you as a Treafure in your felf, thefe two old Gentlemen have no Eyes for either Beauty, or Merit, any farther then they are accompany'd with Riches; and I have fome Reafons to believe that they expect a larger Fortune with any one whom they will confent to my taking for Wife, then fuits either with your Father's Conveniency, or Inclination to beftow on you; wherefore I muft conjure you if my Perfon is not difagreeable to you, to accept of my Vows in private, till either my Father's, or my Uncle's Death, puts it in my Power to confefs my Flame, and efpoufe you publickly.

I muft confefs, Sir, faid fhe, that what you alledge is not altogether without Reafon, my having more Sifters, and my eldeft Brother's running away with the Eftate, makes it impoffible for my Father to give me a Fortune anfwerable to what yours may reafonably expect; wherefore as long as your Vows are honourable, and it can be no Difcredit to me to receive them, I fhall make no Scruple to accept them, till Time caufes fome favourable Alteration in your Affairs, unlefs my Father fhou'd compel me to give my Hand elfewhere: In the mean while I agree with you, that it
will

will be neceffary to be private, or elfe my jealous Aunt will put a Stop to our having any more Meetings by our felves.

I threw myfelf at her Feet, embraced her Knees, and thank'd her a thoufand Times for this generous Condefcenfion, whilft the deluded *Fair One*, believing me fincere, thought herfelf very happy in fo paffionate, and difinterefted a Lover; little did fhe then think fhe was receiving a Serpent into her Bofom, which was fhortly to fting her to Death I continued my Addreffes then at every Opportunity, and my repeated Oaths and Proteftations having banifh'd all Diftruft of my Infidelity, or difhoneft Intentions, fhe began infenfibly to fuffer me to take more Liberties with her then fhe wou'd ever otherwife have allow'd; Love, or call it if you pleafe by a more homely Name, is of an encroaching Nature, never fatisfy'd with what is granted till it has got all, and there is no more to give, fo it was with me.

At firft indeed I prefum'd no farther then a Preffure of the Hand, an Embrace, a Kifs, or fo; but when, by thus toying with her, I had rais'd her Inclinations to the utmoft Height, which I cou'd eafily perceive by her wifhing Eyes, I ventur'd to let my Hands rove farther, and commit feveral Amorous Trefpaffes, (ftill laying the Blame on the Violence of my Love, and faying that as we were as good as Man and Wife in the Sight of Heaven, there cou'd be no Harm in it;) till by Degrees I even proceeded

fo

so far as to invade *Love's tempting Fort*, and let them stray all o'er the Sacred *Mount* of *Venus*.

This was at first a sacrilegious Theft, for which nothing cou'd attone; and I thought I shou'd ne'er have pacify'd her: But Time, which makes all things easy, brought her at last to pardon this also; she kindly imputing it only to the Excess of my Passion, which generally carries its own excuse along with it, among the Fair Sex. I did not however, attempt either to seize, or to sue for, the last Favour, not being sure but I might be surprized, even in the Height of all my Raptures, by the sudden coming of the Aunt, or some of her Servants.

I deferr'd this last Effort then till this Family was to remove into the Country, which was to be in a short Time; not doubting but I shou'd have an Invitation to come and see them, and that during my stay there, some Opportunity wou'd offer, when I might securely commit this Amorous Theft, and rifle all her Virgin Charms, without Fear of Interruption. As I foresaw, so it happen'd; the Family went to their Country Seat, about forty Miles off, and the Aunt invited me very kindly to come and pass a Week or two there; which Invitation, as may be well-thought, I very readily accepted.

Accordingly, after they had been there about a Month, during which I sent my Servant thither twice or thrice, on pretence of enquiring

enquiring after their Welfare; but in (Reality with Letters to my Cousin, that she might imagine she was always in my Thoughts) I took Horse and went down after them; and was received with open Arms by the Aunt, and with all the Raptures imaginable by the Niece, as soon as we were together in private. Fortune, which design'd to befriend me, had so order'd it, that the Chamber assign'd me for my Lodging join'd to that where my Cousin lay; all the other Rooms which were tolerably Furnished, being taken up by some Company, who happen'd to come thither accidentally the Evening before, to spend a Night or two with them.

As the Weather was sultry hot, the Evenings very long and Pleasant, and Opportunities very scarce in the Day Time, by reason the Aunt and Niece were both very much taken up with entertaining the other Company, I begg'd on my Charmer to give me leave to visit her in her Chamber, after all the rest of the House were retired to their Apartments. She consented, and two Nights together I spent some Hours there, without even offering to take those Liberties I had frequently done before. By this means I lull'd asleep all Suspicion of my having any ill Design, and she began even to fancy that my Passion abated, and that I did not love her with that Ardour as before. I perceived her Uneasiness, which did not displease me; and as I was sensible of the Cause, I judg'd she
wou'd

wou'd rather pardon my taking yet greater Freedoms, then that I shou'd still behave in the same Manner, which she imagin'd proceeded from my slighting her.

The third Night I again visited her in her Chamber, as usual; and staid with her till I was sure all the Family were in Bed, after which I took my Leave, as if I intended to go to sleep likewise. But far different was my Intention; for no sooner had I slipt off all my Cloaths to my Night-Gown, but I returned to her Chamber, and knocking softly at the Door, pretended I had forgot something of Importance, which I must of necessity communicate to her that Night: By this Time she was quite undress'd likewise, and just stepping into Bed; but the Coldness of my Behaviour that very Night having left her no Room to suspect I intended any Violence, and being extremely desirous of knowing what I had to say, she slipt on one Petticoat, threw her Gown loose about her, and made no Scruple of opening the Door.

Being entered, I clasp'd her in my Arms, vow'd she never appear'd so enchanting as at that Moment, and let my roving Hands wander over all her hidden Charms, whilst all the While I smother'd her with Kisses: when by this means I found by her short Breath, frequent Sighs, panting Breast, and sparkling Eyes, that I had rais'd her to the utmost Pitch of ardent Desire; I pretended a sudden Concern for her Health, and begg'd she wou'd get into Bed, for Fear of catching Cold; telling her that what I had to say wou'd take up some Time, and that I wou'd sit down by her, and disclose it to her; but that I shou'd never forgive myself, if by detaining her undress'd in the Cold, I shou'd occasion her a Fit of Sickness.

With some little Difficulty she comply'd, having first sworn me not to offer her any Violence; but no sooner was she between the Sheets, then I threw off my Gown, leapt in after her, clasp't her eagerly in my Arms, and stopping her Mouth with Kisses, put it out of her Power either to shriek out, or get away, had she been so inclin'd. As soon as I allowed her the Liberty to speak, she began to expostulate with me about my breaking my Oath, in coming to Bed to her: My Life, my Charmer said I, I have not broken my Oath; I did not swear not to come to Bed, but not to offer you any Violence, and what greater Violence is there in Kissing and Embracing you when in Bed, then when up? I swear again, I will Trespass no farther then your self shall give me Leave, and yet what pity 'tis, now when we are both equally wishing and desiring, to languish out the Prime of our Days, when it lies in your Power to make us both happy! Say my Angel, are you not determin'd to be mine, as I'm resolved to be for ever yours, What hinders then but we may now be blest? O, speak the Word, my Love, and give Consent, and I'll not envy

Monarchs

Monarchs on their Thrones. O prefs me not, my Dearest, to my Ruin, said the half-yielding *Fair-One*; shou'd I consult my Heart, Heaven knows there is nothing, that I cou'd deny thee; but be not thou ungenerous, nor take the Advantage of a Virgin's Weakness, or I too sure, too sure shall be undone; Stay then till *Hymen*'s Knot has made us one, and then I'll willingly resign my Charms, nor shalt thou be denyed thy utmost Wishes. I cannot wait till then, my lovely Charmer, answer'd I; my Blood is all on fire to possess thee, and I were not a Man coud I forego thee; how then can you expect it as I am, an ardent, passionate, impatient Lover! then let us lose no longer Time my Angel, but yield and meet my Love with equal Ardour. And will you then be true, answer'd the quite vanquish'd Maiden, will you be always mine, and shall the Priest in private join our Hands, and give a Sanction to our stolen Embraces? He shall, by Heavens, my Fairest, reply'd I, all in Raptures, if Fate shou'd ever make it necessary, before my Father's Death allows me to proclaim, and glory in my Choice. Then take me, take me, to thy longing Arms, cry'd the Soul-ravish'd, and half-dying Virgin, I am too happy if you prove but true, and shall for ever bless the happy Minute. Tis not in Words to express what follow'd, wherefore I shall only say that she gave me Joys, such as I had never before experienc'd; and that I left her not till the

In-

intruding Sun, which discover'd to me all her naked Charms, told me it was Time for me to retire, if I wou'd be undiscover'd, and not expose her.

For some Time did we continue our Amorous Thefts with mutual Raptures, nor was I at all satiated with her Charms, in short, she pleas'd me to that exquisite Degree, that I should certainly for once have kept my Word, and shou'd have marry'd her, had it not been for her own Indiscretion. Our frequent Embraces had the Effect that was reasonably to be expected; She had some Reason to suspect her self with Child, but was not certain of it, when an intimate Acquaintance invited her Father, at whose House she then was, with all his Family, to spend the rest of the Summer Season with him, at a fine Seat he had in *Nottinghamshire*. The Thing was proposed, resolv'd on, and put in Execution in three Days, so that the unhappy *Fair-One* had no Opportunity to give me Notice of this Journey, or of her Condition; not daring to trust a Secret of that Importance to a Letter, and I being at that Time in the *West*, whither my Father had sent me to settle some Affairs, his ill State of Health not permitting him to go thither himself.

On my returning to Town, I went directly to make a Visit to my beloved Mistress, and was not a little surprized when I heard she was gone into *Nottinghamshire*, for the whole Summer: But my Surprize was greatly ly increased some time after, when one Evening, being at *Hazard*, at a noted Gaming-House near *Covent Garden*, her Brother enter'd the Room, and coming up to me very abruptly, told me he must speak with me that Instant. I was not then in the best Humour in the World, having just lost a considerable Sum, which I was bent upon retrieving: Wherefore not suspecting his Business, I answer'd, that I was engaged for the Present; but if he wou'd let me know were he wou'd be in an Hour or two, I wou'd certainly wait upon him, or I wou'd call upon him in the Morning, if that wou'd be sufficient.

D—mn your Trifling, said the rash hot-headed young Man, I won't be put off so, nor will I leave you, now you once are found; Come then along with me this very Moment, unless you'd have me treat you very ill. I am not used, reply'd I, to such Language, nor know I how I have deserved it from you; I beg you therefore to explain your self, unless you'd have me think you are in Liquor, or, what is worse, distracted. Hark in your Ear then, said he; you're a Villain; you know my youngest Sister, that's enough, then think what you've deserved and what I want.

I know not what you want, reply'd I, all in a Fury, but this I know, the name of a Villain ne'er belonged to me, nor have I e'er deserved it at your Hands; so take it to your self, nor tempt me farther, unless you wou'd

pull

pull Ruin on your Head; thus far I may forgive. So shall not I, thou monstrous harden'd Villain, answer'd the enrag'd Brother, nor is the Injury thou hast done our Family to be atton'd for but by Blood; so without more Delay go strait with me, and give me Satisfaction instantly.

You shall not need to ask it twice, said I, so lead the Way, I'm ready; but know, rash Fool, had you not thus provok'd me, I never meant you or your Sister wrong; But now 'tis past, and she may curse her Folly, and you yours. By this Time we were come into the Street, both equally enraged, and breathing Vengeance; accordingly we drew, and for some Time he push'd on me so briskly, that I began to fear I should be worsted, being slightly wounded in three several Places: At last, however, blinded by his Fury, and eager to dispatch me, he ran upon my Sword, and drop'd that Instant breathless at my Feet.

As I believed him dead, in which Case it would have been unsafe for me to stay; he being Heir to a considerable Estate, and having powerful Relations; I retired into the Gaming-House, went out at the Back-Door, hasten'd down to the Water-Side, took a Boat to *Gravesend*, and made the best of my way to *Dover*, in order to go to *Calais*. From thence I wrote Word to my Father where I was, desiring him to remit me some Money, and send my Cloaths after me as soon as possible; to the End that I might secure myself, till he had confulted whether it was advifable for me to furrender myfelf, or not. In anfwer to this, my Father difpatch'd a Servant, in whom he could confide, with Money, and Orders to me to go for *Calais* forthwith, whither he wou'd fend my Things after me, if I intended to be fecure; for they were every where in purfuit of me, and the very worft was to be apprehended if I fhou'd be taken, fince there was no hopes of my Antagonift's Life, tho' he was not yet Dead. The Servant aded that Time was pretious, that he did not know how foon thofe who were in queft of me might be there, and that he was commanded not to part from me till he had feen me fafe away.

This was a very ticklifh Point; the Wind blew directly in to the Harbour, fo that neither the Packet-Boat, nor any other Veffel, cou'd get out of the Port; and if I ftay'd I did not know but I might be feiz'd every Moment, and what the Confequence of that might be, no Body cou'd tell, confidering, I had fuch powerful Adverfaries to deal with. There was no Way left then but to hire an open Boat, to carry me off at all Hazards; and it was not without great Difficulty, and paying an exorbitant Price, that any one was to be got, who wou'd run the Venture, the Paffage being fomething dangerous. At laft, however, I agreed for a ten-Oar Boat, in which I went off a little above the Town, about Ten at Night, for it was impoffible to

G .get

get out of the Harbour, the Tide setting in at the Peer very strong at that Time.

 The Weather was very calm when we set out, and continued so till we were got about half-way over; when the Clouds gather'd on all Sides, and it began to blow pretty briskly, full in our Teeth. After some Time, it grew so dark, that we cou'd not see a Boat's length, and the Wind rose still higher and higher, till it was a perfect Storm, and our Boat at every Moment was toss'd Mountains high, so that I expected every Wave wou'd break in upon us, and send us to the Bottom. The Boat's Crew themselves began to be pretty much terrified, their Oars being of very little, if any, Use to them, to stem the Tide, so that they were forced to let her drive with the Sea: Hereupon they fell a Swearing at one another, each blaming his Fellow for persuading him to undertake the Voyage, if I may so call such a short Passage, as that between *Dover* and *Calais*. For my own Part, I must confess, I sometimes wish'd I had staid in *England* at all Adventures, and run the Hazard of a dry Death a-shore, rather than have an unconscionable Drench of Salt Water, and make Food for Fish. I put the best Face I cou'd, however, upon the Matter, and opening a large Bottle of Brandy, of which I had taken Care to provide a sufficient Quantity, gave it among the Sailors to drink, bidding them ply their Oars, and be of good Heart, and we shou'd do well enough. The Brandy had a
very

very good Effect upon them, and made them a little Tractable, whereas before there was nothing but Swearing, Cursing, and Confusion to be heard; and the Storm abating about break of Day, we found our selves almost as high as *Boulogne*, eight Leagues distant from *Calais*, where we arrived however very safe about seven in the Morning.

The Manner of my coming over in an open Boat, without any Baggage, but a little Linnen in a Handkerchief, and without any Attendants, altho my Garb, which was pretty rich, shew'd plainly that I was not used to travel in that Manner, made the *French* suspect, and not without Reason, that there was somthing extraordinary in my venturing on such a dangerous and unusual Passage. Accordingly, when I was carried before the Governour, as is customary for all Strangers who land there, he examined me very particularly about my Quality, and the Occasion of my coming. I told him in few Words, that I was an *English* Gentleman, that I had unfortunately had a Quarrel with a young Man of Fortune, whom I had left for dead, and that I was forced to come over in an open Boat, because I was close pursued, and neither the Packet-Boat, nor any other Vessel, cou'd get out of the Harbour.

He received me with abundance of Civility, and seem'd very well satisfied with my Answers, tho' he did not believe me, as I found afterwards. It was much about the

Time of the Rebellion, and he had taken it into his Head, that I was one of those unfortunate Gentlemen engaged therein, and had made my Escape from *Preston*. As all the *French* are naturally well-Wishers to the *Pretender* and his Party, this Suspicion did not turn at all to my Disadvantage, but made him receive me with yet more Respect, than he wou'd otherwise have done, and he gave me a very sensible Mark thereof two or three Days after.

The *French*, tho they are generally well-bred, are apt to be pretty opinionated of themselves, and to have a very mean Opinion of all other Nations, especially the *English*, in comparison with their own. This I found before I had been many Hours with them; and I must confess it provok'd my Spleen, and I was resolv'd, if possible, to give them another sort of a Notion of us. As I spoke *French*, as well as *English*, having been taught it by my Father's Care, even before I learnt my Mother Tongue, I kept Company generally with the *French*, and did not, like the generality of our Nation, who travel, frequent only my own Countrymen.

Being at the Coffee-House then, with some *French* Gentlemen, they were very much surpriz'd at my talking their Language so well, and they were much more so, when I told them, it was an Accomplishment which was very common amongst all the better Sort. Whilst I was there, the Daughter of the House,

House, who was very pretty, was learning to Dance, and some of them whisper'd her, to desire me to dance a Minuet with her, imagining I shou'd do it but very aukwardly; she did so, and they were mightily disappointed; for it having been an Exercise I had taken Delight in, I not only danced very well, but even exceeded any of them, not excepting even the Dancing-Master himself. This done, among other Discourse, they began to talk of the Campaigns in *Flanders* in the late War, and some of them who were in the Army, took upon them to affirm, that they had seen several of our *English* Officers who were in Garrison at *Dunkirk*, decide their Quarrels by Boxing, whenever they had any Difference. I told them, that this was very strange to me, for they did not use to do so at Home; however, I cou'd not contradict them, having never been there; but that it was not very much to their Credit, if it was true, since they had *box'd* them *so soundly* at *Hochsted*, *Ramillies*, and *Malplaquet*, that they *never durst Face* them afterwards.

This Repartee gall'd them a little, and the more, because it was matter of Fact, wherefore they did not attempt to rally the *English* any more at that Time; on the contrary, there being a Ball that Night at one of the Principal Inhabitant's, two of them, who were Officers in the Garrison, offer'd their Service to introduce me there. As I had then no better Engagement upon my Hands, I accepted ed their Offer, and accordingly they came in the Evening to the Poſt-Houſe, where I lodg'd, to conduct me thither. Not expecting them ſo ſoon, I was quite undreſs'd when they came, and had order'd a Fowl to be got ready for my Supper, deſigning to eat a Mouthful before I went. Hereupon I deſired them to foul a Plate with me, beſpoke another Fowl, a fine Sallad, and a Diſh of Soop, without which, a *Frenchman* wou'd think himſelf undone, and in the mean while began to put on my Cloaths, having firſt ask'd Leave of them to take that Liberty.

Supper being brought in, we were very merry, and for ſome Time they were excellent good Company, diverting me with a Hundred pretty Songs, in which the *French* certainly exceed all the Nations in the World. But there being no want of Wine, and they drinking of it pretty plentifully, the Fumes of the *Burgundy* began to get into their Heads, to which their Singing contributed not a little, and they grew very Exceptious; in ſhort, it proceeded ſo far, that they downright quarrell'd, and drew upon each other in my very Chamber.

As I was afraid of this, from the very firſt of their begining to jar, I had interpos'd ſeveral Times to reconcile them, but to no purpoſe, for as faſt as one Difference was made up, ſome freſh Diſpute aroſe. Enrag'd at their ill Manners, and dreading the ill Conſequence of a Quarrel in my Room, which

(which in *France*, is yet more dangerous than in *England*,) I at laſt told them, that it was uſing me very ill; that whoever was the Aggreſſor, I ſhould look upon the Injury done to myſelf, and that if either of them offer'd to draw firſt, I would certainly be the Second. This, however, did not prevent their Drawing, whereupon ſnatching up my Sword, which lay upon a Table, I inſtantly did the ſame, and keeping my Eye upon him who faced me, ſtruck down their Swords, and at and at the ſame Inſtant clapping my Leg behind him who was next the Door, which open'd upon a pair of Stairs that went from the Gallery into the Yard, tript up his Heels, and ſent him from the Top to the Bottom. Well was it for him I did ſo, for the other at the ſame Time making a home Paſs at him, had certainly been through his Body, had not his Fall prevented it, by the Sword's going over his Head; and before he cou'd recover, having over-lung'd himſelf, I cloſed in with him run him through the Arm, and diſarm'd him.

The Fall of the Firſt into the Yard, where he lay for dead, had by this Time brought the People of the Houſe about us, who ſecured us, I willingly yielding up my Sword, and carried us before the Governour to be examined, to whom I very readily told the whole Truth of the Story. My not being both quite dreſs'd, and Sober, and their being Drunk, and having had high Words, which the Servants of the Inn avouch'd, together with

with my Sword's laying in the Scabbard upon a Table, made the Governour very eafily believe I had told him nothing but what was Fact: Wherefore, as foon as Word was brought that the other was come a little to himfelf, being only ftunn'd with the Fall, he releafed me, and committed them both into Cuftody, making abundance of Apologies for the Brutality of his Countrymen. Not content with this, he would have broke them both, but I interpos'd and pleaded for them, thinking them already fufficiently punifh'd for a Drunken Quarrel, the one by his Wound, and the other by his Bruifes: However, he continued them Prifoners for fome Days, nor would he releafe them until they had both ask'd my Pardon, and thank'd me for interceeding in their Behalf. I ow'd this extraordinary Civility of the Governour's, to his entirely believing me of the Pretender's Party, as he told me afterwards.

Tho' I fhou'd have been by no means pleafed before-hand, at having fuch a Quarrel, yet the Cataftrophe was very agreeable to me; as it gave me an Opportunity of mortifying the Gentry, who had affirm'd, that our *Englifh* Officers ufed to decide their Differences by *Boxing* when at *Dunkirk*. Accordingly, I went to the Coffee-Houfe next Morning, and the Difcourfe turning about our Quarrel, which had made fome Noife, *Well Gentlemen*, faid I, with a difdainful Smile, *You fee the Englifh don't always box.* They did not much

much like the Banter, notwithstanding which, they carried it off very well, thinking that better than to run the Hazard of the same Fate with their Countrymen; and one of them answer'd very gallantly, laughing; *Well then, since you talk French so well, dance so well, fence so well, and in short do every Thing so well, What the Devil do you come here for, as so many of your Nation do every Day?* What do you think we come for, reply'd I, laughing in my Turn, *but to help drink your Wine, and Kiss your Wives?*

As my Cloaths, and some Remittances which I expected, were not yet come from *England*, and *Calais* is not a Place that affords much Diversion, I resolved to take a Trip to *Dunkirk*, and St. *Omers*, to see the Fortifications of the one, and the *Jesuit's* College at the other. I must own, both of them satisfied my Curiosity very well, altho', the one was in a great Measure dismantled; but I met with an Adventure at the other, which for its Singularity deserves particularly to be recounted.

There was then quarter'd at St. *Omers*, a Brigade of *Irish* Officers, who were upon Half-Pay, or reform'd as they call it: Some of these happening to be about half a League out of the Town, diverting themselves in a little Hamlet that lay upon the Road, and seeing me as I rode by, paid me an extraordinary Respect, as I then thought, they being absolute

H   Strangers

Strangers to me; for they got all off their Seats to a Man, and made me each of them a very low Bow.

I reflected upon it, however, no more, and it was quite out of my Head, when, about two Hours after, being in my Chamber at the Post-House, where I had taken up my Lodging, my Servant, whom I hired at *Calais*, came and inform'd me, that about a Dozen Gentlemen, who seem'd by their Garb to be Officers, desired to know if I was to be seen.

Being very sure there was no Body in St. *Omers* who could have the least Knowledge of me, not having been above five Days out of *England*, and it being the first Time I had ever been abroad, I could not imagine what their Business could be: As I had no Reason, however, to apprehend any Harm, I order'd them to be admitted. Accordingly they came in, and were so full of their Ceremonies, that I was quite confounded; whereupon I told them in *French*, that I did not know how I had merited all these Civilities, not having ever seen one of them before, to the best of my Knowledge, and desired they would acquaint me with their Business.

Their Answer was, that they hoped I wou'd not be offended, but that their Business was only to shew their Duty, in paying me their Respects, and to know if I had any Commands for them. Hereupon turning to the Boy that had

had ferv'd me as a Guide, and underſtood *Engliſh*, being Son to the Miſtreſs of the Poſt-Houſe at *Calais*; *The Devil take me*, ſaid I, *if I can imagine what the Men mean, or what they would be at.*

My ſpeaking both *French* and *Engliſh* perfectly well, confirm'd them in their Error, and one of them anſwer'd, Sire, *If it is your Pleaſure to be* Incognito, *we know our Duty; and after having once paid our Reſpects, ſhall take no farther Notice of you then you are pleaſed to allow.*

The Word *Sire*, which is never us'd in *French* but to *a Crown'd Head*, put me out of all Patience; whereupon, thinking they made a Jeſt of me, What! *Gentlemen*, ſaid I, do you come here to banter me, Who the Devil do you take me for? *For our King*, anſwer'd they all with one accord, *If your Majeſty pleaſes, if not, for what you pleaſe.* Heyday! Said I, ſtill more confounded, What! are you all mad, or have you a Mind to make me ſo? *Far be it from your Majeſty's moſt faithful Servants*, replied they, *to have any ſuch Deſign, we wiſh all your Subjects in the three Kingdoms were as well affected to you as our Selves; Then would you, long ere this, have been reſtored to the Throne of your great Anceſtors the* Stuarts, *nor ſhould we languiſh our ſelves in Exile.*

I began then in ſome Meaſure to apprehend what they meant, and who they were, knowing there were a great many *Irish* Officers in the *French* Service; but this served only to heighten my Surprize: *Why sure, Gentlemen,* said I, *you are not serious, and you don't take me in earnest for the* Chevalier de St. GEORGE! *If you do, I'll assure you, you are egregiously mistaken, and I would not have you continue in your Error any longer.*

Notwithstanding this Asseveration, they persisted in their Opinion, as I found afterwards; but thinking I was resolved to be *Incognito*, and that they shou'd offend me by endeavouring to pry more into my Secrets than I was willing, they seem'd to believe me, ask'd my Pardon, and took their Leave. What contributed to lead them into this Error and to confirm them therein, as they own'd afterwards was, that the *Pretender* had at that Time left *Avignon*, and it was not known whither he was gone; that it was expected he wou'd embark at *Calais* or *Dunkirk* for *Scotland*, where they were then in actual Rebellion in his Favour, and that I was much about the same Size, wore a black Wig, and resembled him as they all assured me, to a very great Degree: The Truth of it is, I have seen a Picture drawn for him that was more like me, than one I had drawn on purpose for me.

Be that as it will, their Mistake did me no Prejudice, but, on the contrary, was of great Service, in making me pass my Time,
during

during my Stay there, with all the Pleasure imaginable; for the next Morning, when I was ready to go out, having order'd my Servant to hire me a Coach for the Day, and he going to enquire of the People of the Inn for that purpose, return'd immediately with Answer, that I need not be at that Trouble, for there was a Coach below waiting for me, with Servants to attend me. Surpriz'd at the Novelty, I sent to ask whose Coach and Servants it was, and by whose Order they came: Word being immediately brought me, it was the Governour's, I wou'd have declin'd accepting it, but that the Obligation wou'd have been still the same, wherefore I got into it, and the first Use I made thereof was to go to him, and return him Thanks for his extraordinary Civility, so much beyond my Deserts, Quality, or Expectation. The Governour smil'd, and told me, there needed no Compliments on that Score, since he had so great a Veneration for the *King* of *England*, (meaning the *Pretender*, whom he call'd so,) that he honour'd his Resemblance wherever he found it, which was the Reason of his sending his Equipage to attend me; having been inform'd, and he must confess he was of the same Opinion, that it was impossible any Likeness shou'd be more perfect. This wou'd have been a very well turn'd Compliment, had he not been deceiv'd in me as well as the others; for being pre-
possessed

possessed by what they had told him, he really thought he found the same Resemblance in me, and actually believ'd me the *Pretender*: Nor was either He, or the Officers convinced of the contrary, as they all own'd, till about a Week afterwards, when they heard that he was in *Scotland*.

It was whisper'd then all over the Town, that the *Pretender* was there *Incognito*, which produced this Effect, that every one strove who shou'd first have the Honour of Entertaining me, and every Day some fresh Party of Pleasure was started to divert me. In short, I cou'd never be alone, but was invited daily to Balls, Consorts, and magnificent Entertainments; wherein none signaliz'd themselves more, then those Ingenious Gentlemen the *Jesuits*, who not only treated me very sumptuously in their College, which is very rich and beautiful, but diverted me very agreeably with a Mask, which their Scholars got up in four Days, and acted to Admiration.

Nothing disgusted me, but that I had too many Eyes upon me, and cou'd never be left to my self; for had it been otherwise, I believe on my Conscience, in the Height of their Civilities, I might have commanded any Favour from the most reserv'd Lady there, and she wou'd have gloried in the Conquest.

Nor did their Civilities cease, even after they found their Mistake; the Governour's Coach

Coach still attended me during three Days longer that I staid there, and my Levee was every Morning crowded with Persons of the best Fashion in that City, who came to take me out to some new Diversion. In Return for all this Respect and Civility therefore, I thought I cou'd do no less, than invite them all in general to a handsome Entertainment, which I made for that purpose; and which was closed by a Ball, that lasted till Morning, and at which there was a more numerous and splendid Assembly, than I shall ever see again at any Entertainment of my making: In short, every one went away very well pleased, and with a better opinion of *English* Politeness then they had ever before entertain'd.

The Company being all gone, I took a few Hours Repose, which done, I spent the Remainder of the Day in taking Leave of those who had laid so many Obligations upon me; and especially the Governour, to whom it was not in my Power to make a suitable Acknowledgment. I wou'd fain have presented him with my own Watch which was *Tompion*'s, *English* Watches being very much esteemed Abroad, but cou'd not prevail with him to accept thereof, on any other Terms, than receiving his own in Exchange, which was as good, because he was sensible I had not another by me. What confounded me more then all the Rest, was that I cou'd not persuade any of his Servants to take one Farthing of me, by any Means whatever, he having strictly

strictly enjoin'd them to the contrary, on pain of losing their Places.

The next Morning I return'd to *Calais*, where my Baggage and Servants were by this Time arrived; whereupon I set out in a few Days for *Paris*, resolving to see that famous City before my Return to *England*, tho' I was inform'd by a Letter from my Father, that my Antagonist was pretty well recover'd of his Wound, and was past all Danger, so that I might come Home when I pleased.

So many Accounts have been already publish'd of *Paris*, *Versailles*, *Fontainbleau*, and *Marly*, that I shall say nothing upon that Head, tho' every one who goes there may see fresh Wonders, of which others have taken no Notice: Besides, it wou'd be quite foreign to my purpose, which is only to mention my own Adventures.

I had not been long at *Paris* before I receiv'd News of my Uncle's dying, and leaving me a considerable Fortune, most part in ready Money, which enabled me to set up a splendid Equipage, and take my full swing of Pleasure in that City. As much a Rake as I was however, I had Generosity enough to be concern'd at his Loss, he having always been particularly indulgent to me; but as a fat Sorrow is best, it wore off pretty soon, and I became, by Degrees, a most faithful and zealous Worshipper, at the Altars of the God of Wine, and the Goddess of Beauty.

In

In the Course of these my Devotions, or to speak more intelligibly, in the Pursuit of these Pleasures, I fell into several ugly Scrapes, during my Stay at *Paris*, from which my Purse alone cou'd not always extricate me, but my Person sometimes came off by the Lee, and I smarted in the Flesh for them more ways then one. This did not deter me, however, from going on still at the same Rate, not considering that neither my Body was Iron, nor my Purse inexhaustible, but of this more hereafter, in its due Place.

As I was now Master of a much better Income than ever I had been before, my Views began to be more exalted; and instead of deluding innocent Virgins, or contenting my self with Women of the Town, as I had done hitherto, I look'd out for an experienced Mistress, of some Rank and Quality, in the Conquest of whom I might acquire some Reputation: For I was so true an *Englishman*, that I bore all the *French* a Grudge, and long'd to arm some of them with good Brow-Antlers.

The first I pitch'd upon for this End, was the Wife to a Counsellor of the Parliament of *Paris*; a Lady of incomparable Beauty, whose Sparkling Eyes, which she well knew how to manage, would have tempted a Hermet and put Life and Vigour into fourscore. This inchanted *Syren*, with whom I became acquainted for my Sins, at an Assembly sung

I ad-

admirably, danced to Perfection, and had Wit at will; in short, she was the most agreeable Companion that a Man could possibly wish to spend an Hour with. But with all these Accomplishments, she had a most Mercenary Soul, was by Nature a Coquet, and a finish'd Jilt; in a Word she was able to have given even *Ovid* Lessons in the *Art of Love*, and would have beaten him at his own Weapons.

It is no Wonder then that this She Devil, such as I have describ'd her, led me a pretty Wild-Goose Chase, and in some Measure reveng'd the Injuries I had done her Sex: For after keeping me for some Time in suspence, and draining from me a considerable Sum in Presents, by way of Return for some little Liberties she was pleased to allow me to draw me on, she pretended at last to yield to my Desires, and fix'd a Night for the making me happy.

When the appointed Hour came, I went thither full of Expectations, and found a very handsome Supper prepared, at which she entertain'd me with all the Sprightliness and Good Humour imaginable; this done, she led me into her Bed-Chamber, and desired me to undress and get into Bed, and she would follow, and to make me believe she was in Earnest, did actually undress herself to her under Petticoat: But then putting out the Candle on pretence of Modesty, she conveys

into

into Bed in her ſtead, a common Whore, whom ſhe had planted in her Cloſet for that Purpoſe, and who in Return for all my Preſents, gave me one, which I did not claw off in a Hurry, and which for ſome Time made me abhor the Sight of the whole Sex.

THE END.

Juſt Publiſh'd.

The THEATRIC Squabble; or the PATTENTEES, a Satire.

Stiff Oppoſition, and *perplex'd* Debate,
And *Thorny* Care, and *Rank* and *Stinging* Hate!
While *Ate*, hot from Hell, makes Heroes ſhrink,
Cries *Havock*, and lets looſe the *Dogs of Ink.*
YOUNG'S UNIVERSAL PASSION.

NEW
PAMPHLETS
Just Publish'd,

'And Sold by the BOOKSELLERS in Town and Country.

THE *Scarborough* MISCELLANY; an original Collection of POEMS, Odes, Tales, Songs, Epigrams, *&c.* None of which ever appear'd in Print before. Particularly a Description of the beautiful Situation of that Town; its Diverfions, *&c.* With an Epifode on the Battle of the *Sugar Plumbs.* The Prieft and the Ferryman. Verfes by *Allan Ramfey.* The Miller but a Truftee. Mifs and the Butterfly: A Tale. A Dialogue on Love, by a Lady. The *Italian* Revenge, or the oblig'd Cuckold: a Tale. Verfes on a Snuff-Box, by a Country Parfon. *Quid pro quo,* or the Biter Bit. The Lover's Watch; a Song. The Friar's Advice. Verfes fpoken *extempore* in a Church Yard. Matrimony; a Tale. With other curious and entertaining Pieces, on a great Variety of Subjects. By feveral Hands. Pr. 1 *s.*

The

New PAMPHLETS.

THE MERRY-THOUGHT; or, the Glafs-Window and Bog-Houfe Mifcellany: Taken from the Original Manufcripts written in *Diamond* by Perfons of the Firft Rank and Figure in *Great-Britain*; relating to Love, Matrimony, Drunkennefs, Sobriety, Ranting, Scandal, Politicks, Gaming, and many other Subjects Serious and Comical. Faithfully tranfcribed from the Drinking-Glaffes, and Windows in the feveral noted Taverns, Inns, and other Publick Places in this Nation: Amongft which are inferted, many curious Pieces from both Univerfities.

Gameyorum, Wildum, Gorum,
Gameyorum, a Gamey,
Flumarum a Rumarum,
A Rigdum Bollarum
A Rigdum, for a little Gamey.

Bedlam-Wall, Morefields.

In *Four* Parts. The *Third* Edition. Price of each Part 6 d.

Round about our Coal Fire; or Chriftmas Entertainments: Chap. 1. and 2. Treating of Mirth and Jollity, Chriftmas Gambols, Eating, Drinking, Kiffing, &c. 3. Of Hobgoblins, Raw-Heads and Bloody-Bones, Tom Pokers, Bull-Beggars, and fuch like horrible Bodies 4. Of Witches, Wizards, and Conjurers, with many of their merry Pranks. 5. Of Spectres, Ghofts and Apparitions. 6. Of Fairies, their Ufe and Dignity. To which is added, a Receipt to make Devils and Witches: With a fuitable Prologue and Epilogue to the whole. Adorned with feveral diverting *Cuts*. Dedicated to the Worfhipful Mr. *Lun*, compleat Devil and Witch-maker of *England*, and Conjurer-General of the Univerfe. The Third Edit. Pr. 1 s.

A

New PAMPHLETS.

A PROPOSAL humbly offer'd to the P—L——NT for the more effectual preventing the farther Growth of *Popery*. With the Description and Use of the Ecclesiastical Thermometer. Very proper for Families. By Dr. *Sw-ft*. The *Second Edition*. To which is added, the Humble Petition of the Weavers and Venders of Gold and Silver Lace, Embroiderers, *&c*. As also two POEMS, *viz*. *Helter Skelter*, or the Hue-and-Cry after the ATTORNEYS upon their riding the Circuit, and the Place of the *Damn'd*. *Dublin*, Printed; *London*, Reprinted. Price 6 d.

A View of the TOWN, or Memoirs of LONDON; containing a diverting Account of the Humours, Follies, Vices, *&c*. of that Famous Metropolis; wherein every Offence meets with its due Correction, Fools are scourged, Knaves jirk'd, and the Ladies have a *Stroke* by the Bye: In fine, not to pall your Appetite by a tedious Repetition of Particulars, here is in short as much *Sing Song* as in the *Beggar's Opera*; and more new Whims than in the *Orator's* Advertisements.

My Book a Salesman's Shop you'll find,
 Where civilly I'll treat ye;
To a Fool's Coat of any kind
 You're welcome if it fit ye.

The *Second* Edition. Price 1 s.

The Secret History of Mama Oello, Princess Royal of Peru

Anonymous

Bibliographical note:

This facsimile has been made from a copy in the British Museum (1418.d.40)

THE SECRET HISTORY OF MAMA OELLO, PRINCESS ROYAL OF *England* PERU.

A New Court Novel.

I. The *Inca*'s Proposal to his Daughter of marrying her to *Atabalipa*, Prince of *Quito*.
II. Her Aversion to the intended Match.
III. The *Curaca Robilda* endeavours to reconcile her to it by Promises of a large Dowry out of the publick Revenues.
IV. The Princess's Reflections upon it. In which is contain'd the Character of *Atabalipa*, Prince of *Quito*.

LONDON:

Printed for J. DENT, near *Exeter-Exchange*, in the Strand. 1733. [Price One Shilling.]

a Key

Cusco — Peru	London —	Great Britain
Mama Oello	Ann. eldest daur. of K. Geo. II Commonly called "Princess Royal" born 1709, married 1733, died 1759
Manco Capac	K. Geo. II
Coya Mama	Caroline of Brandenburg Anspach 2. Consort of K. Geo. II.
Cacique Loque Yupanki	Jno. Ld. Carmichael afterwd. E. of Hyndford.
Huxin Capossa	Hanover
Curaca Robilda	Sir Robt. Walpole
Atabalipa P. of Quito	Wm. Chas. Friso, P. of Orange born 1711. died 1751. on the 8th May 1733 – the King signified to the Parliamt. that the Contract of Marriage was forbidden
river Apurimac	river Tweed
Posinki	?
projecting a scheme	the Excise on Tobacco
Quito	Holland
Prince of Quito	Stadholder of Holland
a Revende & Palace	in July 1727 a Bill was passed for settling £100,000 p. ann. jointly with Somerset house & Richmond old Park – on the Q. for life – in case she shall survive the K.
Contracted	on the 8 Octr. 1733 – the King sig the Contract of Marriage bet. the P. of Orange and the Princess Royal
arrived	the P. did not arrive in England until the 7th Novr. following
	Hampton Court
Capac	
Convention of the States	on the 14 March 1733. the Hou. of Commons went into a grand Committee on the Excise Scheme and a Bill was ordered in – which was afterwards postponed for two months
burned in Effigy	on the 11 April – among other rejoicings Sir R. W. was burned in effigy at Temple bar
America	Europe
Araucans	Spaniards
Yaya Napa	?
Marks of Honour	on the 15th July 1733 the P. of Or. was invested with the order of the Garter at the Hague
Sinche – E. of Chesterfield	Cobinqui Ld. Cobham
space of a Moon – the P. of O. arrived on the 7 Nov. :–

To the Right Honourable the
Lady HUMBLE.

May it please Your Ladyship,

THE Translator presents You with the *Secret History of* MAMA OELLO, Princess Royal of *Peru*; but I am afraid, deviates very much from the common Road of *Dedication*; when, instead of writing a fulsome Panegyrick upon Your Ladyship, (whose superior Merits would look down with Scorn on Flattery, and whose Virtues render You sufficiently conspicuous to the World without the Assistance of an Advocate to sound them) he lays before You the Advantage You may gather from the Perusal of it.

The Design of all History in general is to improve Mankind, to stir up a laudable Emulation in us to imitate the good Actions of our Ancestors, and to detest and avoid the bad.

A 2   This

DEDICATION.

This, that I humbly presume to lay at Your Ladyship's Feet, is a Novel form'd from true History found some time ago by the Vice Roy, amongst the Royal Commentaries of *Peru,* and wrote originally by the *Inca Garzilasco de la Vega,* Author of those Commentaries, whose Father was of a noble *Spanish* Family; and in Reality descended by his Mother's Side from the *Incas* or Kings of *Peru.* In which is contain'd Variety of pleasing Amusement. Hence Your Ladyship may learn to prize the Liberty that the *British* Ladies boast of in chusing their own Husbands, and bewail the Misfortune of the fair *Mama Oello,* with the secret Satisfaction to find Yourself free from that Compulsion. The *Curaca Robilda*'s Character will inform You that there were Evil Ministers even amongst the simple *Indians*; and the *Curacas Posinki, Sinchi* and *Cobinqui* point out the true Patriots of their Country. *Atabalipa* Prince of *Quito* will shew you that Marriage by Compulsion, or even Proxy, was altogether distasteful to the *Americans*; and the *Cacique Loque Tupanqui* will demonstrate the wonderful Effects of Love.

But I forbear mentioning any more Particulars to Your Ladyship, and only wish You may receive it with the same Intent as it was written, which was to give the World a Proof how much I am

Your Ladyship's most Devoted

And Humble Servant,

The TRANSLATOR.

The SECRET
HISTORY
OF
MAMA OELLO.

IN the imperial City of *Cusco* lived the charming *Mama Oello*, eldest Daughter of *Inca Manco Capac*, by his Queen *Coya Mama*, a young Princess of admirable Accomplishments, who possess'd a large Share of the Beauties of the Mind, as well as those of the Body, and fortunate in every but Love. How happy was the fair *Mama Oello*, till enslav'd by this inveighling Passion? How did it imbitter her Days, and make her Life become a Burden to her? Not that this lovely Princess had any Reason to complain of the Indifference of her beloved

beloved *Cacique* (for a *Cacique* he was, and one of the noblest Extraction amongst those that adorn'd *Inca Manco Capac*'s Court, that had got the Ascendant over this Lady's Heart) he glow'd with a mutual Passion, and fell a grateful Victim to her Charms: But another Obstacle, and that unsurmountable, nipt her growing Hopes in the Bud, and made her for ever despair of enjoying her Heart's desire.

There had been a Law enacted by the Emperor and the States of *Peru*, that no Princess, of the Blood Royal of the *Inca's*, should be suffer'd to marry a *Peruvian* Subject, or any foreign Prince that was an Idolator, but only one of the reform'd Religion, who worshipped the invisible *Pacha-Camæ*, and their Father the Sun. How could the charming *Mama Oello* relish this severe Restriction, which not only hinders her from being match'd to her dearest *Cacique*, but to any one else that she might like, provided he was not of the prescrib'd Sect? She consults with herself, and contrives, but all in vain; what Method can there be left to get over such apparent Difficulties, as she is oblig'd to encounter with? Distracted with ten thousand Fears she sends for her dearest *Cacique*, to see if between them both any Expedient might be found to accomplish her Wishes, but if it is all in vain, as she has but too great Reason to suspect, yet it will be some mitigation

tigation to her Pain (and that no small one) to sooth her Cares in his engaging Company. To this Purpose she dispatches away her trusty Confidant to acquaint the *Cacique* she had something to communicate to him on which her Happiness and his did depend.

This noble Personage (who constantly attended her Royal Father's Court, as being one of his *Dica Vidida*, that is of those Nobles who belong'd to his Bed-Chamber) receiv'd the trusty Messenger, and with an ominous Concern, first kiss'd, and then unloosed the beloved Seal, which soon discover'd the Uneasiness that his dearest Princess labour'd under. He answers the Fair one's Billet with all the Tenderness he was Master of, and express'd his Design of waiting on her that Evening.

Hardly was this Affair transacted, and the Confidant gone, but one of the *Inca*'s *Curacas* or Counsellors comes to the disconsolate *Cacique* with a Message from his Sovereign, which informs him, that the *Inca* had no farther Occasion for his Service and therefore dismissed him, having received private Intelligence that this *Cacique* was a greater Favourite of his eldest Daugher, the Princess *Mama Oello*, than ever he had been of his Royal Master, and thereupon forbid him the Court. The before dejected *Cacique*, now thunderftruck at thefe Words, ftood for fome time fenfelefs and confounded, not fo much on the Account of his lofing his Penfion (which was very confiderable) but leaft it fhould debar him the Converfation of his dearelt Princefs; but recovering himfelf out of his Infenfibility, return'd the *Curaca* this Anfwer; That it had been his higheft Ambition to ferve the *Inca* with the fincereft Loyalty and Affection, whilft his Majefty had been pleas'd to honour him with his Royal Favours, but fince it feemed good to his Sacred Highnefs to withdraw them, he patiently fubmitted to his Sovereign's Will and Pleafure.

The *Curaca* being gone, the enamour'd *Cacique* had time to ruminate on his prefent Circumftances; And can there (fays he) be fo great a Crime in Love? If Nature has formed me of *Porcellain* Clay (as our Poets term it) of a finer Mould than the Majority of my Fellow-Creatures, how am I to blame? If Fortune has deftin'd me to charm thefe Eyes, which charm the World befides, how is it my Fault? 'Tis decreed, 'tis decreed that I fhould captivate the fair *Mama Oello*, and who can refift Fate? But, alas! rigid Laws, and Reafons of State forbid the Accomplifhment of our Defires, as her Letter too plainly intimates; why thought we not of this when firft we embark'd in the Affair? We launch'd out

in

in the midſt of Sun-ſhine, on a ſmooth Sea, but now too late perceive the gathering Clouds portend the impending Storm, yet my deareſt Princeſs will I hazard all to ſee you once more, to take a long and laſt Adieu, to waſh thy Cheeks with Tears, to bid farewel to Pleaſure, Courts and Love. Then rouſing himſelf out of this melancholy Soliloquy, he bends his Steps towards the well-known Apartment of his deareſt Princeſs; where gaining a ready Admittance, (for as yet the Princeſs had not been forbid the Sight of him) he finds his Fair one bath'd in Tears, but yet charming in Grief. Such a Sight as this ſoon diſheartned the already dejected *Cacique* who perceived by her extraordinary Concern that ſomething more (than ſhe had in her Letter expreſs'd, or he underſtood) diſtracted her Mind. Then ſeizing her fair Hand, and throwing himſelf at her Feet; Tell me, my deareſt Princeſs, ſays he, tell me what other killing News you have to impart worſe than your Billet hinted, for I perceive by your exceſſive Grief, and that Deluge of Tears you pour forth, that you have conceived ſome extraordinary Trouble, which labours within your Breaſt? Ariſe (ſays the fair diſconſolate *Mama Oello*) ariſe, my deareſt *Cacique*, and I will impart to you the Torments of my Soul. When I ſent (proceeds ſhe, deſiring him to ſit) the truſty——to you this Morning, that Letter

con

contain'd the Sum of my Affliction; and was not that Affliction enough to think I muſt loſe you; for ever loſe you, becauſe the Laws of *Peru* forbid? But I was in hopes that I ſhould have greatly alleviated my Trouble by your good Company, if a freſh Cauſe of Grief had not demanded freſh Sorrow. O ye Gods! was it not enough for ye to debar me from the Enjoyment of my deareſt *Cacique,* but muſt ye deſtine me to the Arms of one I hate: Why was I born of Royal Race? Why not rather a ſimple Shepherdeſs, then ſhould I have been happy in the Embraces of my deareſt *Cacique.* Hateful *Peru*! what are your Laws to me? Happier had I been if my Royal Father had never ſway'd this Scepter, nor my illuſtrious Anceſtors left the Province of *Hurin Capaſſa,* their ancient Patrimony for theſe extenſive Dominions, whereby my Sorrows are extended. Then ſhould I have never ſeen my charming *Loque Tupanqui,* or not have ſeen him in vain. I have been rais'd higher only to be reduc'd the lower, and enjoy a miſerable Greatneſs.

Wonder not, my deareſt *Cacique* (ſays the charming Princeſs, purſuing her Diſ-courſe) at what I am going to tell you, for ſince I wrote to you, the *Inca,* my Father, and his chief *Curaca Robilda* have paid me a Viſit, to inform me, That (for what they call Reaſons of State) I muſt ſurrender up my Hand and Heart (which laſt I never

can

can to any but you) to *Atabalipa*, Prince of *Quito*; and to encourage you, says the *Inca*, my Father, chearfully to obey my Commands, I will make you a Present of Jewels of inestimable Value, which I design'd to dedicate to our Father the *Sun*: And I, says the old *Curaca Robilda*, will engage at the next Convention of the *Curacus* and *Caciques* of this glorious Empire you receive an ample Annuity out of the publick Revenues, to render you more acceptable to Prince *Atabalipa*.

Thus you see, my much beloved *Cacique*, says the Princess, giving him her Hand, I must not only be depriv'd of you, the sole Comfort I ever propos'd the Enjoyment of in this World, but be oblig'd to waste a wretched Life in a foreign Country, and another's Arms. And I (reply'd the gallant *Loque Tupanqui*, interrupting his dearest Princess at these last Words) have a fresh Scene of Woe to discover to you. I thank you, says he, O Invisible *Pacha-Camac*, and our Father the *Sun*! that you have made me compleatly wretched; now Fortune do your Worst —— Then after some Pause, recollecting himself he imparted to the weeping Fair, the sorrowful Message he had receiv'd from her Royal Father, the *Inca*, by the Mouth of one of his chief *Curacas*, which enjoin'd him to leave the Court, and return into his own Province Northward, beyond

the

the great River *Apurimac*. That he had great Reason to suspect the *Curaca Robilda* was at the Bottom of it all, as well the Author of his Banishment, as the Projector of her Marriage with Prince *Atabalipa*; that if she could procure this Favourite to be discarded, they might (if not obtain the Accomplishment of their Desires) get some further Respite to their Misfortunes: He likewise inform'd her, that almost all the *Curacas* and *Caciques* of the *Peruvian* Empire hated this *Curaca Robilda*, that the Voice of the whole Nation, and of the Imperial City of *Cusco* was against him, on Account of his perswading her Royal Grandfather and Father to impose heavy Taxes on their Subjects in time of Peace; that even in a publick Convention of the *Curacas* and *Caciques* some of them had not spar'd him, and that altho', by his immense Treasures, he had secur'd the Majority of them to his Interest, yet he did not Fear, but the brave uncorrupted few that were left behind, would soon open the Eyes of those that were dazzl'd with the Splendor of his yellow Mettle. You know, says he my dearest *Mama Oello*, that the *Curaca Posinki* has always attack'd him, and I doubt not but will Second us (as far as lies in his Power) in procuring the Fall of his Enemy and ours. Besides, I know the *Curaca Robilda* is now projecting a Scheme (which I believe

must

must prove fatal to him) since the Convention of States, now assembled, have been petition'd against it by the Provinces of *Caranca Ullaca, Lipi, Chicha, Ampara*, and most of the rest. You know, moreover, adds the disconsolate *Cacique*, that the *Curaca Robilda* is but an Upstart, not one of them, or of their Family, who join'd with your illustrious Ancestors, the first *Incas*, in civilizing these Nations; in diverting them from their superstitious Idolatries; from Adoration of Tygers, Lakes, Rivers, and Serpents, to the true Worship of the Invisible *Pacha Camac*, and our Father the Sun; that altho' it is strongly reported, and by some believ'd, that the illustrious *Inca*, who immediately preceeded your Royal Father, distinguish'd him by some Marks of Honour for his good Services towards him, yet the *Curaca* has never been pleas'd to own his Titles, or to have his Ears bor'd to hang Jewels in, or to cover his Head with a black Tress.——That he, for his Part, had given her the most sensible Proof of his Esteem, since now, even this Moment while he is speaking to her, he hazards his Life, if he is betray'd or discover'd——The fair Princess was going to answer, but both recollecting they had over stay'd their Time, were oblig'd, tho' with the utmost Reluctance, to part. remember, dearest *Cacique*, says the languishing Princess, Remember your *Ma-*

ma Oello, when you get beyond the great River *Apurimac*, and I will let you know by a trusty Messenger, when the Storm is a little blown over, how we may meet again; and as to Prince *Atabalipa*, you know my Heart. Can you be ever absent to your *Loque Tupanqui*, says the enamour'd *Cacique*? No; were I ten thousand Leagues from you, beyond the snowy Mountains of *Challampa*, yet would you be always present to me: Adieu, fairest *Mama Oella*! Charming Princess, Adieu! and sometimes bestow a Thought on your constant *Loque Tupanqui*.

Thus parted these two Lovers; the *Cacique* retir'd to order his Matters so that he might leave the Court and Imperial City of *Cusco* the next Day, which he accordingly did, and departed towards his own Province Northward, beyond the great River *Apurimac*, according to the *Inca*'s Mandate; the Princess to her Place of Rest: but, alas! none of that was to be found; for ten thousand Thoughts distract her divided Mind. The Absence of her belov'd *Loque Tupanqui*, the Thoughts of her losing him for ever are not her only Affliction; a far greater Trouble wrecks her Spirit; there was Hopes of her *Cacique*'s returning, and that Time, which effects every thing, might cool her Father's Passion, and then the Legislature of *Peru* forbid their Marriage,

age, yet she might be happy in the Sight of her dear *Cacique*, and sometimes in his Company. But how could she accomplish this, if she must be wedded to Prince *Atabalipa*, as her Father and the *Curaca* told her in positive Terms she must? She farther pursues her Reflections, and vents her Grief in this melancholy Soliloquy.

Atabalipa *may be a deserving Prince as far as I know, but not comparable to my beloved* Cacique; *but if all be as Fame says, the Beauties of his Mind far exceed those of his Body. I might have been happy in his Arms, had I not before given my Heart to the charming* Cacique: *They tell me moreover, that if Birth, Titles, and Honour had not distinguish'd* Atabalipa, *that Nature had. But stay, thoughtless Princess, 'tis ungenerous to censure natural Defects, which in a great Measure proceed only from the Almighty. Aid me then, all-powerful Love, 'tis in your Cause I engage, to find Fault with the Object that must undeservedly be my Aversion; did all the Wisdom of the past and present Age center in* Atabalipa, *yet should I be insensible of all his persuasive Eloquence, since my* Cacique's *Rhetorick must and does surpass it all.* Prince Atabalipa *may be fam'd for his Parts, which to me seems something strange, since those that instruct my Brothers in the Manners and Customs of the different Nations who inhabit the*

known

known World, and in what they call *Geography*, *informs us*; that the Province of Quito is a low, barren Soil, productive of nothing but Pasturage for Butter and Cheese; the Inhabitants not fam'd for Arts and Sciences, or any thing else but an over-reaching Method in Trade and Commerce; that they were esteem'd a few Centuries ago but a poor and beggarly People, and that they are indebted for their present Grandeur to one or more of our Royal Ancestors. They tell me for Encouragement, that Atabalipa is Prince of Quito; but then I hear from other Hands, that Part of his Principality is still in Dispute, that some of it is diminished; and if he was in real Possession of the whole, yet many of our Bobinquos, or private Gentlemen, in this mighty Empire of Peru, enjoy a larger Estate than all his Dominions put together: Why then must I, who am Princess Royal of the mighty Empire of Peru, leave my Country and Friends to be only Co-partner in the poor Principality of Quito? Did I love indeed Prince Atabalipa, as I do my dearest Cacique, a Cottage with him would be a Palace, but to exchange better for worse, to be confin'd to a Prince I can never like so well as Loque Yupanqui, must be very disagreeable. My Royal Mother, moreover, offers me her Maiden-Plate and Jewels (which to be sure must be of considerable Value) but what is Plate or Jewels to me, or any Thing else, without the Man I love?

Thus

Thus the fair Princess employ'd Part of the remaining Night, till gentle Slumbers at last clos'd her Eyes; but too soon she awakes again to Trouble and perplexing Thoughts; however she endeavours to stifle them as much as possible, and puts on her wonted Gaity: All her Thoughts now turn which Way she may divert the intended Match, and and re-establish her dearest *Cacique* in her Father's Favour. But in this consisted the Difficulty; the Advice of her dear *Loque Yupanqui*, was to attempt the Favourite *Curaca Robilda*'s Fall, which to her seemed impracticable: the Hints which she had received from her Lover gave her some glimmering Hope that it might be effected, but which way to attempt it she was at a Loss; she hated the *Curaca Robilda*, as the Author of her intended Nuptials to Prince *Atabalipa*, but yet believ'd him to be firmly attached to her, and her Family's Interest, even to the Prejudice of his own Country, as she had often observed. Moreover, she knew her Royal Father and Mother to be so wrapt up in him, that his Counsels were always followed, tho' he often abus'd his Trust, and shelter'd himself under the Royal Wing, when he had transacted any Thing base or offensive. That likewise her Royal Mother Queen *Coya Mama* had been particularly oblig'd to the *Curaca Robilda* in many things especially

especially for an ample Revenue, and a spacious Palace in the imperial City of *Cusco*, which he procured for her as a Royal Maintenance after the Decease of her dearly beloved *Inca*, and chiefly by his own Interest; a Maintenance which far surpassed any that the Dowager Empresses of *Peru* had ever possessed; she thought it therefore in vain to attempt a Matter clog'd with so many Difficulties, and chose rather prudently to leave it to Time and Providence (which accomplish every Thing) to extricate her out of these Troubles; and as she was not without Hopes that the Scheme which the famous *Curaca Robilda* was to bring on the Carpet, at the next Convention of the *Curacas* and *Caciques* of the *Peruvian* Empire, might prove his Ruin, she was resolved to wait patiently till a favourable Opportunity offer'd itself. Whereupon she put on all the outward Unconcern she was Mistress of, and seem'd to be entirely resign'd to her Royal Father's Will and Pleasure. Her Marriage with Prince *Atabalipa* was publickly declar'd at the imperial City of *Cusco*, and all over the *Peruvian* Empire, and likewise in the Principality of *Quito*, and in the Seven Provinces of *Havilca, Tuna, Chuncuri, Pucana, Muyuncuyu, Charcas,* and *Collasuyu* thereunto joining. Both received the Compliments of their *Curacas* and *Caciques*, on their intended Marriage,

as

as well as of the foreign Ambassadors; and now Prince *Atabalipa* is daily expected from *Quito*, at the imperial City of *Cusco*, to espouse his charming Princess.

Whilst these Affairs were transacting at the imperial City of *Cusco*, the charming Princess was not unmindful of her dearest *Cacique*, and although she seem'd to pay an implicit Obedience outwardly to her Father's Commands, yet in secret did she earnestly wait for the happy Minute that might restore the lovely *Loque Tupanqui* to her Father's Favour, and her longing Eyes, which some time after offer'd itself; for the Inca looking upon the Marriage of the Princess *Mama Oello* with *Atabalipa*, Prince of *Quito*, as good as consummated, gave the banish'd *Cacique* Leave to return to the City of *Cusco*, and restor'd him seemingly to his Favour, tho' not to his former Places of Honour.

As soon as the Rumour was noised abroad that the noble *Cacique Loque Tupanqui* had Leave to return from his Northern Retirement, beyond the great River *Apurimac*, the overjoy'd Princess was resolv'd he should receive the first News of it from her, and therefore dispatch'd away a trusty Messenger to inform her beloved *Cacique*, that his Doom was revers'd, and how Matters stood (for Prince *Atabalipa* was not yet arrived at the imperial City of *Cusco*, from

his

Principality of *Quito*, altho' he had been for some time contracted to the Princefs, and daily expected, proving, it feems but a flugifh Lover) that the was to move in a little Time to the Palace of *Capuac*, in the Province of *Capuany*, and therefore fhe advis'd him not to come to the imperial City of *Cufco*, but wait her Arrival at *Capuac* : The Meffenger was likewife order'd to deliver the *Cacique* the following Letter, which we fhall infert in this Tranflation, for the Satisfaction of the fair Part of our Readers, and to give a Specimen of the *American* Gallantry in thofe Times.

The Princefs Mama Oello, *Daughter of the* Inca Manco Capac, *and Queen* Coya Mama, *Son and Daughter of* Inca Huafcar (*for the* Incas *of* Peru *commonly married their Sifters*) *of* Huana Capac, *of* Tupac Yupanqui, *of* Inca Palhacutec, *of* Inca Virachocha, *of* Vahuar Huacac, *of* Inca Roca, *of* Capac Yupanqui, *of* Mayta Capac, *of* Sinchi Roca *Child of the Sun*. (*See how fond the* Indians *are of tracing their Genealogy*).

To the Noble Cacique Loque Yupanqui, *sendeth Greeting*.

Moft Illuftrious CACIQUE,

'TIS *with no fmall Satisfaction I acquaint the* Cacique Loque Yupanqui, *he may with Impunity*

(17)

punity repass the great River Apurimac, *and without Danger revisit the Princess* Mama Oello: *Had I been less condescending to my Father's Commands, I had been the longer depriv'd of this happy Opportunity. You shall know what has been transacted in your Absence, when you come to the Palace of* Capuac, *according to the Bearer's Instructions Believe me, noble* Cacique, *I am as highly pleas'd at this good-natur'd Action of my Royal Father, as it i proper for the Princess of* Peru *to declare ; I don't doubt but your own Prudence will so time our next Meeting, that it shall receive no Interruption till that happy Minute arrives.*

I remain Yours,
MAMA OELLO.

Soon was the belov'd *Cacique* inform'd (in his Retirement, where he had now been for some time, diverting the melancholly Hours one while with the Thoughts of his dearest Princess, and at other times with Books and rural Sports) that a Messenger was arriv'd, in Post-haste from the imperial City of *Cusco*, at his Palace Gate: He steps with eager Strides to learn the Reasons of his Journey. But how agreeably was he surpris'd, when, to his great Joy, he found it to be the trusty *Sinchal?* What News, says he, faithful *Sinchal?* What News dost thou bring to me from my Princess; and the imperial City of *Cusco?* Does she live? Is she well, or is she for ever lost in the Arms of *Atabalipa*, Prince of *Quito?* Most illustrious

D

lustrious *Cacique*, replies *Sinchal*, my Royal Mistress lives, and is well, is not yet in the Arms of Prince *Atabalipa*, but how soon she may I know not: But if you will give me Leave to enter your Palace, I will tell you more of the Matter. Dismount, honest *Sinchal*, says the impatient *Cacique* (ordering his Servant to take his Horse) for I long to be inform'd of all that concerns my charming *Mama Oello*, as well as the State of the Court, and of the imperial City of *Cusco*. The trusty Confidant then deliver'd the Letter. Go you, says the enamour'd *Cacique*, and refresh yourself with such a Collation as my House affords, and in the mean time I will retire till that is over, and then will send for you into my Closet. Having so said, he bid one of his Domesticks entertain the Messenger with the best he could procure, and himself hasted away to peruse the welcome Epistle.

And does my Princess, says the transported *Cacique*, condescend to acquaint her Slave that his Doom is revers'd? How prudently must she have acted, so soon to have wip'd off all Suspicion that she had ever cast a favourable Eye on her undeserving *Leque Yupanqni*? but she mentions nothing in her Letter of Prince *Atabalipa*, or the *Curaca Robilda*'s Disgrace; 'tis in vain for me to hope for any Success, whilst that *Curaca* continues in my Royal Master's Favour! he was, and always will be an Enemy to true Merit.

Merit. But I will call for *Sinchal*, and inform myself from him of what has past since my Retirement; he us'd to be conversant in Court Affairs, and is a likely Person to acquaint me what Things of Moment have been transacted at the last Convention of the *Curacas* and *Caciques* of this glorious Empire, during my Absence; then shall I be better able to judge how I must behave in this critical Juncture, and to accomplish my Desires in seeing the Prince's *Mama Oello* at the Palace of *Capuac*.

He rings the Bell, and commands his Servant in waiting to convey the trusty *Sinchal* to him. We'l, says he, faithful Servant, now you have refresh'd yourself, let me hear a little of the present State of the *Peruvian* Empire; what Affairs of Importance have the Convention of the *Curacas* and *Caciques* been busied about, since I left the Imperial City of *Cusco*, the usual Place of their Resort when any National Affairs requires their Attention.

I will answer your Demands, (replies the trusty *Sinchal*) as far as lies in my Power. Know then, that immediately after your Departure, the Scheme which the *Curaca Robilda* had been so long projecting was brought on the Carpet; a Scheme entirely distasteful to the whole Empire of *Peru*, as you yourself must know full well by the many Petitions handed up against it from all the Provinces of the *Peruvian* Empire.

Yet notwithstanding this the *Curaca Robilda* was resolv'd to carry his Point, to effect which he employ'd all his Emissaries to infuse Notions among the Vulgar how advantageous it would be to the Empire of *Peru*, if this Scheme was once to take Place.

In Answer to that, the mercantile Part of the Nation, and especially those of the Imperial City of *Cusco*, plainly shew'd it would be destructive and pernicious to all Trade in general, subjecting them to the Enquiry of every petty Officer; besides many other Inconveniences.

It was particularly oppos'd by a Set of Men amongst whom were several *Caciques* of Note, who had formerly been *Curacas* in chief to some of our *Incas* headed by the *Curaca Posinki*.

Robilda's Party stiled these Men Malecontents, and disaffected to the *Inca*'s Person and Government, because their Arguments were unanswerable; but those of the Imperial City of *Cusco*, and the Generality of the People of the *Peruvian* Empire distinguish them by the honourable Appellation of Patriots, being those who stand up for their Country's Good.

Indeed, if I may be allow'd to give my Opinion of what may be gather'd from

from the Writings of both Parties, these in Reality are as firmly attach'd to our *Inca*'s true Interest as those of the *Curaca Robilda*'s Clan.

Upon a Set-Day then the *Curaca Robilda* procured it to come before the Convention of States of the glorious Empire of *Peru*, and a Majority of Votes (after his usual Method) for its being brought in: but when it came to be canvassed whether it should pass or not, the Superiority inclin'd to the Patriots Side; whereupon one of our waggish Wits compares the *Curaca Robilda*'s mercenary *Bobinquos* to Men *drawn thro' a Horse-Pond befoul'd with Mire and Dirt, and all to no Purpose.*

But give me Leave, trusty *Sinchal*, how did the *Curaca Robilda* himself escape? Was he not entirely discarded the *Inca*'s Service for his wild and ill-tim'd Projects? 'Tis the Belief of many, (answers *Sinchal*) most illustrious *Cacique*, that he is more firmly rivetted than ever in my Royal Master's Favour; which to the wise and considering Part of Mankind seems somewhat surprizing. But the exasperated Populace dealt quite otherwise with him; as soon as the News spread that the *Curaca Robilda*'s Scheme had miscarry'd, the Imperial City of *Cusco* was immediately illuminated, Bonfires and Bells ringing expres'd the general Satisfaction of the Inhabitants: the *Curaca Robilda*

Robilda was hang'd, and burn'd *in Effigie* in feveral Parts of that great Town; and nothing prevented them from venting their Rage on his Perfon but the Refpect and Duty they ow'd to their Sovereign the *Inca*: the other chief Cities and Towns following the Example of *Cufco*, expref's'd their happy Deliverance from this pernicious Contrivance by wonderful Demonftrations of Joy, have moft of them in general return'd Thanks to their refpective *Bobinquos* for their brave and ftrenuous Oppofition of it.

Thus moft noble *Loque Tupanqui*, I have endeavour'd to comply with your Requeft, as far as my fhallow Memory will permit. You have indeed in Part, (anfwer'd the attentive *Cacique*) but I have ten thoufand Queftions more to ask you concerning my Princefs and *Atabalipa*, but will inform my felf from her own dear Mouth concerning that Affair, having already trefpaffed on your Patience after fo long a Fatigue.

I perceive you are tir'd, fays he, and want Reft. Good Night to you, honeft *Sinchal*; whatever you have Occafion of, call freely for it, and I will difpatch you away to-morrow on your Return homewards.

No fooner was *Sinchal* retir'd, but the *Cacique* mufes on what he had heard. I was in Hopes (fays he) to have receiv'd

the

the News of *Curaca Robilda*'s Fall; but if that did not accomplish it, sure nothing will. Unhappy *Peru!* how are you degenerated from what you were in good *Inca Virachocha*'s Time! What a glorious Empire was you then! How formidable your Armies! How terrible your Canoes! How upright your *Curacas* and *Caciques!* You might justly then be esteem'd to hold the Balance of *America*; but how often lately have you shamefully purchas'd a Peace with Money from those who formerly you compell'd to sue for one? Your Trading Canoes are now taken Captive by the sluggish *Araucans* without Recompence or Restitution; your *Curacas* consist only of *Robilda*'s Creatures, who consult nothing but to impoverish your People by insupportable Impositions: A Man that would now arrive at Preferment must commit something deserving the greatest Punishment.

But why do I employ my Time in such useless Reflections, unless I could reform all the Abuses which so flagrantly dishonour my beloved Country; rather let me shift the Scene, and turn my Thoughts to Love and my dearest Princess, I must to-morrow dispatch away the trusty *Sinchal*, and answer the Charming *Mama Oello*'s Letter. It will be better for me, I believe, not to return immediately to the Imperial City of
Cusco,

Cufco, but wait here till I receive News of the Court's Removal to the Palace of *Capuac*; then shall I find Means to see my Princess without Danger. It is now high Time for me to think of inditing her Letter, that it may be in Readiness to give to Sinchal to-morrow Morning; the Contents of it were as follows:

The Cacique Loque Yupanqui *to the Princess of* Peru, *Daughter*, &c.

Most High and Mighty Princess,

HOW happy must the Cacique Loque Yupanqui *be, since the charming* Mama Oello *expresses her Satisfaction at his Return, which, without her Approbation, would have been entirely useless to him: Yes, my dearest Princess, since you graciously permit, I will fly on the Wings of soft Desire, but shall take Care to pay an implicite Obedience to your Directions, both as to Time and Place. But how uneasy shall I be till that bright Day appears which shall give the lovely* Mama Oello *to the longing Eyes of her humble Adorer,*

LOQUE YUPANQUI.

Early the next Morning the happy *Cacique* deliver'd his Answer to *Sinchal* with Orders that he should hasten back as fast as possible to his Princess: he himself thought it advisable to stay behind till he shou'd hear of the Court's Removal to the Palace of *Capuac*, which he in a little time
was

was advertised of it by means of his fair *Mama Oello*.

Now he prepares with all Diligence for his Return to the glorious Empire of *Peru*, and *incog.* enters the Province of *Capuany*. He is inform'd by the Host where he stopt to refresh himself, that Prince *Atabalipa* was not yet come, that it was strongly rumour'd abroad, his intended Journey to *Peru* was entirely laid aside; that, nevertheless the Princess *Mama Oello* was to espouse him by Proxy, and so to be sent to the Province of *Quito*: That in order to which her Royal Highness had but few Days before made Choice of *Taya Napa*, a near Relation of the Noble *Cacique Loque Tupanqui*, (who was sometime ago forbid the Court) to accompany her to the Prince of *Quito*.

The *Cacique* thank'd his Landlord for his courteous Information, thinking it most advisable to send to his Sister *Taya Napa* first, that he might consult with her the proper Means of seeing his dearest Princess; he therefore dispatch'd away an hir'd Servant of his Host's to the Palace of *Capuac*, with a Letter to his Sister desiring her Company. The Messenger soon arriv'd at the Palace of *Capuac*, and deliver'd his Letter to the Lady *Taya Napa*, who immediately comply'd with her dearest Brother's Desires.

After a Meeting full of Brotherly Love and Affection, they began to consult about the main Affair, how the *Cacique* might safely see his Princess. I am acquainted with a *Bobinquo* who lives near this Place, (says the compassionate *Taja Napa*) in whose Gardens my Royal Mistress often diverts herself in an Evening: I have Interest enough with this *Bobinquo*, if you you like my Contrivance, to get you admitted into his House as his Gardener; and under that Disguise you may securely converse with the Princess *Mama Oello*.

I thank you, my dearest *Taja Napa* (says the passionate *Cacique*) for this lucky Thought, which will succeed, I hope, according to my Wishes: let us hasten then, and put our Designs in Execution; for I burn to throw myself at the Feet of the Charming *Mama Oello*. Accordingly the impatient *Cacique* discharged his Host, and was conducted by his Sister to the *Bobinquo*'s House, to whom she introduced her Brother, and unravell'd the whole Secret. The *Bobinquo* receiv'd the *Cacique* in a very kind Manner, and told him he was ready to serve him to the utmost Stretch of his Capacity, although he should thereby incur the *Inca*'s Displeasure.

The over-joy'd *Cacique* thank'd him for his great Civility, and accordingly put on his Gardener's Habit. In the mean Time

Yaya Napa haftens away to the Palace of *Capuac*, to acquaint her Royal Miftrefs of all that had pafs'd, as well of her deareft *Cacique*'s Arrival, as the Stratagem made Ufe of to procure an Interview between them.

In a lucky Hour, fays the fair Princefs (overjoy'd at this agreeable News) did I chufe you, charming *Yaya Napa*, from the midft of the bright Circle of Ladies that adorn this illuftrious Court; O dearer to me than Sifter, tho' I dare not make thee fo: They fhall never tare thee from this Breaft, tho' they do thy Noble Brother. You fhall always remain with me, the only Comfort I fhall have left to calm the Sea of Troubles that now haftens to overwhelm me: But To-morrow-Night I will fee my deareft *Cacique*, and till then endeavour to compofe myfelf. Accordingly fhe bids *Taya Napa* fend her Brother Intelligence that fhe would take an Airing in the *Bobinquo*'s Gardens the next Evening.

How reftlefs thefe impatient Lovers paffed that Night may be eafily guefs'd at; at laft the long defir'd Minute comes, when the Princefs enter'd the Garden, as ufual, difmiffing all her Attendants but the fair *Yaya Napa*, feating herfelf in a Cyprefs-Grove, there expecting her deareft *Cacique*. The tranfported Swain, in a Gardener's Drefs to prevent all Sufpicion, now trembling

E 2

bling draws near, and presents her with a curious Nosegay of Roses and Carnations. The fair *Mama Oello*, lost in Thought, lifts up her Eyes gently, and seeing her dearest *Cacique* so near, being overpower'd at the Sight, closes 'em again in a fainting Fit. The distracted *Cacique* could not forbear taking her in his Arms, altho' had he been overseen, it must have prov'd his utter Ruin; whilst the officious *Taya Napa*, who was the only Person present, hasten'd to the nearest Fountain for Water, and after a second or third sprinkling, the swooning Fair began to revive, and finding her self in the Arms of her beloved *Cacique*; *Oh! ye Gods!* says she, *what do I see! here let me die, and never enter the Palace of* Capuac *more: With what Pleasure could I end my Miseries and Life in these dear Arms! But, what have I let drop?* (somewhat recovering herself) *Expressions, I fear, too unguarded for the Princess of* Peru *to utter. And art thou not contented, most illustrious Cacique, to bring me all the Fragrance the World contains center'd in thyself, but must you give me also the selected Sweets,* (says she smelling to the Nosegay) *that this Garden affords?*

'Tis in Yourself, your own incomparable Self, (replies the transported *Loque Tupanqui* interrupting her) that not only the Sweets of this delicious Place but of the whole

whole Univerſe are compriz'd. Talk not of dying, my Princeſs, 'tis your unfortunate *Cacique* that muſt die: You ſhall live long, and be happy in the Embraces of *Atabalipa*, Prince of *Quito*, while the miſerable *Loque Tupanqui*, not able to endure that hateful Conſummation, will ſoon put an End to his wretched Life.

Why thoſe killing Words to me? (anſwers the fair *Mama Oelio*) why any Talk of *Atabalipa*? You know my Heart is as true to you as the Needle to the Pole; every Thing conſpires to compleat my Sorrows, and there is no Redreſs, nor any Hopes on which my ſhip-wreck'd Love may anchor: But till that fatal Day that will force me from this dear Retreat, and thoſe dearer Arms to the ungrateful *Atabalipa*'s, will I repeat this Evening's Delights, and after that bid a long Farewel to every Thing that's pleaſant.

I know you muſt be ever loſt to me, anſwer'd the amorous *Cacique*, and therefore have been long arming myſelf with all the Philoſophy I am Maſter of againſt that fatal Time; but in vain, I can never ſurvive it. I have heard, ſince my Arrival in this Province of *Capuany*, tho' you, my faireſt Princeſs, have been cautious in diſcovering the diſtaſteful News; that your Marriage with *Attabalipa* is irrevocable, and that an extravagant Character

racter of him has been induſtriouſly ſpread up and down this glorious Empire in the publick Prints: One tells us, Courtesy and Affability *are a Part of his Conſtitution.* But how is this conſiſtent, when you, my Princeſs, on whom, and only whom it ought to have been been beſtow'd, have been entirely inſenſible of it? Had I been Prince *Atabalipa,* had I been that happy *Cacique,* ſwift as Lightning would I have flown to have paid my Devoirs to you; no Compliments of the *Amanta's* or *Vimo's* ſhould have ſtopt me. His Complaiſance, his ingenious Advocate tells us, coſts his Highneſs no Pains; and I believe that indeed to be the only true Part of the Deſcription.

'Tis true, illuſtrious *Cacique,* anſwers the diſconſolate *Mama Oello,* what you ſay is too true; but alas! how can I help it? Who amongſt us all can reſiſt Fate? O inviſible Pachachamac, and our Father the Sun! How can you be ſaid to be juſt, when you are thus partial? How deplorable is my Condition? Under what an unfortunate Planet was I born? But yet, ſays ſhe, this preſent Moment will I enjoy, in Spite of you, O inviſible Pachachamac, or our Father the Sun.

Thus did this faithful Couple paſs the Hours away in ſoft Complaint and amorous Converſe, till the good-natur'd and beauti-

beautiful *Taya Napa* returning from a Walk of Orange-Trees, where she had retreated to favour the Lovers in their Converse, told 'em the Clock had struck One, and it was Time to part. They were oblig'd to submit to pressing Necessity, and after mutual Promises of seeing each other every Evening, whilst the Court remain'd at the Palace of *Capuac*, retir'd, the *Cacique* to his Bed, and the Princess to the Palace of *Capuac*; where musing on her past Evening's Conversation, and admiring the Composure of her beloved *Cacique*'s Present, she observ'd in the middle of it a Paper artfully wrought up: when unfolding it, she found the following Copy of Verses; which we insert, as they are found in the Original, only with this Alteration, that we have changed the *Indian* Names which are rough, and not sonorous in Verse, for some made Use of by the ancient Heathen Poets.

On a NOSEGAY presented to the Princess MAMA OELLO.

I.

FOR once, my Princess, learn to prize
    Thy Beauty by a Flower;
And think how both may charm the Sense,
    Yet neither live an Hour.

Think

II.

Think that Thyself art planted here,
    But to be pluck'd by Man;
And think how short is Beauty's Date;
    If Life is but a Span.

III.

Then MAMA, *seize the flying Bliss,*
    Nor foolishly rely
On Charms that for a Moment's Bloom;
    But ev'n in blooming die.

IV.

Such Roses wanton on thy Cheeks,
    And put such Beauties on;
This blushes with a stronger Red,
    To see itself outdone.

V.

While on thy Breasts the Lillies smile,
    They mourn in secret there,
To see those fragrant Rivals rise
    More soft, and sweet, and fair.

VI.

Think on their Doom, fair Nymph, to thine;
    Then be the Thought apply'd:
And the same Cause at once must raise,
    And mortify thy Pride.

Oh!

VII.

Oh! could thofe Flowers, that once were Boys,
 To know their Blifs attain;
How would they wifh to be transform'd
 From Flowers to Boys again.

VIII.

Had e'er Narciffus view'd that Face,
 He had renounc'd his Pride:
Nor for his own, but MAMA's *Charms,*
 The blooming Youth had dy'd.

IX.

Or, could fair Hyacinth revive,
 And all his Charms renew,
The Boy had fcorn'd Cæleftial Joys,
 And left his God for YOU.

And is it poffible, fays fhe, that Prince *Atabalipa*, with all the Accomplifhments they fay he is Mafter of, can produce fuch a Proof of his Wit and Gallantry as this; when, as my *Cacique* well obferves, he has never given himfelf the Trouble of coming or writing? Unhappy Princefs! Unfortunate *Mama Oello!* Why was I not the Daughter of one who fues for the Scraps of the well-fed Rich from Door to Door? Then might I have fingled out the Man I lov'd; then might I have fhar'd the plea-

F fant

sant Toil of the Day with him, and at Night sate down under the green Turf to what the invisible PACHACHAMAC, and our Father the SUN had granted to our Prayers with Content. O miserable Restraint! O free, yet captive Princess! what availeth thy wide and far stretched Greatness, if you must be a *State-Slave*? I am, indeed, somewhat like the gaudy Vegetable; my charming *Cacique* resembles me too: but the Emblem would have been more exact had it been of the *sensitive* Plant; for, like that, shall I shrink and withdraw myself from the Hand that is to pluck me.

In such melancholy Reflections as these did the disconsolate *Mama Oello* waste away a great Part of the Night, till the God of Sleep with his Leaden Wand lock'd up her Eyes and Sorrows together for some short Interval of Time: but *Phœbus* being now almost half advanc'd to his middle Station, too soon awakens both. The Peerless Fair knocks for her Favourite *Taya Napa*; and rising, adds new Lustre to the Day.

How does lazy Time, says she, my faithful *Taya Napa*, seem to flag his Wings whilst I am absent from my *Loque Tupanqui*? I thank you, however, drowsy God of Sleep, that I have been some few Hours lost to Thought and Woe: The heavy Gloom, that constantly hangs o'er my Soul, has for this short Space quitted Possession;

but,

but, I fear, will soon return: yet muſt I diſſemble, put on the Vizor, gay Looks and pleaſant Mirth; very unſuitable to the preſent Tenour of my Soul! So ſpeaking ſhe bends her Steps with her Favourite to the publick Room of State, with a feigned, but becoming Cheerfulneſs.

The natural Sympathy that is between Lovers produced almoſt the ſame Thoughts in the Breaſt of the reſtleſs *Cacique*; he cou'd not build any Hopes on the Continuance of this Interview with his Princeſs, knowing *Atabalipa*, Prince of *Quito*, would ſhortly, either in Perſon, or by Proxy, eſpouſe the fair *Mama Oello*; both which were confidently reported, and both alike fatal to him: He reſolves, therefore, to inform himſelf, if poſſible, from the courteous *Bobinquo*, whether the Marriage was to be perform'd perſonally or not: To put that Queſtion to his Princeſs, he thought would be ungrateful: And beſides, ſhe was kept in ſo much Ignorance, tho' the principal Perſon concern'd, that it was to be doubted whether ſhe could reſolve him when or how ſhe was to be diſpos'd of.

He therefore after Dinner asks his kind Entertainer, if it would be agreeable to him to paſs an Hour or two away in the Garden? Upon the *Bobinquo*'s Compliance, the diſguis'd *Cacique* intices him to the ſame Cypreſs-Shade, in which he had been so happy the Evening before, and hoped shortly to be so again. Well, says he, my Friend; for I must, and will call you by that Name, since the uncommon Civility you have shewn me highly deserves the Title: What News does the *Peruvian* Court afford? For, tho' I am so near it, which you know has not been long; yet do I wander as much in the Dark, in that Affair, as if my own Province now detain'd me beyond the great River *Apurimac*.

The Eyes and Tongues of this mighty Empire, reply'd the good-natur'd *Bohinquo*, are all now wholly employ'd on this intended Marriage betwixt the *Princess Royal* and *Atabalipa*, Prince of *Quito*; but how, or when, where, or in what Manner it is to be solemniz'd, I don't find that any Dependance can be form'd. Self-Contradiction, in this Case, reigns; our publick Intelligence one while affirming, and at other Times denying what before it asserted: However, this is certain, that it is to be; accordingly, Badges, and Marks of the highest Distinction and Honour have been transmitted to him; tho' it would seem not worth his Acceptance, since not worth coming after: He has been presented with Jewels to hang in his Ears, after they are bored; and the black Tress to tye round his Head: Verses and Orations

tions on his illustrious Self and Family have deduced his Original from the invisible PACHACHAMAC, and our Father the SUN: By them he is already deify'd, and inscrib'd amongst the Number of the Gods.

But you know full well, most illustrious *Cacique*, says he, all these Arts to render him dazling bright and glaring, serve only to darken him in the Esteem of the disconsolate Princess *Mama Oello*: how your Presence may dry up her Tears I cannot tell; but 'tis reported, and that not without some Foundation of Belief, that they incessantly flow from Morning to Night: That Prince *Atabalipa*'s Absence will be no Disappointment to her, tho' it may to several others, where Interest makes his Presence needful: Nay, even Numbers of People, as well *Curacas, Caciques*, as *Bobinquos*, have been so fantastical as to imitate *Atabalipa*'s favourite Colour in their Garbs and Dress; the Colour of *Quito* being now all the Mode.

I must not, however, forget one remarkable Story related in this Affair, which, notwithstanding all your present Gravity, I hope will make you smile; The disconsolate *Mama Oello* being found some time ago by her Sisters the other Princesses in Tears; Why all this Grief, happy Princess, say the young Ladies? Mirth and Gladness should be your Portion now, for you

you are fure of an illuftrious Prince to your Husband. But no one, except the invifible PACHACHAMAC, and our Father the SUN, can certify wherever we fhall have one.

What frefh Materials for News the Court may have furnifh'd out fince I was there I cannot tell, neither is it in my Power to acquaint you with any Thing elfe worthy your Notice, unlefs 'tis the Removal of the wife and learned *Curaca Sinchi*, and the valiant and couragious *Cacique Cobinqui*: But you'll excufe my entering upon the particular Caufes of this our great Lofs; (for I call it fo, it being univerfal to the whole *Peruvian* Empire) being engaged to meet fome Friends this Afternoon at a neighbouring *Bobinquo*'s. I will not make you the Compliment of going with me, becaufe I know you are at prefent indifpos'd to all Company; but beg, illuftrious *Cacique*, you will pardon my Abfence. So faying he departed, and left the *Cacique* to himfelf.

A ftrange Account I think, fays the pondering *Loque Tupanqni*, I have heard, which leaves me as much in the Dark as I was before: It is to be, he fays, but when, where, or in what Manner he knows not, and thereupon forms a Certainty out of an Uncertainty; yet this I am fecure of, as may be eafily gather'd from his Difcourfe, course, my Princess's Love: So far am I happy, but what is Love, if not enjoy'd? The Impossibility of this renders me again miserable. As to the Prince of *Quito*'s Honours, Titles, Dignities, I envy him not the Possession of them, or any earthly Grandeur the giddy World can heap on him, but that of my Princess: Let Orators and Bards make a God of him, I shall not envy him Heaven itself, if he will but leave my Princess here below. But to what Purpose do I dwell on this melancholy Subject, cherish Woe, and contemplate my own Misfortunes? I find I am not the only Man or *Cacique*, that is at present singled out by the invisible PACHACHAMAC, and our Father the SUN, to be the Sport of Fortune; the sage *Curaca Sinchi*, and the brave *Cacique Cobinqui* bear a Part with me: But say what could occasion such a Change, ungrateful I am sure to the *Peruvian* Empire, as well as prejudicial to my once Royal Master? All this must come from the *Curaca Robilda*, that cunning old Fox; for, can *Peru* produce any pernicious Alteration that was not first contriv'd by him? Who, now the Rudder's gone, can steer the Helm? Who can supply the judicious *Curaca Sinchi*'s Place? 'Tis a Weight too heavy for common Shoulders to sustain, and therefore adapted to no one but *Curacas* of uncom-

mon

mon Ingenuity and Penetration, such as *Sinchi* is; but where shall we find such another now he is gone? How long did the ingenious Artist, as History reports, keep his Enemy without the Walls, and maintain a perfect Union within by his prudent Councels and Advice? So long has this *Curaca* diverted our Foes from Abroad by his wise Negotiations, and heal'd our private Differences by a well-temper'd and prudent Moderation, just to his Royal Master, our most sacred *Inca*, true to his Country, indefatigable in serving both; his Affability, Courtesy, Complaisance, and his Capacity in publick Affairs, let the Provinces of *Havisca*, *Tuna Chuncuri*, *Pucana*, *Muyun-Cuyu*, *Charcas*, and *Collasuyu* confess, as dear and agreeable did *Sinchi*'s blameless Conduct render him to them as his matchless Deportment deserv'd.

Again, who shall essay to enumerate the brave Actions of the valiant *Cacique Cobinqui*? What Nation has been able to withstand his victorious Sword? For thirty tedious Winters, and as many sultry Summers, has *Peru* seen him head Part of her Armies, and in all her Wars (since he has been a Commander) given Proofs of an undaunted Courage. Must then the Wise and the Brave truckle to the capricious Humour of this *Curaca Robilda*? Cannot Wisdom secure, nor Valour save? No;
I

I find that the wife Man, who will not come into his Meafures, muft be difcarded; and the couragious Man, that will not run his Lengths, muft quit his glorious Profeffion: But, fure, it wo'n't be always fo. Look down, O invifible PACHACHAMAC, and our Father the SUN, and behold Extortion, Bribery, and Corruption, triumphantly lording it over your Favourite Empire; whilft Virtue, Probity, and true Merit skulk about from Place to Place entirely difregarded: But, foft! methinks, an unufual Fragrance ftrikes my ravifh'd Senfes far fweeter than any that this delightful Place can afford. So faying, he leaves at once his Arbour and Meditations, and advancing fees his Princefs, who was juft enter'd the Garden with the fair *Yaya Napa*, coming towards him.

With the greateft Reftraint upon his Paffion, for Fear of being overfeen, the lovefick *Loque Tupanqui* retires again into the Cyprefs-Shade, and there expects his charming *Mama Oello*.

For many tedious Minutes and Hours, which to me feem Months and Days, fays the enamour'd *Cacique* to his deareft Princefs upon her entering the Arbour, have thefe longing Eyes waited for the Sunfhine of your Prefence? 'Tis that difpels all my Cares, fooths all my Misfortunes; and for the Time it lafts, renders me entirely happy.

Illustrious *Cacique,* answer'd the Princess, I take as much Satisfaction in your dear Company, as 'tis possible for you to enjoy in mine; tho' I can't express myself in such gallant Terms as you: But (added she, letting fall some pearly Tears) how long this Pleasure may last I can't determine. I perceive (says she looking in a languishing Manner upon him) you would be better pleas'd to hear your Destiny and mine from me than any one else, could I but inform you: but alas! my *Cacique,* I am kept so much in the Dark myself, as to that Affair, that I know but very little of it; yet that very little is by far too much.

With less Regret, reply'd the Gallant *Loque Tupanqui,* most adorable Princess, could I hear you pronounce my Doom than any other, because I could for ever dwell with Attention on the soft Musick of your Voice: which in one Respect, tho' it would be piercing and killing; yet in another it would be medecinal and healing.

If I could unravel the whole Secret concerning myself, which lyes so close conceal'd in my Royal Father's and the *Caraca Robilda*'s Breast, yet would the Task be too ungrateful, and my faithful Tongue unwilling to perform so distasteful an Office, would soon faulter in my Mouth.—— But let us shift this Talk, and from so

me-

melancholy a Subject think of somewhat more entertainining. I did not know, illustrious *Cacique*, says the Princess, till very lately that you were a Favourite of the Muses: I thank you for the Present you conceal'd in your Nosegay last Night; the Sight of some more of your Performances would oblige me very much, as well as divert our Melancholly a little.

Charming *Mama Oello*, dearest Princess, answers the enamour'd *Cacique*, I never pretended to Poetry in my Life: but if ever any Thing worth Notice dropp'd from my Pen, 'twas when the Thoughts of my Princess inspir'd me. I am glad, replies the fair *Mama Oello*, I have so much Influence over you; and therefore will exert it, by commanding you to repeat, or shew me some more of your Works: (for more you must have I am certain) those you favour'd me with seem not to be the Flights of a young Beginner, but to flow from a Pen well vers'd in that harmonious Art.

Can I any Ways disobey my Princess? says the brave *Loque Tupanqui*, (putting his Hand in his Pocket) I should have a Copy of Verses, which I compos'd on your own dear Self, when I was in my Northern Confinement beyond the great River *Apurimac*; after (proceeds he, pulling out a Paper) I had ransack'd Heaven and Earth, the Sea and Air, to find out amongst the cœlestial

Inhabitants above, or the terrestrial below, or the Goddesses of the liquid Deep, one that was comparable to my far surpassing Princess; and finding it all to no Purpose, that the four Regions could not produce your Likeness, the following Thoughts presented themselves to me, which I now offer to my dearest Charmer: So saying, he gave her the Paper; I am afraid, if that be the Subject-Matter, answers the Princess, that your good Opinion of me has transported you too far; and, instead of making a *Simile*, you seem by your own Discourse to have soar'd beyond an *Hyperbole*, if that is possible: but pray (returning him the Verses) let me hear you read them, and then I shall be a better Judge. The *Cacique* taking the Paper, and kissing the fair Hand that restor'd it, read as follows. We observe the same Method here as in the preceding Verses.

MAMA OELLO, a SIMILE.

*T*HE *antient Bards who felt Love's piercing Fires,*
And by Enjoyment eas'd their fierce Desires;
Those Charms they tasted, and the sweet Delights
Of Vows by Days, and Ecstasies by Nights.
Each form'd his Muse, as she inspir'd, repaid;
Each form'd his Goddess of some mortal Maid,
Liken'd her beauteous Charms as was his Love,
To all that e're was great and good above.

Thus

Thus fair Corinna *in* Love's *softest Strain*
Brightens as Venus *rising from the Main.*
Thus we find Delia *by* Tibullus *drawn,*
Like silver Phœbe *tripping o'er the Lawn.*
Lycoris *too, as* Gallus *sweetly sung,*
With all the easy Softness of his Tongue,
Had Majesty superior in her Face,
And awful Juno *heighten'd every Grace.*
Feign would I thus my Charming Princess
paint,
But why? alas! those Images are faint;
Those heavenly Beauties are compriz'd in one,
And ev'ry Goddess meets in her alone.
In her shines forth the lovely Cyprian *Dame,*
Youth, Beauty, Vigour, all but the lascivious
Flame:
She seems Diana *with her silver Hair,*
As greatly virtuous, and divinely fair.
Saturnia's *State in all the Nymph is seen,*
She moves a Goddess, and she speaks a Queen:
Then who a proper Simile *can find,*
Since Heaven collected scarce can paint her
Mind:
Her own Antithesis *must match the Fair,*
And none but Mama *with her Self compare.*

Very great Encomiums indeed, says the Princess, and not only superior to my Deserts, I believe, but to those of any Mortal living. She had scarce utter'd these Words but the fair and faithful *Taya Napa* hurry'd into the Arbour with Advice that the Empress

press of *Peru* was just entering the Garden. The affrighted *Cacique* retir'd in Haste by a Back-door into the *Bobinquo*'s House, and the Princess advanc'd out of the Arbour into a Walk to meet her Royal Mother.

You have had a long Airing, Princess Royal, says the Empress; sure this Garden is very tempting, that it engrosses so much of your Time; Night after Night you constantly frequent it, and this Spot of Ground seems to be your sole Delight.

Retirement, please your Majesty, answers the Princess, is sometimes grateful; and indeed, with your Royal Leave, to me more pleasing than the Noise, Hurry and Pomp of Courts. You must talk now, reply'd the Empress, contrary to your own Sentiments; Splendor and glorious Appearances, such as the *Peruvian* Court affords, captivates the Hearts of all young Persons in general, how happy would the Majority of the Universe, that are of our Sex, think themselves, were they but in your Condition; to be Princess Royal of the mighty Empire of *Peru*, to possess every thing that your Heart can wish for or desire, to be happy in the Arms of a young and powerful Prince, as *Atabalipa* Prince of *Quito* is, are Blessings which the invisible PACHACHAMAC, and our Father the SUN, has reserv'd in Store only to bestow on the Princess Royal of *Peru*. The Blessings your Majesty mentions

tions are too valuable for any one Mortal to possess, or even hope for: my Expectations, tho' towering enough, soar not so high as what your Majesty represents. I am, indeed, in the first place, indebted to the invisible PACHACHAMAC, and our Father the SUN, for my illustrious Descent; and next to my Royal Father the *Inca*, and Yourself, for that tender Regard Ye have always shewn; but who I may thank (says she sighing) for matching me to *Atabalipa* Prince of *Quito* I can't tell: It could never be ordain'd by the invisible PACHACHAMAC, or our Father the SUN, it could never be contriv'd by the Royal *Inca* my Father, or Yourself, because all Ye, I am perswaded, firmly interest Yourselves in my Welfare and Happiness. From whence then must it proceed, or who can be the Author but the *Curaca Robilda*, or *Quatzultoult* the God of the Air, and an Enemy to this mighty Empire. I seem, added the Princess weeping, to be *Atabalipa*'s Aversion, since, tho' I have been contracted to him so many Moons, yet have I never receiv'd the least Mark of his Esteem, either in Person or by Proxy; how then can I be said to be happy in his Arms, whilst they seem to be as it were shut against me; and I alas! am constrain'd to force them open much against my own Will, and I believe against his?

No,

No, Princess, says the Royal Empress, he loves you, he's enamour'd with you, altho' he never saw you; your Picture has charm'd his Eyes already, and what must the Original do? The Fame of Beauty flies swift, very swift, and often wounds before the Object is seen. I might add here important Reasons which, were the Prince of *Quito* less agreeable, would be able to outweigh any Consideration. But I think the Air is somewhat cool, 'tis now Time for us to return to the Palace of *Capuac*.

The Princess was obliged to leave her beloved Garden, and much more beloved *Cacique*, without seeing him any more that Night; she wip'd her Eyes, and put on her usual, tho' now feign'd Smiles, she accompany'd the Empress into the Drawing-Room: but how insipid did all the Company appear to her! She was present and absent at the same time. She play'd indeed at *Noveda*, an *Indian* Game, to oblige the Princesses her Sisters, and the other Ladies, but hardly knew what she did, or what she said.

At last the wish'd for Hour of Repose came, and as soon as the faithful *Taya Napa* and she were retir'd into her own Apartment her Thoughts immediately arrest the dear Bower, and her dearer *Cacique*. Why, says she, O invisible PACHACHAMAC, and our Father the SUN! did you permit the Em-

Empress to interrupt me and my lovely *Loque Tupanqui*? Have we drawn down the Envy of the Gods upon us as well as Men? Then is our Fate irreversible. My Royal Mother mentions nothing but Happiness and Blessings, but I fear Misery and Discontent will be my Portion. Tell me, faithful *Taya Napa*, tell me, my sole Comfort, now thy Brother's absent, can you find nothing to sooth my Affliction? No Remedy for my Disease? If to act always by Constraint, to speak, and be obliged almost to think contrary to my Inclinations? If to know nothing at present hardly but Woe, and to expect nothing for the future but Uneasiness? If these are Blessings, then are they plentifully bestow'd on me. 'Tis the Part of a desponding Mind to be so very much dejected, answers the good-natur'd *Taya Napa*, Things may fall out, my Royal Mistress, beyond our Expectation; you see *Atabalipa* is not yet come, and perhaps, may not come at all. What if he is not, or what if he shou'dn't? reply'd the Princess hastily, yet shall I be sent over to him like a Victim to the Altar. It may be so, says the soothing *Taya Napa*, but then you know there are strong Dissentions Abroad now at *Policany*, occasion'd by their electing a new King, in which all the Powers of *America* seem to be concern'd. Should a lucky War now break out, it might be,

H per-

perhaps, of some Service to you, by diverting *Atabalipa* from the inglorious Pursuits of Love (as he terms it, to be sure) to the more glorious Profession of Arms. What the Fate of War may produce, no one (except the invisible PACHACHAMAC, and our Father the SUN) can foresee: *Atabalipa* may fall in Battle, or *Atabalipa* may return victorious; if the former, it eases you of the heaviest part of your Misfortunes at once: if the latter, whatever Trophies he brings home will be thrown at your Feet, and add a brighter Lustre to the intended Nuptials.

You talk extravagantly, answer'd the Princess, I ha'n't Patience to hear you any longer; *Atabalipa* has nothing to do in the Affairs of *Policany*: that will do us no Good. Death! nothing but Death, either mine or his, can put an End to my Misfortunes. O ye Sea-Gods, if he does prepare for *Peru*, whilst he is on your Element bury him in the Deep.

But stay, wicked Princess, as well as unfortunate, why do you imprecate an undeserved Fate on an innocent Prince, rather let the ravenous Billows swallow me up in my Passage, if I must be sent to him, or drive me to some unknown part of the World, where I may never see *Quito* or *Peru*. Thus did the disconsolate *Mama Oello* vent her Complaint to the faithful *Taya Napa*,
till

till Nature at laſt prevail'd, and ſhe fell into a Doze.

In the mean Time the moſt melancholy Thoughts exercis'd the now half diſtracted *Cacique*; he foreboded ſome extraordinary Misfortune attending for which he could give no Reaſon. To be thus interrupted in his Happineſs was almoſt Death to him; but alas! a far greater Tryal of his Patience was immediately to enſue.

The next Morning he receiv'd a Note from his Siſter *Yaya Napa*, which expreſs'd that Prince *Atabalipa* would certainly be at the Imperial City of *Cuſco* in leſs than the Space of a Moon, in Order perſonally to eſpouſe his deareſt Princeſs; that the Empreſs entertain'd ſome Suſpicion of her Daughter on his Account, becauſe ſhe had of late ſo often frequented that *Bobinquo*'s Garden, who was a particular Acquaintance of the fair *Yaya Napa*. Surpriz'd, aſtoniſh'd, and confounded, he firſt curs'd his Fate, and then the *Curaca Robilda*, as Author of his Misfortunes. * * * * * * *

Here the Original breaks off, but to be continued as ſoon as the Remainder comes to Hand,

F I N I S.

Just Publish'd,

THE *Oxford Act*. A new Ballad-Opera. As it was Perform'd by a Company of Students at *Oxford*. Dramatis Personæ, Vice-Chancellor, Proctor, Haughty and Pedant, Two Fellows of the Colleges reduced by the Act, Terreæ Filius, Thoughtless, Spendthrift, and Sprightly, three Extravagant young Students. Flippant, Hainessa, Vinessa, Ruella, four Oxford Tosts, who made a grand Appearance at the Publick Act.

Sold by the Booksellers of St. Paul's Church-Yard; and at the Pamphlet-Shops of London and Westminster. Price 1s.

Where also may be had,

I. The *Terra Filius's Speech*. The Third Edition Price 6 d.

II. The *Oxford Toast's* Answer to *Terra Filius's* Speech, wherein she confutes his scandalous Aspersion, Paragraph by Paragraph. Price 6 d.

III. The History of *Harvides* and *Donna Lupella*. Containing, The Family of the Harvides. His Amour with a married Lady of Distinction, call'd Harriot. His Marriage with Lupella, and many other diverting Adventures.

And in a few Days will be Publish'd, The *Court Medley:* Or, The *Deceitful Marriage*. An Opera.

The Masterpiece of Imposture

by

Elizabeth Harding

Bibliographical note:
This facsimile has been made from a copy in the Yale University Library (Nvq70 734h)

THE
MASTERPIECE of IMPOSTURE;
OR THE
ADVENTURES
OF

John Gordon and the Countess of *Gordon*, alias Countess *Dalco*, alias Madam *Dallas*, alias Madam *Kempster*.

CONTAINING

The Reality of an HISTORY, and the Amusement of a ROMANCE; being an Answer to the late MEMOIRS of the said *John Gordon* of *Glencat*. Done from authentick Accounts.

By ELIZABETH HARDING.

LONDON:
Printed for the AUTHOR, in the Year MDCCXXXIV. Price 1 s. 6 d.

THE

Masterpiece of Imposture, &c.

I Could wish I had not had the hard Fortune to buy the Knowledge I have of these two Impostors at so dear a Rate as I have done; but since it was God's holy Will and Pleasure to make me the happy Instrument of putting a Stop to their wicked and base Designs, when I was with them in *Scotland*. I think it my Duty to publish it to the World, and particularly in this Place, for Abroad, both in *France*, and in *Scotland* they are further known than ever they will be trusted again, it was my hard Fortune to be acquainted with this said *John Gordon*, ever since the Year 1728. He lived then in good Reputation to all outward Appearance; but ever since the Year 1730, that he unfortunately came acquainted with that wicked and base Impostor which he now Lives and Cohabits with, he has ever since liv'd a most scandalous and wicked Life, given himself up to all manner of Villany, this I can assert for Truth, for I am very well acquainted with several Persons of Distinction both in *France* and in *Scotland*, who has been Sufferers, both by *John Gordon* and his sham Countess, who has been a national Cheat for many Years, but now it's to be hoped that she is almost got to
the

the End of her self now; but however, since *John Gordon* and his Lady has lived so long together in so dishonourable a Manner, I am not at all surprized that he should leave out without taking the least Notice of the last 4 Years of his Life, when he wrote his own Memoirs, where he had the Impudence to say in his Title Page, that he had been 13 Years at his Study's in the *Scotch* College in *Paris*, when at the same Time he knew, in his own Conscience, that he had been but little more then half the Time, this I prove from the authentick Registers of the College, sign'd with his own Hand; he was admitted into the *Scotch* College the 12th Day of *November*, in the Year 1722, and he was extruded the 11th of *August*, in the Year 1730, this being Fact.

I beg my Readers will consider what Truth can be expected in the rest of his Book, that was begun with a Lie in his Mouth; nay, he has the Impudence to say that he is in *London*, ready to vindicate what he has written in his Memoirs, which shews to me, that the Impudence of some People must be very great; however, the best Construction can be put upon this Challenge, is, that he was ready to justify the Doctrinal part of his Memoirs, and that no Objections of any Moment could be made against the Exceptions he had made, to those Points of Doctrine which he had condemn'd; as to that I am no Divine, I am a Woman, and of no extraordinary Learning, and indeed, by what I have heard, his Adversaries and he are well agreed, since the Points of Learning which he has

has objected against are either generally Condemn'd by the Church of *Rome* herself, or allowed by very few; and consequently the Subject of a pure School-Dispute, but that a Man should give a general Defiance, both as to Fact and Speculation, and have but a tolerable Surmize, that his Book would even be Subject to my Eyes (as he must have) is what I have call'd an Impudence, and must call it so once more an Impudence, greater then what belongs to Man, to my Grief I speak it, for although I have been acquainted with him, and have known him but too well, the occasion was Innocent and Honourable; tho' as I conceive, not necessary to be related with many Circumstances; the Injunction will lie on *Gordon* to demand an Account of my Credit, which I am ready to give; but neither will the Affair I have with him turn upon that, since my Memoirs will consist of undeniable, authentick Accounts, ready to be produced, if call'd for; the chief View I have in this Work, is to expose a Villain, and do Justice to the Publick, that a Rogue may find his due Discouragement in the World, and honest People be preserved from his Designs, by which, I myself have been but too great a Sufferer, I am not asham'd to own that I am a *Roman* Catholick, neither do I think that the World will think the worse of my veracity, purely for my Profession, it being allowed by all, that there are good and bad of all Professions. This short Account of myself is a necessary Introduction to my Acquaintance with *John Gordon*; for in a Sickness, with which

which it pleafed God to vifit me at *Paris*. I was lett by Mr. *Smith*, who was then my chief Director under God, to the Care of this *John Gordon* for 3 or 4 Days, Mr. *Smith* being oblig'd to go into the Country about Bufinefs belonging to the *Scotch-College*, where *John Gordon* liv'd at that time, and I being thought dangeroufly ill at that Time; he vifited me at all his Leafure Hours, and I can't fay but after my Recovery, I was delighted and much edified by his Converfation, I being but a little Time then a *Catholick*, was wont to ask him feveral Queftions, which he anfwer'd to my Satisfaction and Improvement in my new Profeffion, he explained the Scriptures to me, he compared thofe pafs Ages of the new Teftament with the old, which feem'd to relate to my Purpofe, and indeed in fuch a Manner and Senfe, as I had never been Inftructed in before; fo that his Company was fo agreeable to me at that Time, that we promifs'd to keep a friendly Correfpondence, when his and my Affairs fhould call us into *England*; but a little before I came to *England*, *John Gordon* became acquainted with one *Elizabeth Mathews*, who was under the Care of Mr. *Holden*, fhe was defign'd for a Religious, and Mr. *Holden* had the Charity to get her into a Religious Houfe, but fhe having but little or no Vocation to that holy and retir'd Life, fhe was taken from the Convent, and Lodg'd in the fame Houfe that I Lodg'd in, but yet fhe was not content, by reafon fhe was lodg'd with another Perfon with whom fhe told me fhe could not agree with, therefore fhe beg'd of me, if

it

it was in my Power to get her into a Chamber-maids Place; but as I was every Day expecting to come to *England*, I told her that I could not be serviceable to her, so *John Gordon* hearing *Betty Mathews* daily making her Complaints both to me and him, he promised to get her a Service himself, for he said that he had much Interest and Acquaintance amongst the Quality, this was very agreeable to *Betty Mathews*, but then she was still at a loss, for she wanted several fine Things in order to fit her out for this great Place, and daily exclaiming against her best Benefactor, because Mr. *Holden*, wou'd not allow her to wear Ribbons upon her Head whilst she was living upon Charity, which indeed was nothing but what was very reasonable, if she had but Grace to have thought so, however, *John Gordon*, who was resolv'd to do all things effectually, gave this said *Betty Mathews* a Pair of Scarlet Stockings, with fine Clocks, and a pair of brocaded Slippers, richly Embroidered, and Ribbons flowered with Silver and Gold, a Pair of Mittens Embroidered upon the back of the Hands. Now all these things *Betty Mathews* shew'd me before I left *Paris*, but I did not know who gave her them untill I was upon my Voyage, going to *Scotland*, and then to my Sorrow I heard that base Woman who came from *France* with him, upbraid *John Gordon* with the many Favours he had bestow'd upon *Betty Mathews*, so I learn'd by that, that if she had stay'd longer at *Paris*, there would have been nothing but Jealousy betwixt the poor sham Countess and *Betty Mathews*, that indeed poor Monſieur *Labbey*, as he once call'd himſelf, would have had a very hard Task to pleaſe both his fine Ladies; for by what I hear he has had Trouble enough with the ſham Counteſs alone, not but that ſhe Acts very prudantly for him ſome Times, for ſhe takes ſpecial care who ſhe admits to ſee him. I can compare *John Gordon* and his Lady to nothing more like then to Sir *W. Penn* the Quaker that I have heard of, who had got ſo much in Debt, that he was afraid to ſhow his Head, even amongſt his own Friends, except he lik'd them; the Quaker being oblig'd to betake himſelf to his Room, he lock'd himſelf in, and made a Hole in the Wainſcoat to look through, that he might ſee every Body that came to his Houſe, and then he gave orders to his Family that no Perſon ſhould be admitted to ſee him until he ſee whether he lik'd them; now the Creditors hearing how difficult it was to get to the Speech of their Friend, one of them thought to Out-wit the Quaker, and ſo he bought a Piece of Cloth and cauſed it to be made up in the Quaker's Faſhion, to fit a Bailiff, who had orders to Arreſt the Quaker, in caſe he could get admitted into his Room; ſo the Bailiff went and deſir'd to ſee his Friend, the Servant went and told her Maſter that there was a Friend deſir'd that he would be pleaſed to ſee him that Day, but the Quaker immediately ſent Word that he had already ſeen his Friend, but he did not like him; now this I am afraid was *John Gordon*'s Caſe but a few Days a go, for a Friend of his went to pay his Reſpects to him and his Lady, and *John Gordon* would

not

not see the Gentleman, nor his Lady would not acknowledge that ever she had seen him, although the Gentleman had been in Company with her several Times when she was in *Paris*, and knew her when she went by the Name of Madam *La-countess-de-Gordon*, yet for all this, that Jilt had the Impudence to tell him that she never was in *Paris*, nor yet in *France*, nor in *Scotland* in all her Life-time; but this I suppose, she said, for fear the Gentleman should expose her in this Place; for if she had not been afraid of being taking Notice off, she would not have gone to my Lord *Bishop* of *London* with another Fellow, in order to clear herself, that she was not that Impostor who went by the Name of *Gordon* in *France*; however, I believe she will find it a difficult Piece of Work of it, when it comes to the rest, for if Sir *Robert Walpole* is pleas'd to Revenge his Brother's Cause or his own, he may very easily do it, for here is several Gentlemen in *London* who has seen her in *France*, and knows her very well, even some that was in Company with her when she play'd the Hypocrite at *Lyons*, and pretended that her Pocket was cut off with all her Money in it, now by this Projection, she mended her Pocket very well, but at length she was catch'd napping, as *Moss* catch'd his Mare; so that I am confident, that her going to my Lord *Bishop*, rather expos'd her, then being of any Service to her. However, before I go any further, I must acquaint my Readers who that Gentleman was, who thought to have renew'd his Acqaintance with *John Gordon* and his Lady; it was one

Mr.

Mr. *Couper* who lives in *Paris*, but is lately come from *France*, and is now in *London*, he knew this sham Countess perfectly well when she was in *Paris*, although she had the Impudence to tell him that she was never there, nor yet in *Scotland*, although she went to see her old Neighbour at *Edinburgh* not 2 Years ago; and as for *John Gordon*, this same Mr. *Couper* kept him from starving in *Paris*, after he was disgracefully turn'd out of the College, he not only fed him at his Table, but he also gave him his Lodging, purely for God's sake out of Charity, without expecting any Reward, and that ungrateful Rogue *Gordon* to make such a base Return as he did, it's unpardonable, for when Mr. *Couper* call'd at his Lodgings, he desired nothing of him but one Hours Conversation with him, and when he found that he could not have it, he desired only the Favour of a Line from his old Friend *Gordon*, to know when he should do himself the Honour to wait upon him again, which indeed was granted much sooner then he expected according to the rest of his Treatment. *John Gordon* wrote a Letter to Mr. *Couper*, and directed it to the care of one Mrs. *Doggett*, an Acquaintance of his, who lives by *Golden-Square*; the Contents of that impertinent Letter, is as follows:

SIR,

IF you'll Speak with me, it must be at ten in the Morning, or at five in the Evening, for I am always out till past Eight at Night, and this is but for three or four Days whilst Lent comes

comes in, for after that I shall not have one Moment of Time to speak with any Man, a Due,
I am, S I R,
Your Humble
Servant,
John Gordon.

Now if *John Gordon* had not had an impudence greater then belongs to Man, he could never have sent such an impertinent Letter to a Gentleman, to whom he was owing so many Obligations; but for my part I am surpriz'd at nothing that he doth. I know him but too well, and has been a very great Sufferer by him as will afterwards appear.

And now I have given here a short Account of these too Impostors of the late Proceedings, I will return to my first Subject again, just when *John Gordon* was so full of Business, serving *Betty Mathews*, I came to *England*, and I heard no more of them for some Time; I left *Paris* the 21*st* of *June*, and arriv'd here the 8th Day of *July*, in the Year 1730, and as soon as I found what reception I met with here, and how my Affairs stood, I wrote to my Friends at *Paris*, and sent a Packet of Letters by a Gentleman of my Acquaintance who was going there, and directed them to the Care of Mr. *John Gordon* at the *Scotch College*, I not knowing then that he was turn'd out of the *College*, and when my Friend went to ask for him, one of the Students told him that *John Gordon* was no more there; but he gave him a Direction where to find him, so the Gentleman went by that

that Direction to the *Hotel, Deallemagne, rue dufour,* where *John Gordon,* and the poor Countess of *Gordon* was then living together; O what woefull change had that miserable Man made to forsake God, to serve the Devil, for when my Friend ask'd for *John Gordon,* the Countess appeared and desir'd to know what his Business was with *John Gordon,* and she would tell him of it, my Friend told this fine Lady that he had a Message from *London,* that he could not deliver to any Body but himself, and therefore he told her sham Ladyship that he must see him, so then *Monsieur-Gordon* appear'd muffled up in a most deplorable Condition with the Pox, as the Gentleman told me when he return'd to *London* again, but this I did not belive, then I had too great confidence, God knows, in my old Friend *Gordon* at that time, then to believe any thing so scandalous of him, however, when *John Gordon* had receiv'd my Letters, he found only one for himself which he answered in a very friendly manner, the Words are as follows:

Paris, the 7th of *September,* 1730.
MADAME,

I Recived *your kind Letter, and was overjoyed to understand from the Bearer of yours, that you was in good Health, I am sorry you cant give me no exact Account about your Affairs; however, I hope, that as soon as they are settled, you will grant me the Satisfaction of a Line from you, I belive you will be surpriz'd to hear that I am no more in the* Scotch College, *I was oblig'd to leave it upon Mr.* Holden *and your*

your Friend Panton's *Account*, *they so spoke and molested the Superiours of the College, that they gave me my Dismission, and that upon a quarter of an Hours Advertisment, the only Cause they had was for acting for* Betty Mathews, *and standing up in Defence of a Lady of Quality, who, they in vain endeavour'd to blast and ruin her Reputation, I am still in* Paris, *and Blessed be God, I want for nothing, I shall write to you again, after I am settled, all I can say at present is, that I shall not have the Satisfaction of seeing you so soon as I expected, for if my Affairs go right, I shall leave* Paris *for some time, and go down to* Burgundy *in* France, *after which I may go into* Italy, *however, I will give you my Address in* Paris, *where you may write to me, for they will always know where I am, and they will send a Letter to me, this is all I can say at present, only assure you that I take great concern in all that Regards you, I am Dear Madame,*

A Monsieur, Monsieur　　　*Your*
Gorden Chez Madame,　　*Sincere Humble*
La-countess Dalco,　　　　*Servant,*
Sur le quay des,　　　　　*John Gordon.*
Theatins, a Paris,　　　*the Address in* French.

Now when I had read this Letter, I did not think the worse of my old Friend *Gordon*, for his being turn'd out of the *College*, for at that time I was not capable of thinking an ill Thing of him, and what made me the harder to belive any thing against him, was, that I knew that there was some little Difference betwixt

Mr.

Mr. *Holden*, Mr. *Panton*, and *John Gordon*, but a little before I left *Paris*, which I thought might have been the occasion of all that Trouble, which I was in great hopes would soon be at an end, and *Gordon* be restor'd to his *College* again, I not knowing then how double Dilligent he had been to *Betty Mathews*, in serving her and the sham Lady of Quality. However, I am now very well informed, that it was neither Mr. *Holden*, nor yet my Friend *Panton*, as that Rogue *Gordon* was then pleas'd to call him, that was the Occasion of his being turned out of the *Scotch* College; it was his own Disobedience to his Superiours, who forbid him to go any more to that sham Countess, and he refusing to Obey, they turn'd him out, and then he intirely liv'd with his Countess.

I heard of a pleasant Story which happened soon after, whilst they was living together in the *Hotel d'allemagne rue duforu*, a Gentleman among the *Gensdes Arms* made Love to that fine Lady, till one Day he found her in Bed, and *John Gordon* with another Person sitting by her, then he Cain'd her as she well deserv'd, she threw at him a Candlestick, which broke in Pieces a large Looking-Glass, which one Mr. *Lauder* a *Scotch* Man, who happen'd to go in at the end of the Fray, lent the Lady sixty *Livers* to pay for it; but that is not all, they got Seven and Twenty Pound *Sterling* of that same Man. Just after that, *John Gordon* and his Countess was forc'd to flee out of *France*, to escape Transportation

tion during their Life-time; now I only beg my Readers will be pleased to consider well the aforesaid Letter, and the following Account which I have given of my old Friend *Gordon*, and that abominable Impostor, which he still keeps Company and Cohabits with, and then compare them with what I am now going to relate.

These Misfortunes had no sooner happen'd to the poor sham Countess, but there came more, and much greater Troubles upon her, as I shall make it appear hereafter, for after she had play'd all Legidemain Tricks that she could, and *John Gordon* had used all means possible to assist her in forging of Letters and false Bills and the like, to Cheat and Trick the *Jesuits*, who was endeavouring to recover the considerable deal of Money which she had got from them; they was both Banished out of *France*, and then they came to *England*, where they stay'd but a short Time. But however, whilst they stay'd here, they made good use of their Time; their whole Study then was to forge Letters, and compack a thousand Lies together, to Cheat and Trick me out of my Money, and when they found that I would lend them no more, they then went to *Scotland*, and being then got to their last Shifts, was forc'd to fall upon new Projections, and as the Lady then pretended to be a Daughter of my Lord *Sutherland*, she was visited by the Ministers and several Gentlemen of Distinction at *Edinburgh*, so the Lady having more Eloquence and Impudence then poor Monsieur
Labby

Labby had, she acquainted those Gentlemen of the Affair they was come upon, and told the Ministers that *John Gordon* was born of *Popish* Parents, but was left very young to the Care of the Laird of *Barrack*, who was his Uncle, and a *Roman Catholick* also; but she said that *John Gordon* never had any confidence in the *Popish* Religion, but was always desirous to imbrace the *Protestant* Faith, for which Reason she told them that the Laird of *Barrack* banished *John Gordon* out of his own native Place against his Will, and sent him to the *Scotch* College at *Paris*, in *France*, where he was kept like a Prisoner nine Years; so that he had no Opportunity of getting away to make his Escape from that Place, untill she found an Opportunity to steal him away out at a Window of the College, and so took Care of him untill she got safely arrived here in *England*.

Now when those worthy Gentlemen had heard this Story, they all with profound Reverence made their Compliments to the sham Lady, and thanked her for their great Proselite, and they rendred Thanks to Almighty God for so safe a delivery of such a bright Man as they look'd upon him to be at that Time, untill he was discovered; however, as soon as those Gentlemen was made sensible of all this, and had Discourse with *John Gordon*, who declared to them that he had no other Business in *Scotland*, but to Renounce *Popery*, and imbrace the *Protestant* Religion, then the Day appointed was for his Abjuration, where that miserable Man *John Gordon* had the Impudence to declare in the Presence
of

of God, at the Profession of his new Faith, that he was banished out of *Scotland* by his Uncle *Barrack*, when he was but a Boy, and was sent to *France* to be bred up in the *Popish* Religion; he also told the Ministers and other Gentlemen at that Time, that he was kept like a Prisoner at the *Scotch* College in *Paris*, nine Years against his will; and kept very strict to the *Popish* Religion, which he never had any Confidence in. He told them that he oftentimes had endeavoured to make his escape out of the College, but he was always disappointed; for he said, that those Villains, the Superiors of the College, kept such a strict Eye over him, that he could not make his escape, untill Madame *La Countefs de Gordon* stole him out at a Window of the College; after she had procured a Guard, to secure his Person whilst she got him into a Cart, covered with a Blanket, and so she brought him all the way through *France*.

Now when this lying Villain was telling this dismal Tail to those Gentlemen, he little thought that I should bring his own Hand writing before them, to be an Evidence against him; for when these Gentlemen told me this last Story, and I shew'd them the aforesaid Letter; I leave the World to judge how like a Rogue and a Fool the new Proselite look'd, whilst these Gentlemen was upbraiding him in the Judgment-Hall, when his own Hand-writing condemned him, and I made it plainly appear to all our Hearers, that poor Monsieur *Labby*, as he then call'd himself before that great Change, had

B much

(18)

much more Difficulty to get out of *France*, then to be brought in a Cart cover'd with a Blanket; for if that Rogue, and his sham Countess had not trudged it a long in another sort of Manner, they had both been imprisoned during their Life, as it will appear by my following Discourse.

For as soon as *John Gordon* was disgracefully turned out of the *Scotch* College, he went to that wicked Woman, whom he now Lives and Cohabits with, for she at that Time was at a great loss to find out a new Title; these *Jesuits* having then discovered that she was no Branch of the Duke of *Gordon*'s Family at *Edinburgh*, as she had had the Impudence to call herself for many Years, so the poor Countess having a great Veneration for the name of *Gordon*, was loath to part from it; and therefore she call'd herself Daughter to the Lord *Sutherland*, his Lordships original Name being *Gordon*; she also gave it out that she had married one Colonel *George Hambleton* of the *English* Dragons, and that she had Possessions both in *Scotland*, and in *England*; but she said that the *Whigs* in *Scotland* persecuted her so much upon the Account of her Religion, that she was forc'd to flee to *England*, where further Difficulties arose, for she said that the Lord *Sutherland* was so much exasperated against her, for turning *Roman* Catholick, and marrying a Gentleman of so mean Extraction, for a Lady of her Quality; that he had caused her to be banished out of *England*, and two Children, a Boy and a Girl was left to be taken Care of by the

the Government; the reſt of her Affairs were left to the Care and Management of Alderman *Couper* of this City, and ſeveral Letters was counterfeited in his name by *John Gordon,* ſign'd *Couper,* to amuſe and blind the World, and make her Creditors believe that ſhe could command Money from *England* and *Scotland,* when at the ſame time that Jilt had no Pretention to one Farthing; however, all their Projects would not do; for at that time the Eyes of her Creditors was opened, and none of them believ'd that ſhe was a branch of that Family; ſo John Gordon being reſolved to be ſatisfy'd, wrote two Letters, one directed for me, and the other for Mr. James Shirley, Junior, in Dean-Street; they were both upon her Account, the Contents of my Letter is as follows:

MADAME,

' AS you are there upon the Spot, I beg
' you'll pleaſe to inquire whether the
' Lord Sutherland has a Daughter or not, and
' whether in Scotland or in England, or in
' France; and whether or no ſhe did not mar-
' ry one Colonel George Hambleton of the
' Engliſh Dragoons; he alſo deſired me to en-
' quire whether ſhe had any Eſtates, either in
' Scotland or in England to depend upon; for
' he told me that the Reaſon why he deſired
' that Favour of me, was, that not only
' he, but there was ſeveral Perſons of Diſtinc-
' tion who had lent this Lady a conſiderable
' deal of Money, and they was doubtful whe-
' ther they ſhall get one farthing of it again,
' ſo

'so he beg'd that I would grant him the Sa-
'tisfaction of a Line from me, as soon as pos-
'sible, and that would oblige my old Friend
'and Humble Servant,

John Gordon.

Now this Letter I kept in my Pocket-Book, until I got to Aberdeen, where Madam had the Impudence to take upon her again the Title of Countess of Gordon, and Daughter to the Lord Sutherland, which much surprised me, for whilst they stay'd in *London*, John Gordon told me that she was that Impostor's Chambermaid, and that made him fear that this Letter would be an Evidence against his poor Lady, so to prevent the Danger, John Gordon took the Letter out of my Pocket-Book, as it lay upon the Table in my Lodgings at Aberdeen; I see him take it, but if I had known then what Villany they was going to enact, I would have taken more Care of it.

However, now I have given a short Account of these two Impostors; I will first prove what Extraction this sham Countess did derive from, and then I will acquaint my worthy Readers how that unfortunate Man John Gordon came first acquainted with her.

Her counterfeit Ladyship was born in *Edinburgh*, of very honest Parents, who liv'd decently by their Labour, and her Father was a writer in the Council Chamber, and his name was *More*, as their Magistrates told me before John Gordon's Face; when I had him before them, she has two Sisters who lives in the Canongate,

Canongate, in good Reputation, and one of them I was in Company with at her Lodgings, but this sham Countess at the Age of 16, was kept by a Captain, until he thought fit to Part with her; and then he promised a poor Man a Lieutenant's Place, in Case he would marry her, so then all Parties being agreed, they were married, and she liv'd sometime with her Husband, until she had 3 Children by him, but when she found that her Husband could not maintain her so well as the Captain had done before; her Husband being absent, she told her Friends that she would go to London and beg her Husband a better Post.

So she left her Children with Mr. *Edey* a-writer, who lives at the High-Cross in *Edinburgh*; and his Wife and she told them that she would be back again at such a Time as she then appointed; but if any thing should happen contrary to what she expected, so that she could not come according to her Expectation, she would leave with them a Trunk full of very rich and valuable Things, in order to supply all her Childrens necessary Wants; but she beg'd that they would not be too hasty in opening of the Trunk, for she would certainly return as soon as possible she could, although it's much to to be feared, that she never intended it; however, Mr. and Mrs. Edey did not open the Trunk, until there was due to them upon the the Account of their Children, betwixt 20 and 30 Pounds; and then finding that Madam did not return, nor give them any Account when they might expect her, they opened the Trunk,

Trunk, and found nothing in it but o'd Pewter Plates and Pots, with Holes melted in them, wrap'd up in Rags; fuch was the Treafure the Trunk was fill'd with, fo Mr. and Mrs. Edey finding themfelves bit, they went to the Parfon of the Parifh, where their Children was born, and defired that he would give them from the Regifter their Names and Date of their Ages of thofe Children, and then they carefully fent their Children to London after their gracelefs Mother, who had the Impudence to deny her own Children, adding, that fhe never knew what it vvas to bear a Child in her Life, and fo fhe vvent on abufing the poor Man at a very great Rate, until he fhevv'd his Authority, and prov'd the Children to be hers; nay, he alfo told her, that if fhe refufed to take care of them he would certainly fecure her; then Madam finding herfelf trapan'd, fhe took her Children and put them to a Nurfe immediately, for fear fhe fhould be difcover'd, for at that time fhe was a-kept Miftrefs, and liv'd very Grand; fet up for an Heirefs, and went to Court frequently, in which time fhe got acquainted with feveral Perfons of Diftinction, but particularly with Sir *Robert Walpole,* for that was not long before fhe went to *France,* fo fhe thought that would be an introducement to her Acquaintance with his Brother, who was then in *France,* for fhe was not long there, before fhe appeared at the *French* Court, in which time fhe got acquainted with the honourable *Horatio Walpole,* but fhe took care to be well furnifhed with counterfeit Letters and falfe Bills;

Bills; firſt, upon which ſhe prevailed upon his Honour to advance her ſome Money, ſo he ordered Mr. *Alexander* his Banker to let her have One Hundred Pound *Sterling* upon her Bill on Demand; and I have been informed ſhe had the Impudence to draw upon Sir *Robert*; but whether it was ſo or not, the Money ſhe had, but they are not the only worthy Gentlemen that has been Trick'd out of their Money that way, not by many Hundreds, by that wicked Woman; for which reaſon I have took this Trouble upon me, to put a Stop to her wicked and baſe Proceedings, that other honeſt People might not ſuffer as they have done; however, ſhe had no ſooner got that hundred Pound, but ſhe made a very great Figure, and was no leſs Ambitious of Greatneſs, then to claim a Right to Quality, and took upon her the Title of Madame *La-counteſs-de-Gordon*, in order to make her grand Viſits amongſt the *Catholick* Nobility, for her great Zeal for the *Proteſtant* Religion, was all over as ſoon as ſhe had got the hundred Pound from the Honourable *Horatio Walpole*; then on the other Hand ſhe went to the Head Miniſter, his Eminency the Cardinal *de Fluery*, with as much pretended Zeal for *Popery*, and acquainted his Eminency what Family ſhe was of, and alſo the great Difficulties ſhe had undergone, on Account of her Religion, not only by their Perſecution ſhe met with in her own native Place, by their *Presbytery* of *Edinburgh*; but alſo by the Epiſcopal Church of *England*, for which ſhe was baniſhed, and forc'd to flee to that Place where she hop'd to enjoy the *Catholick* Religion in more Peace then she had done before, she being perfectly perfuaded it was the only Religion, by which she at time could be faved; therefore, when she had told this, and proclaim'd herself in such a manner, not only to his Eminency, but there was several other Persons of Distinction, who out of Compassion to a Lady of that Quality as she pretended to be, and in great Distress, they made her counterfeit Ladyship such large Presents of Money to supply her necessary Wants, that she trump'd up her Coach and Six, and kept an Equipage so Grand, that she appear'd like a Princess of the Blood, to those that did not know her; but her Money being then far spent, she began to think it was time to make some more of those profitable Visits; so she then went in her Coach and Six to his Eminency the Pope's *Nuncio* with her old canting Tale, for under a Pretence of Religion, she had always a Cloak for her Villany; however his Eminency had the like Compassion as the rest of the Nobility had for the poor banish'd Lady, who was always in Distress, and therefore he presented her with a Purse of Gold, and desired that she would not Want, but let him know; but his Eminency took care to inform himself, whether or no she was a Branch of the Duke of *Gordon*'s Family or not; and by that means the sham Countess was discovered after living a long time in those wicked Practices, but she still continued to be a strong Catholick; and to confirm that she

provided

provided herself with a Jesuit Chaplain to sound her Trumpet, and bring her in Favour with their Fraternity, and very good Use she made of her Time then, for she cheated the Procurator of the *English* Jesuits of twenty thousand Livers; and so she continued 'till the Year thirty before she was discover'd, and then about that time the unfortunate *John Gordon* became acquainted with this sham Countess; the first Reason was occasion'd by placing *Betty Matthews* with her to serve her as Chambermaid; and as I am inform'd, *John Gordon* at that time was too much inamour'd with *Betty Matthews*; and because Mr. *Holden* oppos'd his wicked design, both to preserve him and the Girl from Ruin, he has ever since been imbitter'd against Mr. *Holden*; however, *John Gordon* improv'd his Accquaintance with the Countess of *Gordon*, and us'd to go and spend whole Days with her; his Superiors in the *Scotch* College not approving of this his Conduct, forbid him to go any more to her, and he refusing to obey, they turn'd him out of the College, and then *John Gordon* intirely liv'd with his Countess, and remain'd with her above eight Months, during which time he went about getting Money for her; but at length she was put into Prison by the King's Order, and then *John Gordon*, finding himself destitute of all Comforts of Life, pretended to become Penitent, and wrote to Mr. *Holden* a Letter, wherein he declared he was very sorry for what he had done, and desir'd mightily to speak with him, which Mr. *Holden*

den consented to, and was glad to find *Gordon* in that Disposition, after almost a Years wandering, he went to him, and confirmed by word of Mouth what he had before wrote by Letter; and he told Mr. *Holden* how great an Impostor his Countess was, and that she had cheated the Procurator of the Jesuits of above twenty thousand Livers, by pretending to have Money in *England*, and gave this said Jesuit false Bills; and in fine, he related such Stuff to him of her, that he did not think it was worth his while to attend to it; for all Mr. *Holden* desir'd, was a Proof of *Gordon*'s Sincerity; who to convince Mr. *Holden*, desir'd to go to Confession to Mr. *Holden*, and did so for above six times in ten Days, which to any impartial Reader, is an evident Proof that what he says, Mr. *Holden* told him of the *English* Nuns is a Lie, and *Gordon* knows very well, that what is heard in Confession, is never told on any Account; or else, if *Gordon* really thought Mr. *Holden* was capable of what he says of him, he would not dare to provoke him, after he had made a general Confession of his whole Life to him; however when *John Gordon* went thus Penitent to Mr. *Holden*, he, out of Charity, sent *Gordon* to the College of St. *Lazars* to make a Retreat, where he stay'd for almost a Month at Mr. *Holden*'s Expence, which cost him above six Pound sterling; now *Gordon* desir'd at that time to engage in that House, but they would not take him, then he pretended that he could be admitted amongst the *Oratonians*; but that proved

a

a Lie, and at length, when the Countess came out of Prison, *John Gordon* went to see her, and Mr. *Holden* never saw him any more; for then *John Gordon* began his old trade of Forgery again, he counterfeid Letters, false Bills and the Like; for his poor Countess, she having then lost her Coach and Equipage, and was oblig'd to walk without, as honester People, then she was did; however their counterfeit Letters was of little use to them at that time of the Day, for they was better known then trusted; but *John Gordon* having a great share of Impudence, he forged two Letters, which I my self have had to Read, one of the Letters is now in Scotland, but I took a Copy of the Address before it went, and the other Letter I kept.

The Address is as follows,

A *Monsieur, Monsieur* Ogiluis, *chez Monsieur* Arbuthnat Banqier, *onglois dans la Rue, neuve St.* Thomas *au coin de la Rue, vivienne a* Paris.

Now the following Letter which I have by me, was not address'd, but had been inclos'd, Sign'd *Couper*, and Dated *London* the 7th of *August*, 1733.

MADAME,

I am heartily sorry that a Lady of your Pro-
' bity and Experience should have acted
' with so little Consideration, as to put your
' Person, and even Effects, as I am credibly in-
' form'd, in the Hands of a set they call Jesuits,
' Your

(28)

'Your Ladyship cannot be ignorant of the
'Character thofe People have in the World,
'even amongft thofe of their own Religion; in
'a Word, Madam, all I can fay of them is,
'that they are a People intrufted, and will do
'nothing without Intereft; I wifh to God you
'may not find the Expreience of what I fay,
'your Ladyship has known what Effects you
'had from this Place; I defire you will manage
'well, becaufe I do not fee how I can advance
'you more; fo foon as my Son fet out for *Eng-*
'*land*, he left this Place laft Week, and will be
'with you very foon, mean time you may have
'an intire Confidence in this young Gentleman,
'who underftands Affairs perfectly well, he
'will fee your Ladyship get Juftice in that
'ftrange Country you are in, againft all Rogues,
'who may endeavour to do you harm, your
'Daughter is well, my Wife offers her humble
'Refpects to you, as alfo doth my Son, who
'was impatient until he fet out to wait upon
'you, the Bearer of this will inform you any
'other Particulars, I remain.

Madam.

Your moft Obedient,

and ever obliged Servant,

COUPER.

Now

Now it plainly appears that *John Gordon* began this Trade of Forgery before he was turn'd out of the College, for the aforesaid Letter was dated *August* the Seventh, and he did not leave the College until the Eleventh Day of *August* in the Year Thirty; however, he being then extruded from the College, he continued in these wicked Practises until the *February* following, and then there was a Letter *de Caſſet* granted from the King of *France*, to banish the poor Countess out of the Nation, and then she was forc'd to flee, and that silly Rogue, *John Gordon*, had no more Grace left then to follow her, and when they came to *Rouen*, and found themselves short of Money, *John Gordon* went to my Lord Stafford, who was then there, and finding his Nephew Mr. Plowden, whom I knew to be a Student in the *English* Seminary, *Gordon* tells him that he had been reconciled with his Superians of the *Scotch* College, and was going by their Orders to *Scotland*, and to prove this, he shew'd him a Letter he had counterfeited from Mr. *Thomas Inneſs* to a Gentleman in *Scotland*; as also another Letter from the Procurator of the *Scotch* College in *Paris* to Doctor *Wachop* in *London*; he added that his Superiors had given him a hundred Livers for his Journey, but being obliged to stay at *Diepe* for Captain *Moore*, his Money was spent, and therfore he begg'd of Mr. *Plowden* to lend him sixty Livers, which he did, and that Rogue *Gordon* had the Impudence to send a Letter to the Procurator at *Paris* to pay Mr. *Holden* that Sum for Mr. *Plowden*;

Plowden; and *John Gordon*, at that time, faid many bitter Things againſt his Lady *Gordon*, although fhe was actually with him at *Rouen*; and ſo they fold *France*, without being brought in a Cart covered with a Blanket; but before they came off the Spot, the Lady *Gordon* got acqainted with one Mr. *de Lange*, a high *German*, who is now Porter to Count *Kinsky*, by Hannover-Square; and I am very credibly inform'd that he had ſerv'd his Excellency before, and had ſaved an hundred Pounds, which he carried to *France* with him to buy Goods with to improve that Money, in order to ſettle himſelf in ſome way of Buſineſs, for he had promis'd Marriage to a young Gentlewoman, who then liv'd in *Red-Lyon-Street*, before he went to *France*; but its much to be fear'd the Counteſs of *Gordon* eat him up more then his Profit, or at leaſt fhe took care to give him the Pox to ſome Purpoſe, as fhe had done to *John Gordon* before: However, this ſaid Mr. *de Lange*, in gratification for the Favours the Counteſs had granted him, he agreed with a Fiſherman to bring them over in his Boat to Haſtings in Suſſex, where they landed, but neither *Gordon* nor the Counteſs had a Farthing to pay their Paſſage, therefore the high *German* was oblig'd to pay for all; after which he hir'd a Horſe, and took the Lady up behind him, and away they went to *Tunbridge*, and *John Gordon* was their running Footman, which fhew'd very much Humility in him; now they was no ſooner got to *Tunbridge*, but the Lady's Head was at work, and

(31)

and so falling upon some of her old Stratagems, she after one Nights Refreshment, prevail'd upon Mr. *de Lange* to go along with her four Miles out of Town to a Gentleman's Seat, where she pretended to have a considerable deal of Money due to her there.

Now this Story gave Mr. *de Lange* some hopes that he should get back the Money which he had been out of Pocket by her, so he got a Horse ready, and away they went, the Gentleman being at Home, order'd his Groom to take care of their Horse, and entertain'd these Strangers with such as was left at his own Table at Dinner, there was cold Ham and Fowls, two or three Bottles of good *French* Wine, and the like; but there was no Money in the Case; however, after the Lady had entertain'd the Gentleman with her foreign Discourse, and had very well refresh'd her self, she tip'd him with a Wink, and he went with her into another Room, where Mr. *de Lange* thought they was gone to settle their Accounts, although it was thought afterwards that she had no pretention to expect one Farthing; however, when the Gentleman and Lady return'd to Mr. *de Lange* again, she look'd as pleasant about the Mouth, as though she had received five hundred Pounds; so after taking another Glass of Wine, she told Mr. *de Lange* that she had nothing more to do then but to take Horse and return to *Tunbridge* again to her old Friend *John Gordon*; but by the way, she told Mr. *de Lange*, that she got only five Guineas then, but was to receive the rest in a

Fortnight's

Fortnight's Time, and she also expected to recieve some Money that Evening at her Lodgings in *Tunbridge*; so they was no sooner got in there, but the Marchioness *de Gordon*, as she then call'd herself, order'd a great Supper to be made ready, and every thing to be done in great Form, for she expected some Persons of Distinction to Supper with her that Evening, so all things was made ready, but the Gentlemen did not come as Mr. *de Lange* expected; so to put the better gloss upon the Matter, the Marchioness order'd Supper to be set back for half an Hour, then after they had waited for some time, and found that no Body appear'd, the Lady and her two fellow Travellers went to Supper, and eat very plentifully, and drank Wine until they could not well stand; but at length they all retir'd, and the next Morning the *Marchioness* was observ'd to be in some Disorder, so one of their Servants was sent into the Lady's Chamber, to know what her Ladyship wanted, or what was the matter with her, she told the Maid that she had only five Guineas to bear her Charges up to *London*, and she had unfortunately put them in her Bosom the Day before, and at Night having drank a little too much Wine, she forgot her Money, and had drop'd it somewhere in the House, but she could not tell where; however, desir'd the Maid to look well for that Money when she sweeped the House, so they all went to sweeping, whilst that lying Hypocrite seemingly let fall some of her old chrocodile Tears to deceive the World; then

Mr.

Mr. *de Lange* finding himself Bit, pay'd all their expences in that Place, and then he resolved to make the best of his way to *London*; so the next Day they all took Horse and rid Post, 'till they came to the *Whitehart* in *Southwark*, it was *Saturday* Evening when they came there, and on *Sunday* Evening, *John Gordon* and his sham *Countess* came in a *Coach* to *Lincolns Inn Chapel*, where she call'd for the Reverend Mr. *Alexander Middleton*, Chaplain to the *Sardinian* Envoy, to inform themselves where I lodg'd; so Mr. *Middelton* was so complaisant to his Country-Man and the *French* Lady, as he suppos'd, that he went along with them to my Lodgings, but I was not at Home, therefore they drove back again, set Mr. *Middleton* down where they took him up, and then return'd to their Lodgings again; but they was with me the next Morning by eight o'Clock, where I receiv'd that graceless Rogue with all the Respects and Pleasure in Life, believing him to be a true and faithful Servant of Jesus Christ, as I had never heard any thing to the contrary then; and he at the same time told me that he was going to *Scotland* to take the Orders of Priesthood from Bishop *Gordon*, which Discourse was very agreeable to me, I asked him what *French* Lady that was which came along with him, and he said that Woman was the Countess of *Gordon*'s Chambermaid, whom he told me was then in *Paris*, but had sent her Maid to *England* with a present of a Purse of Gold to the Lord Chancellor, in Case he would examine the Rolls, and take out her

C   Lady's

Lady's Name that was Register'd there, that she might return from her Banishment without any Danger of being imprison'd, during her Life, as the Law had determin'd; however *John Gordon* said, that he would not have brought her Chambermaid to me, but that he had been oblig'd to borrow two Guineas of her at *Diepe*, or else he could not have proceeded on his Journey to *England*, for his Pocket was pick'd of all his Money at *Diepe*; therefore he desir'd me to lend him two Guineas to pay the Chambermaid her Money again, or else he should be like a Prisoner to her, for she would not allow him to go out of her Sight until she was pay'd that Sum, therefore I very readily pay'd her one Guinea then, and I gave her the other Guinea the Day following, at the *White-Hart* in *Southwark*, and thankfully acknowledg'd all Favours done to my Friend; the Chambermaid was as thankful to me for her Money, and said, that if poor *John Gordon* had not found a Friend, like me, she did not know what he would have done, for he would have been destitute both of Money and Friends in this strange Place; nay, she had the assurance to tell me that she never was in *England* before herself, so she beg'd the Favour of me that I would take her a Lodging in *London*; so in gratification for the Service she had done my old Friend *Gordon*, I took her a Lodging in *Red-Lyon-Street*, the next Door to the *White-Swan*, at four Shillings *per* Week; but I little thought then that my Money was to pay for it; however

I

I took my leave of the Chambermaid, and did not see her again for some time, and I went with *John Gordon* to Mr. *Shirley*'s, in *Dean-Street*, where I had placed that Rogue in a good Lodging, and I had promis'd payment for that and every thing else that he should have occasion for whilst he stay'd in that House, for *John Gordon* had told me before, that he had wrote to his Uncle *Barrack* in *Scotland* for fifty Pounds, and expected an Answer in three Weeks time, which would be either Money or Bank Notes, to pay me all that he should be indebted to me, and therefore he beg'd of me not to let him want in this strange Place; so I assisted him with Money to buy every thing that I thought he had occasion for; he said he should set out for *Scotland* as soon as he had got an answer to his Letter, and the Chambermaid was to stay in *London* whilst he return'd from *Scotland*, to settle Accounts with Alderman *Couper*, for her Lady expected there would be a considerable deal of Money due to her from him.

So when *John Gordon* return'd to *London* again, the Chambermaid and he was to steal two Children away from the Government, and take them to *Paris* to their graceless Mother, to be brought up in the *Catholick* Faith; and the better to confirm her Son in that Religion, *Gordon* said, she would take him to *Italy* the Summer following, and put him into the *Scotch* College at *Rome*, to go thorough all the Studies there; and *John Gordon* said, that the Countess of *Gordon* had offer'd him one hundred Pounds

Pounds Sterling *per* Year to go along with her to be her Chaplain; for he said, she had parted with her Jesuit Chaplain, and would never have any thing to do with them any more.

Now all this while I believ'd every Word the Vilian told me to be true, as I had never known him guilty of Lying before; he injoin'd me to Secresy of all this, for he told me, that if the Goverment should get the least Jealousy of what their Intention was to do, they might all suffer either Imprisonment, or be Banish'd during Life, and Alderman *Couper* might be in great Danger of forfeiting his Estate, for acting underhand betwixt the Government and the banished Lady; now I cannot say, but this last Story gave me some concern; for I thought that a Gentleman of that Character, which I thought he bore at that time, ought not to be concern'd in a Plot like that, therefore I beg'd of him to have no share in it, but come to me again the next Morning, which accordingly he did, and we went together to *Lambert*, where I d liver'd two Ton and half of cast Iron, at five Pounds ten Shillings a Ton, and some other Goods, for which I received the Sum of sixteen Pounds twelve Shillings: and although Mr. *Gordon* kept an account of the Weight of those Goods, and wrote the Receipt I gave for that Money, he would, after some time, as you will find, have sworn that he never saw any of my Goods, or one Farthing of my Money; however, when I had receiv'd that Money, we return'd to *London* again, and at my Lodgings I lent Mr. *Gordon*

Gordon some of that Money; and now before I proceed any farther, I will give a just Account to the World of the Friendships Mr. *Gordon* receiv'd from me, and how ungrateful a Return he made me for it: First of all, Mr. *Gordon* desir'd me to lend him two Guineas to pay his Chambermaid, and half a Guinea to pay the Coachman for bringing them twice to my Lodgings; I lent two Guineas more to buy him Stockings, Shoes, and other Necessaries; then he wanted to change too old Perry-Whigs for one new Perry-Whig, and therefore he pray'd me to lend him two Guineas more to pay for the exchange of them, and to buy him a Hat; and every Week I lent him half a Guinea to put in his Pocket, and I pay'd for his washing and Lodging at Mr. *Shinley*'s besides: Now all this I did for him, and much more as you'll find hereafter, believing him to be a Man worthy of all the Service I could render him, for he appear'd as such, not only to me, but to all my Acquaintance, or else I should not have done so much for him as I did; but his Behaviour to every Body here was such, that they all look'd upon him to be a Saint, although at the same time his daily Study was to do the Works of the Devil, for after I had assisted him in this manner five or six Weeks, I then asked him what he intended to do, and if he thought there was any hopes of getting an Answer to his Letters from *Scotland*, which he pretended to have wrote to the Laird of *Barrack* his Uncle, he told me that he had got none as yet, but he should
certainly

certainly have a Letter by the next Post; so then he went from me and counterfeited a Letter as from his Aunt *Barrack*, who had been dead fifteen Years, and gave it to his Chambermaid to write a Woman's Hand, she having been but too long Mistress of those black Arts: so when she had done, he folded up the Letter, seal'd it, and directed it for himself, he broke it open, and then brought it to me at my Lodgings, where that Rogue *Gordon* put on such a melancholy and dejected sanctified Look, that it is impossible to make the World truly sensible of the Impostor; for I thank God, that I never knew such an Hypocrite before.

He was no sooner sat down by me, but he told me that he had got a Letter God help him, to his sorrow; I was at Dinner, but indeed I had soon done, for the very first Sight of him gave me enough, without that dreadful Speech, I was impatient until I had heard that sorrowful Letter read to me, it was dated *May* the tenth, one thousand seven hundred and thirty; now my worthy Readers may observe what the Lady writes to her Nephew, after having been fifteen Years dead.

May the Tenth, 1730.

Dear NEPHEW,

'WE are overjoy'd to hear that you are so
' far advanced on your Journey for
' *Scotland*, we have wrote three times to the
' Scotch-College at *Paris*, but never yet got
' any Answer, which very much surprised us,
' you write to us for fifty Pounds, but your
' Uncle

'Uncle lies a dying, he is given over by the
'Physicians, and has receiv'd all the last Sacra-
'ments of the Church, in order to prepare him
'for his long expected Change; so that I did not
'think it proper to mention a thing of that Im-
'portance to him, knowing that he was incapa-
'ble of taking Notice of any thing more in this
'World, and we are perfectly perswaded that
'there is no Churchman there upon the Spot,
'but what will lend you so much Money as
'will bring you to your own native Place, where
'you have always Money enough at your Com-
'mand upon your Arrival here; I doubt not, but
'it's endless to desire you to offer up your Prayers
'for so good an Uncle as you always had, but I beg
'you'll always remember me in your Prayers a-
'long with him, and pray make all the haste you
'can to this Place; and if you can possible do it,
'bring me a mourning Hood, and a Handker-
'chief, and in so doing you'll oblige,

Dear Nephew,

your loving Aunt,

BARRACK.

Now, when this Rogue had read this counterfeit Letter to me, he shaked his Head, and said that nothing greived him so much as that his Uncle died under the Care of a Jesuit, for he would insinuate himself into his Uncle's Favour so much, that he would get half what he had, and that would be the worse for him, he being the next Heir to all that he had after his Aunt's Death, which would not be long before, for she was very old, and had walked with a Stick a many Years, and his Uncle had gone upon two Crutches above twenty Years: Now, when I heard this, I did not doubt but that the Gentleman would be dead before his Nephew could possibly get to *Scotland,* but I found it to the contrary, for I had not been in *Scotland* long, before the Laird of *Barrack* did me the Honour to come to my Lodgings at *Aberdeen,* to satisfy himself in regard to his Nephew, who had then fill'd the Nation with Amazement and Discourse of him and his Countess: I was much surpris'd, I must own, when I saw the Laird of *Barrack,* who appear'd to me to be as clever a Gentleman as most I saw in *Scotland,* and not more then five or six and forty Years of Age, and he himself told me that his Lady had been dead fifteen Years, and that he enjoy'd as perfect good Health when that Rogue his Nephew said he lay a dying, as he had done for many Years. And to shew farther the Hypocrisy of the Vilain, when *John Gordon* had read that counterfited-Letter to me, he seem'd very full of Grief, to think which way to get to *Scotland* before his Uncle

(41)

Uncle dy'd, to prevent the Jesuits doing him any Prejudice ; and also for fear that he should not get time enough there to provide his Uncle a secular Clergyman to make his Peace with God, and to serve him 'till his ancient Bones was laid in the Dust, from whence they came ; now whilst that vile Rogue was telling me those canting Stories with his grim Looks, he was in expectation, all the while, that I would put him Money into his Pocket to bear his Charges to *Scotland*; but I told him, that he must Address himself to some Body else, for I had done a great deal for him, and could not conveniently let him have much more, least I should have occasion for my Money before he could return it to me again ; but as for what he had then borrow'd of me, I did not in the least question but that he would have restor'd it to me as soon as he could conveniently ; so then Mr. *Gordon* told me that he was acquainted with one Mr. *Garnes*, a *Scotch* Gentleman, who then liv'd at *Greenwich*, and he would go there and endeavour to borrow some Money of him upon his Bill, and by the way, he would enquire whether there was a Captain going off for *Aberdeen*; so then I gave him Money in his Pocket, and away he went.

Now at that time there was Letters come from *France* to several Gentlemen in *London*, which gave an account of his ill Conduct th , but I did not know of that until it was too late, for although Mr. *Middleton* was so good as to come to me at that time, he only desir'd me to
take

take care of him, for he said he was no better then he should be; now I could not tell what to make of this; for when I asked Mr. *Middelton* what he meant by that, he said it was no matter, we muft be careful what we fay in fuch Cafes as thefe; but ftill he perfifted in it, that he was an ill Man, and therefore he faid take care of him. Now although I preft him over and over to tell me what his Reafon was for faying this, and told him that I had lent him a confiderable deal of Money, yet Mr. *Middelton* would not grant me any farther Satisfaction, and therefore this Advertifement was too fmall to take any Root in me, that had never known that Man guilty of the leaft ill Action before, which gave me but too much Confidence in him; however, I hope that I have nothing to anfwer for before God, in regard of that Man; for although I refpected him very much, it was purely for God's Sake, in regard to that Character which I thought he bore at that time; and again, I thought I could never make a return for the Favours I received from him when I was in *Paris*, in a mor fuitable time then to relieve him in his Neceffity.

However, Mr. *Middleton* was no fooner gone from me, but Mr. *Gordon* came in, and found me very much concern'd about what I had heard, he very preffingly defir'd me to tell him what had happen'd, fo then I told him that by fome Information which I had that Day from a Friend of mine, I had reafon to fear that he was not the Man I took him for, but I did not tell

tell him who was my Author, but that he presently judg'd; after which, he wrote a very scurrilous Letter to Mr. *Middleton*, who sent a true Copy of that Letter to Bishop *Gordon* in *Scotland*, where I first heard it; but until I left my own native Place to go with Mr. *Gordon* to *Scotland*, I could not entertain an ill thought of him, for I reason'd with myself, and did believe that the Man was unborn that was without some Scandal or other, whilst our blessed Lord and Saviour did not pass this mortal Life without Scandal, who was God as well as Man; therefor I thought some Person or other, perchance might have pick'd a Hole in his Coat undeservedly, so under these Sentiments I rested myself contented, and continued my Friendship to him, knowing that his Time was but short here, for he had then told me that Captain *Brown* was almost ready to go to *Aberdeen*, and that Mr. *Garnes* had promised to lend him so much Money as would carry him to *Scotland*, but that was a Lie; however, he had borrowed, some time before, a Silver Snuff-Box of Mr. *James Shirley*, Junior, and it was made in the shape of a Cardinal's Hat; and this Box he had kept some time, until Mr. *Shirley* demanded it of him, and then the Vilian said he had left it with me the Night before; so then Mr. *Shirley* came to me the next Day following, and desir'd to know whether Mr. *Gordon* had left such a Box with me, I told him that he had not, but I had seen Mr. *Gordon* have such a Box in his Hand some time before now; at this Mr. *Shirley's ley'* Countenance chang'd, which very much surpris'd me, so that I began to think something was in the Case more then ordinary, I rather equivocated then Mr. *Gordon* should be prov'd a Liar, for I thought he perchance might have left the Box in some other Place, and so told Mr. *Shirley* that to make him easy, and therefore I told him, that if the Box was with me, I did not doubt but that he would believe it was very safe; and again, I told him that the same Person that brought the Box to me, should bring it to him the next Day; and so Mr. *Shirley* left me very well contented, believing still that I had the Box; but he was no sooner gone, but Mr. *Gordon* came to me, and I asked him what he had done with the Box, and what his Reason was for saying that he left it with me; now he never being unprovided of a Lie, very readily told me, that one Day he was short of Money, and was going to *Chelsea* to the Lord *Sutherland* about Business for that sham Countess, which he said was then in *Paris*, and therefore he was oblig'd to leave the Box at a Publick-House for a Crown, I then gave him that Money, and desir'd him to bring the Box to me that night, but he did not think that would answer their wicked Designs, to give me the Satisfaction of seeing that Box so soon, and therefore he came not to me 'till the next Day, and then he told me that he had got the Snuff-Box, but he had unfortunately met with Mr. *Garnes*, who would not be denied the lending of the Box, in order to take a Model of it, it being such a Beautiful Box;

Box; adding, that Mr. *Garnes* had sent his Compliment to me, and had promis'd to come in two or three Days time and take part of a Dinner with me at my Longings, in order to to bring the Money that he had promis'd to lend Mr. *Gordon*, and the Box along with him.

Now I being very well acquainted with Mr. *Garnes*, believ'd the Rogue, and I provided a Dinner for him; but the Gentleman never came, then Mr. *Gordon* pretending to have met with such a great Disappointment, reproach'd Mr. *Garnes* very much with falsifying his Word, when at the same time the Gentleman knew nothing of all this, nor had not seen Mr. *Gordon* of a long time, neither did he ever promise to Dine with me; but all Mr. *Gordon*'s whole Study was to spunge Money out of my Pocket, to supply his Chambermaid's Necessity; however, I being still not contented about the Box, I then gave Mr. *Gordon* a Crown more, to go to *Greenwich* to fetch the Snuff-Box and the Money, but he came without either Money or the Box, and told me that Mr. *Garnes* happen'd to be gone out of Town with his Master, and they was not expected back until the next Day, so *Gordon* pretended to have lost his Labour again; but, however the Rogue said that he would be even with Mr. *Garnes*, for he would go the next Day to know when Captain *Brown* would be ready to go, and he would send one of the Captain's Men to *Greenwich* with his Note for the Money and the Box to Mr. *Garnes*;

nes; and in cafe he fhould not be return'd, then he would order the Man to ftay all Night at *Greenwich*, rather then lofe the lending of the Money or the Box; but his Money being fhort, he beg'd of me to lend him another Crown, and then he hop'd that would be the laft, and all that he fhould have occafion for from me.

Now this hypocritical Rogue that he could fay that to me, when at the fame time he had no expectation of getting one Farthing of any Body elfe befide me; however, his Difcourfe at that time pleas'd me fo well, I gave him the Crown he defir' of me, and away he went, and I faw him no more until the Ship was almoft ready to go off for *Aberdeen*, and then he came to me, and faid he had got the Box, and had reftor'd it to Mr. *Shirley*, but he had got no Money; which to all outward appearance made him very angry with Mr. *Garnes*, and faid how ill he had ferv'd him, by putting him to fuch Expences as he had done; and alfo, he reproach'd Mr. *Garnes*, with making him run after his Tail expecting he would make good his Promife to him, when at the fame time *Gordon* pretended to fay, he believ'd that Mr. *Garnes* never intended to lend him any Money, but made that pretention to cheat and trick him out of the Snuff-Box, and all this time that Gentleman never faw the Box, nor did not know any thing of the Matter, neither was there one word of Truth in all that treacherous Rogue had told me; for, in the firftplace the Cardinal's Hat was never pawn'd, and in the next place, Mr.

(47)

Mr. *Gordon* did not restore the Box to Mr. *Shirley* until the very Morning he went off from this Place to go to *Aberdeen*; now it doth not belong to one of my Sex to wear a Cardinal's Hat, although I have pay'd well for one, and if it did, that would be too great an Honour for me; but I may put on the Fool's Cap, and wear it 'till the last Day of my Life, since I have publish'd my Weakness to the World, except my Readers is pleas'd to put a more favourable Construction upon me then to call me a Fool, for my good Intention to serve a Minister of Jesus Christ, in gratitude for the Favours I had receiv'd from him before; and as I did not know of his dreadful fall I Thought, nothing was too much that I could do to serve him, who was at the last most ungrateful to me of all Persons in the World, as 'twill appear hereafter; for in this time that he had been playing his legerdemain Tricks to get my Money from me, he and his Chambermaid projected a new Scheme to lay before me, which was very pleasing, and but too soon took Place with me; the Chambermaid being indebted to her Landlady near thirty Shillings, was ran away from her Lodgings as far as the Hermitage Stairs, in her Landlady's Riding-Hood, and she had took up her Lodging at the *Edenburgh Castle* Ale-House, in order to wait there, and to be ready to go when the Ship went off; then the Landlady missing her Lodger, enquir'd of Mr. *Gordon* where she was, and he told her that Madam's Absence was occasioned by an accidental Strain on her Ancle;

Ancle; but he told her that she would be able to come to her Lodgings again in two or three Days time he hop'd, but at that time her Ancle was so bad, that she could not stand, for which Reason she was oblig'd to stay at a Friend's House; however, with this Story the Landlady was not content, and Madam being gone, made others suspect Mr. *Gordon*, for he was then endeavouring to gain his Point with me, so I had more of his Company than usual, but I knew not the Reason of that then; so Mr. *Gordon*, to bring his Matters to bare, came to me, and said, Madam, I have oftentimes heard you say, that if it pleas'd God you liv'd you would go to *Scotland*, to see good Mr. *Smith*, whom I long to see as well as you, and as there are some Accounts betwixt you and him that you are desirous to make up with him, I know very well that you will not be easy until that be done; and therefore, said he, if you will please to go to *Scotland* along with me, I do assure you, that for the many Favours which I have received from you, it shall not cost you one Farthing; now this, I own, was a great Inducement to me to go, for I thought he would treat me with the same good Manners as I had us'd him; but yet I told him that I thought I could not conveniently go with him, upon account of my Affairs here; but my friend *Gordon* told me, that we should both return to *London* again in a Month or six Weeks time at the most, and therefore he beg'd of me to consider of it, for he promis'd to take all the Care
of

of me that he possibly could, and said I should not want for any thing *Scotland* could afford me, and he said that I should certainly receive all my Money of him in two or three Days after we arrived at *Aberdeen*. Now all this, I thought, seem'd very feasible, and it was no more then what I might reasonably expect from his Hands, and therefore I but too readily consented to go along with him, and the Ship being ready to go off the next Morning, he desir'd me to pack up my Cloaths in all haste, and be sure to take enough Linnen to serve me, during the time I should stay in *Scotland*, for he said their Women in his Country were very nasty, and he was afraid they would not wash my Linnen to please me; but I rather thought since his chief concern was, that I should take enough for his poor shabby Countess to rob me of, as indeed she had almost gain'd her Point, but was once outwitted in her Life-time; however, I fill'd my Trunk with good things, every thing that was necessary for me, and I took too large silver Spoons, one double guilt with Gold along with me, that at least we might not get sore Mouths by eating after them; but as for Madam *Forbus*, as she call'd herself here, I did not know any thing of her going along with Mr. *Gordon* and me to *Scotland*, until I saw her in her Landlady's Riding-Hood, waiting for our coming at the *Hermitage* Stairs; but now observe the canting Speech that hypocritical Vilain made me when I had repremanded him for dealing underhand with me, that had been so true a Friend to him, and he to bring an impudent Woman,

D   like

like that, in Company with me, and not to advertife me of it, when he knew that my Pocket muft pay for all; in fine, I did give him fuch a Lecture, as I believe he had not had for fome time; he begg'd of me not to be uneafy at any thing for he fhould have Money enough to anfwer all, my Demands, and tentimes more; for, faid he, dear Madam, you know very well, that Gentlemen of our Character is not to fet our Hearts upon Money, but a contrary; we are oblig'd in Duty and Confcience to do all the good we can with what we have, we muft feed the Hungry, and cloath the Naked, or elfe Woe, Woe be to them that doth it not fo far as it's in their Power to do it, he would not have that Lie at his Door for all the World; no Madam, faid he, I will do all the good I can with what I have whilft I live, and then I fhall be fure of an eternal Reward, but he believ'd that many Thoufands of Priefts damn'd themfelves by that very thing; but, Madam *Forbus* did not want his Charity, for what ever he did for her, he faid, the Countefs of *Gordon* would return it to him double when he went back to *Paris* again, and therefore he pray'd me to lend him two Guineas more, that he might pay the Chambermaid's Lodging, and go off handfomely, for Madam had left her beft *French* Robe at her Lodgings in *Red-Lyon-Street*, and could not get it without paying her Lodgings there; but if I had known that, then fhe fhould have gone to *Scotland* without it, and then fhe would have made but a very mean Figure there, for a Countefs tess having nothing but one shabby Gown on her Back, and that Mr. *Gordon* took for her from Mr. *Trantham*'s at *Roune*, when they was both there; however, I gave Mr. *Gordon* two Guineas, and some odd Money, and they both went togeher, for ought I know, for I saw no more of them until I was almost got to *Gravesend*, and then they came in a Boat by themselves, which cost me eight Shillings more; and the next Morning for our Expences in the House, and Provisions for our Voyage, I pay'd eight and twentry Shillings more, before we went off from *Gravesend*; but the Night we stay'd there, Madam was in her Airs, because I did not shew Respect enough to her, as she thought; for what I order'd for our Suppers, was what I lik'd my self; for, as I found that I must pay for all, I thought there was no reason that I should consult with her what we should have; however, she was so much affronted, that she eat no Supper, but call'd for Pen, Ink and Paper to write, as she pretended, to her Lady at *Paris*, and then she said I shou'd soon see who would pay for all in the end, but that gave me no concern at all, and therefore I told her, that if she would eat her Supper she might, or she was as welcome to let it alone ; for what gave me the most concern at that time was, that I thought I knew that hand-writing to be the same that *John Gordon* brought to me in that counterfeited Letter; however, I was resolved to see it out, and so all things being provided, away we went for *Scotland*, and arrived there the sixth Day,

Day, but the laſt Morning all my Tea was gone, but I thought it would be no great hardſhip to go without one Morning, as the Captain ſaid we ſhould be in *Aberdeen* by eleven o'Clock; but Madam order'd the Water to be ready according to cuſtom, and then ſhe aſked me for ſome Tea, but I told her I had none, but ſhe ſaid I had a quarter of a Pound of ſuper-fine Green Tea in my Trunk, would I not have it taken out, I ſaid, no, but ſhe call'd down *John Gordon*, with as much command, as though he had been her Footman, and commanded him to open my Trunk and take out the Tea; but I told him that if he did, it was at his Peril, for I would make them both to ſuffer for it, as ſoon as we got to Land; ſo then they thought it was beſt to keep their Tempers, leaſt they ſhould be at a greater loſs then the wanting of a Breakfaſt.

So we being landed at *Aberdeen*, moſt of our Company went along with us to Mr. *Andrew Moore* to ſalute me with a hearty welcome to *Scotland*, as I had never been there before, and to refreſh our ſelves; ſo the Gentlemen call'd for Scotch *Tipany* in abundance, and a Buſhel of Sea-Sallad, call'd *Dulce*, with hard Cakes and Bonnacks, ſmoak-reak'd Haddocks, and old dry'd Cod, Butter and roaſted Eggs; now ſuch a regale as this I had never ſeen before, I ſat and admir'd to ſee how like to ſo many Swine they all tore and lug'd it to pieces, but I could eat nothing there was, but at length I took courage, and call'd for a glaſs of good *French* Brandy,

Brandy, and a piece of better Bread, if it could be had, and it was brought to me immediately to revive my drooping Spirits, and make me chearful under my Afflictions; for at that time I had trouble enough; however, our Entertainment being at an end, *John Gordon* then wanted Money to pay for what we had in that House, and for want of other change, I was obblig'd to let him have another Guinea, but I told him that I must have half of the Money again into my own Pocket, but he did not design to give me any at all, for after the reckoning was pay'd, he gave one part of it to his Countess, and the rest he kept in his own Pocket, to assist him until he got to his Aunt *Barrack*, who was then risen from the Dead; but as for the Laird of *Barrack* I did not expect he was alive; however, the next Day Mr. *Gordon* went to see how all things were, but before he went from me, he was so just and honest to me, that he spoke to Mr. and Mrs. *Moore,* and desir'd them not to let me want for any thing that place could afford me, and he would pay them for all when he return'd; so I being very well provided for in that House, he placed his Countess the same way in another House, for I would not allow her to be in Company with me any more, so then he desir'd me to lend him my Velvet Cap to ride in, that he might appear a little genteel amongst his Friends.

So I lent him that, and away he went to his Uncle *Barracks,* where he stay'd five Days, and I all that time was as full of Pleasure, as an Egg

D 3   is

is full of Meat, expecting to receive my Money from him when he return'd, but I was much mistaken, for that Rogue had no Pretention to expect one Farthing from his Uncle, except he gave him any out of pure Charity; but all that time I was wanting my Trunk from Captain *Brown* until the last Day, and then I being almost out of all Patience about it, I asked the Captain what his reason was for keeping my Cloaths so long, the Captain's reply was this, Madam, I really do not know who the Trunk belongs to, for the other Lady that came along with you, says the Trunk and Cloaths is all hers, and you'll Pardon me, Madam, said the Captain, if I tell you that she says you was only her Cookmaid when she liv'd in *Paris*, and that she always thought of parting with you as soon as you was arrived here; and at the same time she declared herself publickly to be the Countess of *Gordon*, and Daughter to the Lord *Southerland*.

Now I cannot say but this very much surprised me, to hear of the Impudence of that impertinent Woman, but yet I could hardly believe but that there must certainly be some mistake betwixt the Captain and she, but he assur'd me of the contrary, and gave me an account of all my things that I had in my Trunk, as she had told him; she told the Captain there was all her best *French* Robes in the Trunk, Holland Sheets for her own use, and fine Damask Table Linning, and a great deal of very fine Linning for her own Wear, a Fan worth ten Guineas, and some Plate.

Now

(55)

Now when I heard this, my Blood began to be in a ferment, to think that that Rogue *Gordon* should deal so treacherously with me as to betray me into the hands of such a Jilt; I then call'd two Witnesses, and charg'd the Captain not to part with my Trunk to any Body but my self, and told him that if he did not send it to me that Night, I would have him before the Magistrates the next Morning, and then he sent me my Trunk immediately, and *John Gordon* came from his Uncles that Night, but did not see me until the next Day, by reason he had got no Money from his Uncle to pay me as I expected, therefore he went into the City, in order to see young Doćter *Gordon,* whom he had seen in *Paris,* and pretended to him that his Purse and Silver Watch had been taken from him by Robbers at *London,* and that he was hastning to see Doćter *James* then at *Edenborough,* but was oblig'd first to clear his Skipper, and therefore he pray'd Doćter *Gordon* to give him five or six Guineas upon his Bill, but Doćter *Gordon* gave him but one; yet when he went to Doćter *Ross* with the same Tale, he having being acquainted with him also at *Paris,* he advanced five Guineas upon *John Gordon*'s Bill, and then *John Gordon* came to me, and shew'd me those six Guineas, and told me that was all the Money his Uncle had at that time; but he said, that the *Midsummer* Term was nigh at hand, and then his Uncle would have Money enough for him to pay me all.

In the mean time, *John Gordon* said he would go to *Edenborough*, to finish his Affairs there, and leave me and his Countess at *Aberdeen*, although, at the same time, his design was to take her along with him; but the Night before he went he came to me at my Lodgings, and pay'd Mr. *Moor* for what I had had in their House, and pass'd his Word for what I should have occasion for until he return'd from *Edenborough*; then he told me he had got a very sore Mouth by eating with a Wooden Spoon after his Aunt *Barrack*, which made him think the People in that part of the Country were very unwholesome, and therefore he pray'd me to lend him one of my Silver Spoons until he return'd; so I lent him one, and he took the other, and a fine *Chince* Handkerchief which cost me six Livers in *Paris*, he took it out of my Trunk, and a Velvet Cap which he borow'd of me when he went to his Unclec, which he never return'd to me, but kept it to put upon Madam's Head, to make her appear the more like a Countess; so when he had got all that he could from me, he went to his own Lodgings, but left word by the Family that he would Breakfast with me in the Morning before he went his Journey, so I waited whilst eleven o'Clock, and he never appear'd, and then I had lost all hopes of seeing him that Day, and at three o'Clock in the Afternoon, Captain *Brown* came to me, and told me he saw my old Friend, *John Gordon* and his Lady at *Stone-hive* going to *Eden'orough*, and Madam had my Velvet Cap on her Head, which he thought no ways became her;

her; but what gave him the moſt concern, was, that his Lady had told him, that *Gordon* had got my two Silver Spoons and given them to his Counteſs, who had expoſed them in her Lodgings, and told every Body there, that they Spoons was hers, and that I had Stole them from her, although there was W. H. M. upon them, which was my Husband's Name and his late Wives, whoſe Name was Mary; and yet for all that, her Impudence protected her ſo far, as to ſay, that the Spoons were hers, and ſhe would make me to ſmart for what I had done to her, by keeping her Spoons and her Trunk, ſo that ſhe could not dreſs herſelf, to appear like a Lady of Quality as ſhe ought to do; and ſhe ſaid in ten Days time they would all be ſatisfy'd about her, when ſhe return'd from *Edenborough*, attended out of Town by all Perſons of Diſtinction and their Equipage, in reſpect to her Family; then, ſaid ſhe, all the Gentlemen at *Aberdeen* will meet me at the Bridge of *Dee*, which is two Miles out of *Aberdeen*, to celebrate my Arrival to that Place, with no leſs Attendance then the King's Guards, with their Guns, Kettle-Drums, and Trumpets, Hautboys, French-Horns, Flutes, and in fine, all ſorts of Muſick for her Honour and Service, and then woe be to me, for ſhe would cauſe me to be whipt through the Town for my ill Behaviour to her.

 Now ſo great was the Impudence of that wicked and baſe Impoſtor, to amuſe thoſe People with ſuch Stories as that, whilſt ſhe was picking their
Pockets;

Pockets; and to compleat her Story, she asked her Landlord, he being Captain *Brown*'s Shipmate, whether he would rather accept of being made Master of a Vessel himself, or to have all Debts pay'd, which I understood then was pretty many, for she promis'd him that she would either make him Captain of a Sea-faring Ship to *France*, or pay all his Debts when she return'd from *Edenbourgh*: Now which of the two poor Mr. *John Moor* made his Choice of for his Preferment, that I could not tell, but it gave the poor Man so much Pleasure (the thoughts of being once more rais'd again in the World) that he could not keep his own Counsel, but publish'd it so much, that he was afterwards laugh'd at for his Pains; for instead of the Lady performing her promise to him, she slipt away privately out of the Town fourteen Shillings indebted to him for Meat, Drink, and Lodging, which Story diverted me much, for poor *John Moor* was so proud of his Rise, that he began to be insolent; however his Lady then being gone to *Edenborough*, she did not return back to *Aberdeen* whilst I stay'd there, for if she had, I was resolv'd to Imprison her until she had made me satisfaction for all Damages done to me; but she thought it was better to stay with her favourite Swain at *Edenborough*, where they continued together three Weeks, in which time *John Gordon* had Apostatized his Religion according to the former Account which I have given of him, and then, when he had done that, he publish'd it in the News-Papers, which

coming

coming to my hand to Read, and finding there *John Gordon*'s Advertisement, I was so much surpriz'd and seised with Grief, that I could hardly tell how to contain myself, my Grief was so great that my very Heart was ready to break, for I thought that whilst he was capable of doing that, he was abandon'd by God, and then I thought there was but little hopes remaining for me to expect any Justice done to me by such a Rogue as that, who out of Revenge to his Eldest Brother, who was a Catholick, and belonging to the Society of the Jesuits, sold his Soul to the Devil, to cheat him of his Birthright, it being the Law of the Nation that the Protestant Heir should inherit the Land.

So *John Gordon*, as soon as he had Apostatized his Religion, call'd himself Laird of *Glencat*, and the sham Countess, at the same time, had the Impudence to add to her former Tittles, Baronness of *Barrack*, which Title she took from the Laird of *Barrack*'s Estate, which *John Gordon* expected to be the next Heir to, but in that he is much mistaken, for the Laird of *Barrack* told me, when I had the Honour to see him, that *John Gordon* should never enjoy one Pennyworth of his Estate.

However, these are the only Motives which induced *John Gordon* to renounce his Religion, it was not his ill Usage he met with amongst the Catholicks, nor the weakness of his Faith, or any confinement that he had in his College; for to my knowledge he had all the liberty that he could desire at all his leisure Hours, which was

time

time enough sufficient for any Person to have made their escape; therefore it is plain that he never offer'd to make any attempt to leave the College, until he, for keeping Company with the Countess was extruded from it; and then, because he still persisted in his Wickedness, all his Friends abandon'd him, for his whole Study then was to counterfeit Letters, false Bills, and the like to supply the pretended Countess of *Gordon*'s Necessity, which was then very great; for it was but in the Year twenty Eight that she had very justly been imprison'd for her Behaviour in the *South* of *France*, where she began to play some of her Pranks again to trick the Jesuits there, but it seems they outwitted her, but she was too sharp for some other Gentlemen there; in those Parts she got then three hundred and fifty Pounds from one Mr. *Dowdal*, who hath lost all hopes now of ever seeing the Lady again, and Mr. *Baujan*, a Merchant in that Place lent her six *Louis Dores*, but he expected to be pay'd by Mr. *Alexander*, a *Banqaier* at *Paris*, by reason he recommended the Lady to him; she went then by the Name of Madam *Dallas*.

The Gentleman who gives this Account of her, lent her only three and twenty Livers, which he gives heartily for lost, and was glad it was no more; he said she was in but very poor Condition then much engaged to her Landlord, and had not one sousé to pay him, and then she contriv'd a Trick to come of, which was to make the Jesuits believe her design was to become a Catholike, therefore she was oblig'd to keep in Cognito;

nito ; this went on for some Days, and in the mean time the Jesuits writ several ways to know whether she was right or no, and they found she was *une avant urvie de* Profession ; so that did not take with the Jesuits, and therefore she was oblig'd to make her escape from that Place, and then she went to *Lyons*, where she succeeded much better, for a little time she past there for the Dutchess of *Gordon*, and was visited by several Persons of Distinction, till one Day that a Gentleman of my acquaintance happen'd to be in company with her Grace, as she was coming from the Church, and all on a sudden, she with seeming Surprize, said, Oh! Sir, I am ruin'd, the Gentleman was much concern'd for her, and said, God forbid, Madam, what has happened to your Grace: She seem'd to make some difficulty to tell him, but at length, she said, her Pocket was cut off in the Church, and all her Money was gone, so that she did not know how to proceed on her Journey; but what griev'd her the most, was, that she had a very rich Seal in her Pocket, with the Coat of Arms of the *Gordons*, which had been in her Family many Years, that she would not have took a thousand Pounds for it, and a Purse set with Dimonds. Likewise, a Gold Snuff-box and Gold Watch, and several other valuable things worth a great deal of Money. However, she said, that if she could, but get to *Montpilier*, she had a Daughter there with a Gentleman who would lend her Money enough; but when my Friend understood who that Gentleman was, he knew she Ly'd, for it was but

few

few Days before that happen'd, that my Friend came from that House, where he had stay'd some Days to rest himself upon his Journey: So then he began to think the fine Lady was an Impostor, and he gave her nothing, but she went to a Merchant in that Place the next Day with the same tail, and he out of compassion to a Lady of Quality, as he took her to be, and in distress, lent her a considerable deal of Money to assist her on her Journey, and the Gentleman took so much concern for her great loss, that he put himself to a pretty deal of expence to catch the Thief. So if the Lady had been content with her welfare with him, she had not been so soon discover'd; but she going to several other Merchants in that Place, with the same tail, and showing them all how her Pocket was cut off, they had the like compassion on her, and lent her a considerable deal of Money amongst them; after which she hir'd a Chaise, and away she went for *Paris*, but the sham Lady was no sooner gone from thence, but the Gentlemen began to compare their Notes together, and finding themselves bit, they sent after her, and took her upon the Road, carried her back to *Lyons*, where they Imprison'd her for some time, and several Letters were sent after her, which gave account of her Pocket being cut off where ever she went; so then the Gentlemen finding there was nothing to be got back of their Money, they turn'd her out of Prison, and away she went, this was in the Year One Thousand Seven Hundred and Twenty Eight; and in the Year Thirty, she was banished

nished out of *France* by the King's Order, and that Rogue, *John Gordon*, had no more Grace then to bring that abominable wicked Impostor to me, who had only heard of her vile Character she bore when I was at *Paris*; but I had never seen her before to the best of my Knowledge, till she came to *England*; where she past for the Countess of *Gordon*'s Chambermaid, and went by the Name of Madam *Forbous*, to deceive me whilst she got to *Scotland*; where she openly declared her self to be the Countess of *Gordon*, and Daughter to the Lord *Sutherland*, to the Surprize of all our fellow Travellers, for they all thought I was the better Gentlewoman, and indeed it was with good reason, for they see that my Pocket pay'd for all. I wish I had known as much before as I did then, I would have made the poor Countess have begg'd her way to *Scotland*; and her running Footman too, and put a stop to their wicked and base Designs there, much sooner then I did; however since, by the order of divine Providence, I went along with them to *Scotland*; and although it cost me a great deal of Money to put a stop to their base Proceedings, I never yet repented of any thing that I did in regard to them I cannot say, but that it was a little shocking to me, when I heard that Woman had declar'd that she was the Countess of *Gordon*, whom I then supposed to be in *Paris*, and that I was only her Cookmaid. However, to do the Devil Justice, I must say, notwithstanding my old Friend *Gordon* had betray'd me into the company of such a Jilt, and had got all the Mo-

ney

ney I took with me; he afterwards took care that I should not want for neceſſaries of Life, for he promis'd Mr. *Moor* and his Wife to pay them for every thing that I ſhould have occaſion for, during the time he ſhould ſtay at *Edenborough*, when he went to renounce his Religion: So he left me at *Aberdeen* three Weeks, in which time he not only renounc'd Popery, but he alſo renounc'd all good Morality, for when he return'd to *Aberdeen* again, altho' he had promis'd Payment for my Board, he lodg'd in the Town and never intended to come nigh me; but he being very well known by the Character he left behind him, when he and his ſham Counteſs left that Place to go to *Edenborough*, his Landord where he log'd ſent me Word privately, That my Friend *Gordon* was come to Town, and was then in his Houſe, if I deſired to ſee him; ſo I went immediately to hear what the Rogue could ſay for his not coming nigh me; when I was not only expecting the Payment of all Charges I was at in Mr. *Moor*'s Houſe; but I expected upon his return from *Edenborough*, the full Payment of that and all the Money which I lent him here in *England*, where he muſt abſolutely have ſtarv'd if I had not aſſiſted him; yet notwithſtanding all that, when I went to him, he had the impudence to tell me that he had nothing to ſay to me directly or indirectly; but told me, that he was then Proteſtant, and had declared himſelf ſuch before the Preſbitery of *Edenborough*; adding, that he was under no obligation to me, but I was owing many to him, he was nothing

in-

indebted to me, nor noth'ng he would pay me; however, when I heard this, I did not spare him, I made him know before I had done with him, that he was under ten thousand times more obligations to me then ever I was to him, like an ungrateful Rogue as he was, to tell me such Stories as that: Although I got no more recompence that Night from that Vilian, but the next Day Mr. *Andrew Moor*, took out a Writ against *John Gordon*, who getting notice of it hid himself, and set Spies to watch, least he should be apprehended and Imprison'd, for he had no Money, and therefore he had determin'd to leave *Aberdeen* the next Morning, and return to *Edenborough* to secure himself from me, but to his great Surprize the Bailiffs being order'd to search for him, they found him in Bed and secur'd him, whilst such time as he could give Mr. *Moor* Security for his Money, and then away he went after his Morning Cogg of good *Scotch* Tippenny Yael, which he drank with a heavy Heart, instead of mull'd Sack, which he us'd to drink in a Morning with his Lady. However, when the Bailiffs return'd along with Mr. *Moor* to my Lodgings, they told me that my Friend *Gordon* had got another Religion, for, by fear and trembling he was that Morning become a Quaker; but what diverted them the most was, that they fear'd the Quaker had spoil'd his Bed, for he was observ'd to be in such a Condition with the fright, that he could scarce find his way out to dress himself: However, a

F.   so soon as the Quaker had recover'd his self a little, he went to *Edenborough*, where he he'd Forth by the motion of the Spirit, but the Subject of his Discourse was taken from *Aberdeen*, which Discourse did not take well with his Countess. However, they was oblig'd to make the best they could of a bad Bargin, and they being got together, I will leave them there, whilst I acquaint my Readers how I dispos'd of my self, I being then left at *Aberdeen*, without any hopes of getting one Farthing of my Money again, which I expected to have received there, before I came back to *London* again; however, as I had nothing more to do at *Aberdeen*, then I wrote a Letter to the honourable Lord and Lady *Pit Foddals*, who had some time before given me a very kind invitation to go to their country Seat, a Place call'd *Mary Couther*, and they sent a Man and a Horse for me immediately, after which I went to pay my Duty and Respect to that worthy Family, where I stay'd two Months and wanted for nothing that *Scotland* could afford me, and for their kind Entertainment to me, who was a Stranger and a Traveller in distress, the Memory of them shall not cease although I die; but now, all that time *John Gordon* and his sham Countess play'd their legerdemain Tricks and met with no interruption, until the Ministers at *Edenborough* wrote some Letters and sent them to *Aberdeen*, which gave an extraordinary account of their new Proselite, and Protestant

testant Heir; and of all his Dexterity, they not knowing the blackness of his artful Ways. However, I being then determin'd to return to *England* again, I was resolv'd, if possible, to know the Contents of the Letters at *Aberdeen*, before I came away; so I went to a Gentleman, whom *John Gordon* was so highly recommended to, when he went North to take possession of the Land of *Glencat*, which is in the Parish *Birss*, in the County of *Aberdeen*; and the Gentleman gave me a very just Account of all the villianous Behaviour of those two wicked Impostors, and seem'd to take very much concern for the poor young Man, who had been so great a sufferer by his Popish Relations, and also, his catholick Brethren abroad, who had kept him so close a Prisoner for so many Years as they did, that the poor sufferer, although he had made many attempts to make his Escape, he could never accomplish his desire, until that Lady of Quality who came along with him, took an opportunity to steal the young Man out through a Window of the College, and bring him in a Cart, cover'd with a Blanket all the way through *France*; and in fine, the Gentleman thought the new Proselite ought to be very thankful to God for so safe a deliverance from his Enemies, and for his part he thought his escape was most wonderful; now when I had heard this, I was much Surpriz'd, and could not help telling him, that I should have been of his Opinion, and thought the same, in Case there had been one word of Truth in all

E 2   that

that his Letter contain'd, in regard to those two Impostors; but to the contrary, I presently made appear to the Gentleman, that all those Stories was nothing but Lies and Calumny that *Gordon* had made to insinuate his self into their Favours, in order to get some Preferment by them, and to confirm that, I shew'd him a Letter which I had in my Pocket, that *John Gordon* had sent me from *Paris*, soon after he was disgracefully turn'd out of the College; and this said Letter gave him account of every particular, how he had determined to dispose of himself, after being at his own Liberty, and abandon'd by all his Friends. Nay, I shew'd two more Letters of the same Hand-Writing to him, after which he was thoroughly convinc'd that *Gordon* was a very great Impostor, and told me that it was but just in me to make the Rogue a publick Example; and again, he said, that it would be doing Justice both to God and Man, to expose them both, knowing well how far it was in my Power to do it; and the Gentleman assur'd me, that he would write to *Edenborough* himself, to the Ministers there, and acquaint them with what he had heard and seen from me, that they might no longer be deceiv'd by such vile Hipocrites, and to prevent the wicked Proceedings of that sham Countess, by whose lying Tongue many has been deceiv'd: So then our Converse being at an End, I took my leave of the Gentleman and return'd to *Mary Couther* again, where I staid but few Days longer, and then I hired a Horse and a Man to go alongwith me to *Edenborough*, where I went to see me old Friend *Gordon* once more, who would much rather have given all the Shoes in his Shop, then to have seen my Face there. However, I was no sooner got to that Place; but *John Gordon* came to the Knowledge of it, and then the Countess and he retir'd into a Baudy-House, where they stay'd some Days before I could get any Knowledge of them, any further then that they was just gone from one Lodging fourteen Pounds indebted to their Landlady, one Mrs. *Scot*, who Lives by the Trone *Kirk*, who told me a pleasant Story of what happened frequently to the Countess and her running Foot-man, in the time which they stay'd in her House. Now, although the Countess was very poor, yet her proud imperious Spirit would not allow her to let her necessity be known to any, but particularly in the House where she Lodg'd: So when it happen'd, as it did very often, that they had neither a Farthing of Money or Bread to eat, the Countess on those Days always went to Dinner with the Lord Chief Justice *Clark*, or else with Sir *Dunken Forbous*, the King's Advocate, as her Grace was pleas'd to tell her Landlady; but she being always very hungry when her Ladyship return'd Home to her Lodging at Night, it made the People suspect whether she had been with those Gentlemen or not, notwithstanding all her Eevnings Discourse was, in telling her Landlady how many Dishes of Meat came to the Table that Day where she Din'd, and how many Sorts of Wine, and either Coffee or Tea, with a Glaſs of good *French* Brandy to conclude with, which gave the Lady always ſuch an Appetite, that ſhe could eat at Night Six Eggs, with only a little Salt and hard Bonnox, in caſe Mrs. *Scot* would give her them upon Credit, and then the Footman got the like Portion; but Mrs. *Scot* was reſolv'd to ſatisfy her Curioſity, and therefore ſhe ſent her Servant after the Lady one Day, when ſhe ſaid, that ſhe was going to Dine with the Lord Chief Juſtice *Clark*, and at the ſame time ſhe was only going her own walks into the Fields, where ſhe had wont to ſtay whole Days, and return to her Lodging at Night, as full of Lies, as an Egg is full of Meat, after ſuffering on thoſe Days both hunger and cold; and again, it was in that ſame Houſe that they Lodg'd, when *John Gordon* renounc'd his former Principles, and took up none, for the very Sunday following when theſe Gentlemen might very reaſonably have expected to have ſeen their new Proſelite at their own *Kirk*, to make his firſt Appearance amongſt that Congregation, the fooliſh Rogue went to a Quakers-Meeting to hear their Nonſence; after which he return'd to his Lodgings again, where he held forth as furiouſly by the Motion of the Spirit, as tho' the Devil had been in him, to the great Surprize of all his Hearers. So now I will leave my Readers to conſider what Religion that miſerable Man has in him now.

However,

However, Notwithstanding he began to Act so foolishly then, he had so much wit remaining, as to consider where his chief interest lay; therefore to make his Friends amends, he promis'd them to write a Book against the Church of *Rome*, for which Reason the Lord Chief Justice *Clark* was pleas'd to make the new Proselite a Present of twenty Pounds, which he heartily repented; for soon after, now all this, and much more of the like Proceedings, I was entertain'd with as soon as I came to *Edenborough*, where I had been but few Days, before Doctor *Ross* had took out a Decreet against *John Gordon* for the five Guineas which he lent him upon his first arrival at *Aberdeen*, for which Money the Doctor laid an Arrestment upon the Land of *Glencat*, and as soon as I heard of that I lost no Time, for then I got Knowledge of the House, where the Laird of *Glencat* and his poor Countess Lodg'd, and then I went to a Lawyer and laid my Cause before him, and he wrote my Bill over in Form, and sent his *Clerk* along with me to another Agent, who immediately drew me up a complaint against *John Gordon* of *Glencat*, and he went along with me to the Council Chamber, and read my Complaint before the Magistrates; after which they granted me a summery Warrant, in order to bring *John Gordon* to Justice the next Day, the Magistrates seem'd much concern'd for me, when they understood who I was by my Husband's Name, as he had been very well known there, and had also been made a Freeman of that City; but yet the Gentleman could not help telling me, that they was a little Surpriz'd to think that a Woman like me, should have been so much tricked and beguil'd of both Money and Goods, in the Manner as I was, for they was pleas'd to say, that I appear'd to them to be a Woman of more Sense. However the construction they put upon that, was, that they believ'd the Catholicks would Sacrifice their Lives to serve their Church-men; but they was soon convinc'd of that, after I had laid before them all the black artful Ways and Means, that Rogue had us'd to me, and the Lies and Stories he told them, at the Profession of his new Faith, and also his forged Letters to me and others; then the Gentlemen began to think, that whilst *John Gordon* was capable of such villiny, as I had laid to his Charge, he would not stick at taking a Purse on the High-way; so they order'd four Officers to be call'd in, and gave them the Warrant into their own Hands, and order'd them to bring *John Gordon* before them the next Morning, and they found that he had not been in his own Bed that Night; but searching for him in the Countess of *Gordon*'s Room, they found him under her Bed, with only his Breeches on; and this coming to the *Kirk* Treasurer's Ears, he made it his Business to come after them to the Council Chamber, in order to examine *John* and his Countess, about their honesty, which God knows there was but little of that on either Side. However, the *Kirk* Treasurer and the poor Countess was order'd

to

to withdraw, and go into another Room, whilſt John Gordon and I had our Trial over; but firſt of all the Magiſtrates deſir'd John Gordon to tell them ſincerely, whether he was Married to the ſham Lady or not, and John Gordon declar'd, as in the preſence of God, that he was not Married to her, nor never intended any ſuch thing, but as he had neither Friends nor Acquaintance, or Intereſt with any Perſon there, but what he had made by her Means, he was oblig'd to live with her, till ſuch time as he could get ſettled in the World, and then he told the Gentlemen, that he would never ſuffer the Jilt to come nigh him any more: So then the Door was order'd to be ſhut, and the Lady kept out whilſt John Gordon and I had our Trial over, then the Magiſtrates deſir'd their Clerk to read my Complaint which I had made: So then it was read to them before John Gordon's Face, that they might hear what Objections he would make againſt it.

The Clerk *Reads in the following Manner and Form.*

'HERE is a Complaint made againſt Mr.
' John Gordon of *Glencat*, made by Mrs.
' *Elizabeth Harding*, Widow, and relict of Mr.
' *William Harding* of *London*, who liv'd in
' *Lambeth*, in the County of *Surrey*, he was
' a Freeman of *London*, and was made Bur-
' geſs and gil'd Brother of this City of *Eden-*
' *borough* ; and this ſaid Mr. *William Harding*
' went to *Paris*, in the Year One Thouſand Se-
' ven Hundred and Twenty Five, by a Con-
' tract made betwixt Monſieur *Paris* and this
' ſaid Mr. *William Harding*, who liv'd at
' *Paris*, until the Year One Thouſand Seven
' Hundred and Twenty Eight, and then this
' ſaid Mr. *Harding* was viſited with Sickneſs, and
' made his laſt Will, and made his ſaid Spouſe,
' Mrs. *Elizabeth Harding* his ſole and only Exe-
' cutrix of his laſt Will and Teſtament, in *Sep-*
' *tember* One Thouſand Seven Hundred Twenty
' Eight, and this ſaid Mr. *William Harding* di-
' ed the Thirteenth Day of *February* following,
' new Stile ; and then this ſaid Mrs. *Elizabeth*
' *Harding*'s Affairs occaſion'd her to ſtay at
' *Paris* ſome time after, in which Time, this
' ſaid Mrs. *Harding*, became acquainted with
' Mr. John Gordon of *Glencat*, who then
liv'd

(75)

'liv'd in the *Scotch* College in *Paris*, and they be-
'ing acquainted there, they promised each other
'to keep a friendly Correspondence with each o-
'ther, when his and her Affairs should call them
'into *England*; so this said Mr. John Gordon be-
'ing coming to *England*, and he having his Poc-
'ket picked at *Diep*, he was oblig'd to borrow
'some Money of this said Mrs. *Elizabeth Hard-*
'*ing*, who was then in *London*, until such time as
'he could have a return of his Letters from
'*Scotland*, and then the said Mr. John Gordon
'promis'd to pay this said Mrs. *Elizabeth*
'*Harding* all that he should be indebted to
'her: So this said Mrs. *Elizabeth Harding*,
'lent this said Mr. John Gordon the Sum of
'four and twenty Pounds Sterling, in Money
'and Goods.

'First of all this said Mrs. *Elizabeth Hard-*
'*ing*, lent this said Mr. John Gordon two
'Guineas to pay the Woman that came a-
'long with him from *France*, for he said,
'that he was oblig'd to borrow two Gui-
'neas of her to pay his Passage from *Diep*;
'so Mrs. *Harding* paid the Woman One Guinea
'at Mrs. *Barns's* near *Tottenham-Court*, *Lon-*
'*don*; and the next Day, she paid the other
'Guinea at the *White Hart* in *Southwark*;
'and half a Guinea to the Coach-man, for
'bringing John Gordon and the Woman to
'her Lodgings twice.

The

The Magistrates said,

'MR. *Gordon*, the particulars are so plain, that there must certainly be Truth in this, we all know the *White-Heart* in *Southwark*; and its not so far from this Place, but that we can soon know whether you was at that House or not, therefore Mr. *Gordon*, you had much better be ingenious and acknowledge your Debt, and either pay Mrs. *Harding* her Money, or give her your Bill for that Sum to be payable at such a time as she is pleas'd to except off.

' But, John Gordon denied the Debt, or that ever he saw one Farthing of my Money, although he went along with me, where I received sixteen Pounds twelve Shillings for two Ton and a half of Iron, which John Gordon kept an Account of the Weight, and wrote the Receipt which I gave for that Money; yet, notwithstanding all that, he would have given his Oath, that he never saw either Money or Goods.

The *Clerk* Reads,

'THIS said Mrs. *Elizabeth Harding*, lent this said Mr. John Gordon, two Guineas more at different times to buy Stockings, Shoes, and other Necessaries.

John Gordon denied it.

' The

The Clerk,

'AND this said Mrs. *Elizabeth Harding*,
' lent this said Mr. *John Gordon*, two Gui-
' neas more to pay for the exchange of two
' old Perriwhigs, and to buy him a Hat, but
' John Gordon denied that.

The Clerk,

'AND Mrs. *Harding*, lent Mr. John Gor-
' don fifteen Shillings more, at three dif-
' ferent Times, to redeem a silver Snuff-Box,
' which he borrowed of Mr. *James Shirly*, Ju-
' nior, and this said Snuff-Box was made in the
' shape of the Cardinals Hat, which Mr. *Gordon*
' told Mrs. *Harding* he had Pawn'd; but John
' Gordon denied it, he only acknowledg'd he
' knew the young Man when he was in *Paris*,
' and went there by the Name of *Cortney*, alias
' *Shirly*, during the time he was a Student there.

The Clerk,

'MRs. *Harding* lent Mr. *Gordon* a Holland
' Shirt, valued half a Guinea, and two
' Guineas more for to pay his Lodgings, and the
' Womans that came along with him, who
' when she was in *London*, lodg'd with a Gen-
' tlewoman in *Red-Lion-Street*, until she was
' near thirty Shillings indebted to her Landlady,
' and then she run away privately in her Landla-
' dies Riding-hood; but she left her Black and
' White *French* Robe at her Lodgings, and
' therefore Mr. *Gordon* borrowed that Money

' of Mrs. *Harding*, to pay his Ladies Lodgings,
' that she might get her Gown away, and re-
' store her Hood; but John Gordon denied
' all this.

The Clerk,

' Mrs. *Harding*, at different Times, lent
' Mr. *Gordon* four Pounds for Pocket
' Money, and Mrs. *Harding* lent Mr. *Gordon* five
' Guineas more, to bear his Charges to *Scot-*
' *land*, and Mr. *Gordon* promis'd Mrs. *Hard-*
' *ing*, that he would pay her all the Money
' that he had borrowed of her, as soon as they
' came to *Scotland*; he also told Mrs. *Harding*,
' that he would pay all her Expences to *Scot-*
' *land*, and till she return'd back again to the
' Place where he took her from, by Reason she
' came to this Place to serve him; and also,
' for the many Favours which he had receiv'd
' from her, when he was in *England*, but
' *Gordon* denied it.

The Magistrates said,

' MR. *Gordon*, we are very much Surprized
' to hear you deny every Thing, when the
' Particulars seems to us, to be of undeniable
' Truth, for it is morally impossible, that ever
' any Person could make up such a Story as
' this is out of nothing, without varying or any
' Equivocation in the least; and again, Mrs.
' *Harding* seems to us all, to have laid her
' Cause before us, with so much Sincerity, that
' we cannot but believe that there must cer-
' tainly be Truth in what she lays to your
' Charge,

'Charge, and we really think that we see
'something in your Face that shows you are
'Guilty.

'The Clerk,
'Mrs. *Harding* lent Mr. *Gordon* a Velvet Cap, after they came to *Scotland*, to ride in when he went to his Uncle *Barracks*, which he never return'd, valued one Guinea, but *Gordon* denied that.

'And two large Silver Spoons, one of them double Guilt, valued five and thirty Shillings, which Mr. *Gordon* took from Mrs. *Harding* at *Aberdeen*, and a large fine *Chince* Handkerchief, he took at the same time, valued six Shillings, and one Guinea which Mrs. *Harding* lent Mr. *Gordon* in Mr. *Moor*'s House in *Aberdeen*.

The Magistrates said,
'Mr. *Gordon*, now consider well what you do, Mrs. *Harding* we believe has made you a very just Bill, and also, has given us so just Account of every particular, that we have all reason in the World to believe that Mrs. *Harding* hath been a very great sufferer by you, but it is not too late to make her amends, 'Therefore, now deal justly by her, and either pay her the Sum of four and twenty Pounds Sterling, or else give her your Bill to pay her, at the time she will please to consent to for the Payment of that Money.

'But

'But *John Gordon* refus'd to give me his Bill, and said, that he never saw any of my Money, or any of my Good, and he desir'd to give his Oath upon the same.

'But the Magistrates refused to give *John Gordon* his Oath; and they told him, that they could not in Conscience do it, as they was so thoroughly convinc'd of all his villany, that they believ'd John Gordon would not make any scruple to Swear that Black was White, or White was Black, since he had not the common Principle of Honesty in him, for if he had, he could never have had so much Impudence as to deny so many Truths, as were so justly laid before him; notwithstanding most of our hearers was of the Opinion, that the sham Countess of *Gordon*, had taught him his Lesson. However, the Magistrates being resolved to try how far his Impudence would protect him, they desired me to shew them that Letter which John Gordon wrote to me, after he was turn'd out of the College in *Paris*, that they might see whether he would deny his own Hand Writing; And I then gave that Letter to Mr. *Dinn*, the Clerk, who held it before John Gordon's Face, and asked him whether he knew that Hand Writing; and *Gordon* said, yes, Sir, it is my own, and then the Gentlemen upbraided him with villanous Lies, that he had told the Ministers

'nisters and other Gentlemen at the Profession
' of his new Faith; they said Mr. *Gordon*, how
' could you say that Woman stole you out at
' a Window of the College, and procur'd a
' Guard to secure your Person, whilst she got
' you into a Cart cover'd with a Blanket, and
' that she brought you through *France* in that
' manner, when at the same time you knew it
' to the contrary, which is prov'd here by your
' own hand Writing, you say here that you
' was turn'd out of the College, and that
' upon a quarter of an Hours Advertisement,
' by your Superiors; and that the only Cause
' they had, was for acting. For Mrs. *Mathews*,
' and standing up in Defence of a Lady of Qua-
' lity, who they endeavour'd to Blast and ruin'd,
' her Reputation; then the Magistrates desired
' me to tell them who these Women were, and
' my answer was, that Mrs. *Matthews* was a
' young Woman that wanted a Service, and
' *John Gordon* was endeavouring to get her to
' be Chambermaid to this wicked Woman that
' he keeps Company with here in *Scotland*;
' who, when she was in *Paris*, went by the
' Name of Madam, *La Countess de* Gordon;
' and she was known there to be an Impostor;
' therefore the Superiors of the *Scotch* College,
' knowing of *John Gordon*'s ill Conduct, they
' forbid him to go any more to his Lady, and
' he refusing to obey, they extruded him from
' the College.

F ' Now,

'Now all this time *John Gordon* stood Mute, and had not one Word to say for himself, but looked with so much Shame and Confusion in his Face, that several People who was there, thought that the poor fellow wou'd have dropt down in the Place where he stood.

'However, Mr. *Dinn* read out the rest of the Letter, which Gordon heard with grief enough; for there he declared, that he determin'd to go down to *Burgundy* in *France*, soon after he wrote that Letter to me; and he said that he did not know but that he might go into *Italy*, for some time after he had been in *Burgundy*; which Story was so different from that of John Gordon's being brought from *Paris* through *France*, in a Cart cover'd with a Blanket, that it made a Subject of Laughter to all our Hearers.

'Then the Magistrates desir'd to hear from me what Gordon had wrote in his forg'd Letter, which he Counterfeited to me in *London*; which he pretended came from his Aunt *Barrack*, who had been dead fifteen Years: So then I read that Letter by roat before Gordon's Face, to his great shame and confusion, even in so much, that he was not capable of speaking for some Time, which gave me no little concern, least, through his wickedness, he had drawn down God's Judgment upon him; but
'at

(83)

'at length he faltering, made a very foolish
'Speech, and said Gentlemen, this Woman has
'been laying her Head together with the Jesuits
'in the North, and I am afraid, said he, that they
'have conspir'd Mischief against me; so that
'I look upon my self to be in such Danger, that
'if they should meet me in the Street they will
'knock my Brains out.

'I then looked upon him with Grief, and
'said, thou Villian, what a foolish Speech hast
'thou made, it had been much better for thee
'that thy Brains had been beat out two Years
'ago, and that thou had'st not seen a Day like
'unto this.

'Now the Gentlemen hearing this silly
'Speech, they told me, that that they was
'very sorry, that a Woman like me, should
'ever have been brought to so much trouble
'as I then was, by such an empty scull'd Fel-
'low as that, but my answer to that was,

'Worthy Gentlemen, whilst this Man serv'd
'God and kept his Commandments, he was
'not thought to be an empty scull'd Fellow,
'and therefore as he hath been but a short
'time Apprentice to the Devil, he cannot as
'yet be perfect in his Works.

''Then the Magistrates said Mr. Gordon,
'since we have known what it is to sit here to
'do Justice, we have not had a Trial laid be-

F 2 'fore

'fore us like unto this, nor never heard of the like villany which you have Enacted to this Gentlewoman, that kept you from starving in a strange Place, and has brought you to *Scotland* all at her own Expence, out of respect and good Will to serve you, hoping to receive the Money which you promis'd her as soon as you got to *Aberdeen*, or in two or three Days after; and you like a base Man, after you had brought her into a strange Place, and also got what Money you could from her, you then abandon'd the poor Gentlewoman, without either giving her any Satisfaction, for either her Money or her Goods, which was the most ungrateful Thing that ever was done by Man.

And all that time John Gordon stood Mute, and had not one Word to say for himself; all he desired was, that he might give his Oath, that he owed me nothing.

Then the Maigistrates desir'd to know whether I could prove any thing of my Debt, to which I answer'd in the following Manner.

Gentlemen,

'AS for the Money that I lent Mr. Gordon, I can only prove that I lent him Money in Mr. *Shirley*'s House, to buy him Stockings, Shoes, and other Necessaries, and also, that I paid for his Lodging and Washing
'and

'and every thing that he had in all the time that he stay'd in Mr. *Shirley*'s House, and I can prove that Mr. Gordon had the Silver Snuff-Box, called, the Cardinal's Hat, which cost me fifteen Shillings to redeem it of Mr. *Shirley*'s Son.

'And I can also prove, that I had my two Silver Spoons after I came to *Aberdeen*, and that I us'd them at my Table five or six Days in Mr. *Moor*'s House, and Captain *Brown* and his Lady saw me take them out of my Trunk, with my Husband's Name upon them; and since I came to *Edenborough*, I have been in Company with several Persons, who has had the two Spoons as a Pledge for Money they lent John Gordon and his sham Countess, and as to my Velvet Cap, Captain *Brown* knows very well that it was never seen off of my Head in all the time that I was upon my Voyage, but I never had it on my Head after I got to *Aberdeen*, now all this I can prove.

'The Gentlemen told me, that if I could prove all these things, or but one or two things, that would be sufficient to bring me all the rest, since Mr. Gordon had denied every thing which proved much for the better on my side.

'Then the Magistrates desir'd to know what time I would take to write to my Friends at *London* and *Aberdeen*, in order to prove part of

'my

'my Debt, and it should be granted me; I
'desired no more then a Months Time, which
'accordingly was granted me, after which the
'Magistrates order'd Mr. Gordon to send for
'Bail sufficient for me to except of for my Secu-
'rity, for the Appearance of John Gordon's Per-
'son that Day Month; the Magistrates asked
'Mr. Gordon who he knew in that Place, and
'he told them, that he was very well acquaint-
'ed with Sir *Dunken Forbous*, the King's Ad-
'vocate, and the Lord Chief Justice *Clark*;
'but altho' he knew these Gentlemen so well,
'as he pretended, he durst as soon take a Bear
'by the Tooth as to send for either of them;
'however, his poor Countess, was all the time
'of our Tryal, waiting in the *Parliament-*
'*Close*, to know how her favourite Swain
'came off, till he was oblig'd to send to her to get
'him Bailed, and then the Countess found that
'she must either stir her Stumps, or lose her
'Bed-fellow, and therefore she us'd her utmost
'endeavour to get him a Release, altho' it pro-
'ved to little Purpose, for they was too well
'known then for any Person to be bound
'Security for such a Fellow; till at length the
'Day being far spent, and the Magistrates want-
'ing to break up to go to Dinner, those Gen-
'tlemen, out of compassion both to him and
'me, offer'd themselves to be my Security for
'the Sum of four and twenty Pounds Ster-
'ling, until the *Monday* following, and then
'they would oblige Mr. G*ordon* to find fresh
'Bail,

' Bail, or elſe to go to Goal: So then I excepted
' of thoſe Gentlemens Security for that Sum,
' and was well content; but whilſt the Clerk
' was Writing for Mr. *Gordon*, his ſham Counteſs
' came into the Council-Chamber, and made a
' very great Figure there; ſhe ſaid, Gentlemen,
' what is it that you want with poor Mr. *Gor-*
' *don*, do you want caſionary, that is, what we
' call Bail, or do you want a hundred Pound, they
' ſaid no Madam, we want nothing but Security
' for Mr. *Gordon*'s Appearance this Day Month;
' then Madam ſat down by them, and was ſo
' full of Venum, that ſhe look'd over the
' Shoulder and Spit towards me, and ſaid
' Gentlemen, I will have a Warrant to take
' this Woman up, the Gentlemen ſaid, Madam,
' there is no need for that, you need not fear
' Mrs. *Harding* running away from ſo juſt a
' Cauſe as hers is; therefore we will all be Se-
' curity for her Appearance; but the Counteſs
' ſtill perſiſted in it, that ſhe would have a War-
' rant to take me up, then the Gentlemen ſaid
' Madam, what will you take this Gentlewo-
' man up for, ſhe that kept you from ſtarving
' in a ſtrange Place, and has brought you here
' all at her own Expence, and that very Gown
' upon your Back ſhe has paid for it; nay, they
' told her that I pay'd more to clear her Lodg-
' ings, then the *French* Robe was worth, the poor
' Counteſs hearing of this, and ſhe not having
' her Liberty there to vent her Paſſion, turn'd as
' pale as Death, and walked off the Stage with that
' affront, to my great Satisfaction; and then Mr.

F 4 ' *Dinn*,

'*Dinn*, having finifh'd our Affair, we all departed in Peace; but altho' Madam had made fuch a blufter with her hundred Pounds, poor Mr. *Gordon* had not fo much as one Shilling to pay the Clerk for writing his Bail.

'However, Monfieur *Labbey*, as he was pleas'd to call himfelf in his own Memoirs, returned home to his Lodgings again, after doing the greateft Pennance that ever he had done in the whole courfe of his Life, and I am confident that I brought my old Friend *Gordon* on that Day to more Repentance then ever either the Reverend Mr. *Alexander Smith* did, or all the Confeffors that ever he had any thing to do with.

'But, yet notwithftanding all that had happened, *Gordon* ftill kept on his old Trade of Lying, although he had been then fo lately well reproved for it; for he was no fooner got home to his Lodgings, but he told his Landlord and his Wife, that he had been at the Parliament Houfe, in order to meet me there but he found that the Magiftrates had nothing to fay to him, and for my own Part, he told them that I had nothing to fay for my felf, and therefore he faid, that he immediately got a Warrant granted to him to fend me to Prifon, and now, faid *Gordon*, I have lock'd Mrs. *Harding* faft, I will eat my Dinner in comfort, which Story feemingly gave
'all

'all his Hearers great Satisfaction, for they never
'doubted in the least the Truth of it; but they
'all believ'd that every Word the Villain had told
't'em was Authentick, till the *Monday* follow-
'ing that I met *Gordon*'s Landlord in the *Par-
'liament Close*; who was almost astonished to
'see me there, he came up to me, and said
'Madam, is it you or your Ghost, I ask'd him
'what he meant by that, or whether he would
'not believe his own Eyes; and then he gave
'me the above Account, and told me all that
'*Gordon* had said after he had return'd from
'the Council-Chamber, where I was then
'a going, and expected to meet him there
'with fresh Bail; but I was much mistaken,
'for he liked his Bail so well, that he never
'intended to go there again, to give the Gen-
'tlemen a Release; but in three or four Days
'thereafter, as *Gordon* had never appear'd, the
'Magistrates sent out a special Warrant in
'search for him, in order to bring him to Ju-
'stice the next Day, which accordingly was
'done, *Gordon* was brought to the Council-
'Chamber again; but instead of bringing fresh
'Bail, he brought an old Solicitor to speak for
'him; but the Gentlemen soon sent him away,
'then the Magistrates demanded of *Gordon*,
'what his reason was for disobeying their Or-
'ders and Command, that he did not appear in
'so many Days, *Gordon* told them that he did not
'know any occasion there was for his appear-
'ing at all, but the Magistrates soon made
'him

'him sensible of the necessity there was, for
' they told him, that if he did not get Bail suffici-
' ent for me to except off very soon, they would
' send him to Goal, and then the sham Coun-
' tess was oblig'd to bring their old Landlord to
' be bound for his Appearance; but I would
' not except of him alone, and then *Gordon* of-
' fer'd me a Bond along with him, that he had
' for the Payment of the Money, which he
' was to receive for the Land of *Glencat*,
' which he had sold but very little time before,
' so then I excepted of their Landlord and that
' Bond for my Security, in Case it was found
' to be good; therefore, I beg'd the Favour
' that the Bond might be Read up before all
' our Hearers, that the Bailiffs might pass their
' Judgment upon it; for as I had found by wo-
' ful Experience, that *Gordon* had so clever a
' Hand at Forgery, he was no more to be trust-
' ed by me, until he mended his Manners, so
' the Bond was read, and it being found good,
' I excepted of it, and then we all departed a-
' gain in Peace.

' But *John Gordon* had little Peace or rest, un-
' til he sent for me, to give me his Bill, he
' being very well assur'd that the Magistrates
' would have a very just Account of all their
' wicked and base Actions upon the return of
' my Letters, particularly those from *Aberdeen*,
' for those only was sufficient to cast him at
' Law, and therefore he went to Mr. *Dinn*,
' who

'who was Clerk in the Council-Chamber, and had heard all our Trial, and beg'd the favour of him, that he would send for me to meet him at a Coffee-House in the *Parliament Close*, and that he would be there also, in order to settle our Accounts, and he would content him for his trouble; so accordingly we all met that Evening at the Place appointed, and Mr. *Dinn*, then read over my Bill again to Mr. *Gordon*, to hear what Objections he would make against it; but indeed he made very little then, which much Surpriz'd Mr. *Dinn*, who had before that time heard him deny that ever he had any of my Money, or saw any of my Goods; and then to hear him acknowledge at once no less then thirteen Pounds, which he had of me, Mr. *Dinn* declar'd afterwards, that he did not know which way to look to keep his Conntenance, for he blush'd for the Rogue. However, as Mr. *Gordon* said, that there was only thirteen Pounds due to me when he and I made up our Accounts together in *London*, I acknowleg'd that to be Truth, but that was a Fortnight before we left *London*, and then I made it appear that he had more then ordinary Money of me, in the two last Weeks to finish his Affairs as he told me; besides fifteen Shillings that I pay'd for the Cardinal's Hat, and two Guineas that he had to pay his Lady's Lodgings, and his own five Pounds that I lent him after all

'to

'to pay our Paſſage to *Scotland*, and one Gui-
'nea after our arrival there, and he was charg'd
'only five and thirty Shillings for my two ſilver
'Spoons, although that which was Guilt coſt
'five and twenty Shillings, and the other coſt
'fifteen, and one Guinea for my Velvet Cap,
'half a Guinea for the Shirt I lent him, and ſix
'Shillings for the Handkerchief; all which *John*
'*Gordon* then acknowleg'd to be juſt and true;
'Nay, he told Mr. *Dinn* that he actually pro-
'mis'd me in *London*, that he would pay all my
'Expences that I ſhould be at from the time that
'I left *London*, to the time that he ſhould
'bring me into *London* again, which I muſt
'own was more than ever I expected to have
'heard from him, who but few Days before had
'ſo often defir'd to give his Oath, that he never
'ſaw one Farthing of my Money, or any of
'my Goods; however, notwithſtanding, he did
'me ſo much Juſtice in the End, as to acknow-
'ledge the Truth of all that I charg'd him with,
'he at the ſame time expoſ'd his villany ſo
'much the more, and made the blackneſs of
'his Crimes appear almoſt as odious in the
'Eyes of the World, as his Conſcience will one
'Day appear before God; however, we agreed
'ſo well, that he gave me his Bill for the Sum of
'four and twenty Pounds Sterling to be payable
'ſix Months after Date, excepted on both Sides;
'after which I Signed an Order for his Landlord
'to deliver up the Bond to him, ſo then we had
'finiſhed our troubleſome Affair; but good
' Mr.

'Mr. *Dinn* was never paid for his trouble
'from that Day to this; however, it being
'pretty late in the Evening, my old Friend
'*Gordon* offer'd his service to wait on me home
'to my Lodgings, which I could not well re-
'fuse, least Mr. *Dinn* should send his Foot-
'man with me, and go alone himself, as he
'had before offer'd it; but when he was gone,
'Mr. *Dinn* was very sorry that he had not
'took *John Gordon* to wait on himself, and
'sent his own Servant along with me, for he
'greatly fear'd that Mr. *Gordon* would Mur-
'der me, and pick my Pocket, if it was but
'only for the sake of my Writings; for it could
'not be supposed that I should have much Mo-
'ney at that time; however, notwithstanding
'I had the hard Fortune to meet with such an
'unexpected Disappointment, as I did, yet God's
'Goodness was so great to me, that I did not
'want Money to pay for every thing that I had
'occasion for, or to pay all Persons whom I
'employ'd to Act upon all Accounts for me,
'and to bring me back to my own native Place
'again, which was a great Satisfaction to me
'then; however, when *John Gordon* and I
'went into my Appartment, as I was laying my
'things upon the Table, he watch'd his oppor-
'tunity to get my Pocket-Book, and as he was
'opening of it I took it from him, and asked
'him what he wanted out of it, or how he could
'be so impudent as to open a Pocket Book of
'mine again; and he told me, that he wanted
'nothing

'nothing out of it, but that Letter which I
' expofed before the Magiftrates; for he faid,
' that he had rather have given twenty Pounds
' then ever that Letter fhould have been feen
' in that Place; but I told him that he fhould
' never have it, for whilft that Letter will
' hang together, I told him, that I would keep
' it to be a Witnefs againft him, and fo wifh'd
' him a good Night, and away he went; but
' the next Morning he came to me again, and
' defir'd to Breakfaft with me, which very
' much Surpriz'd me, to think that any Man
' alive fhould have fo much Impudence as to
' come to me to beg Favours, whom he had fo
' much abus'd; but when I underftood that it
' was neceffity that forc'd him to it, my Heart
' relented, and I wept for him, when I thought
' of the mifery that wicked Man had brought
' himfelf to, for he affur'd me that Day, that
' he had neither Fire to warm him by, nor
' Bread to put in his Head, or a Farthing of
' Money to buy him any thing with, and there-
' fore he pray'd me to lend him Six-pence; fo
' after I confider'd how hard a thing it was to
' fuffer hunger and cold, I gave him a Shil-
' ling, which I never expected any return for,
' and which, if he had but had one fpark of
' Grace remaining in him, that was enough
' to have mortified him to think how much
' he had abufed my good Nature and great
' Charity to him, who was the moft un-
' worthy of all Men in the World; however,

' I

'I defir'd him to come no more nigh me, un-
'til he kept better Company; fo then we took
'our leaves of each other, and I faw him no
'more; for, in two or three Days thereafter,
'he and his fham Lady was forc'd to flee into
'the Abbey of *Holy Rood Houfe*, to keep their
'felves out of Prifon; for as I had made them
'appear in their own Colour and Shapes, the
'reft of their Creditors began to look fharp about
'them, fo that there was feveral Arreftments out
'againft *John Gordon* and his Countefs, which
'oblig'd them never to, appear upon the Streets
'any more; and again they being then known
'to be two fuch bafe Impoftors, they was ever
'afterlooked upon to be no better then Vaga-
'bonds; but however, as foon as I had got
'*John Gordon*'s Bill, I went to an Attorney at
'Law, who liv'd in the *Land Market*, and I
'defired him to raife me an Inhibition, and
'fend it to *Aberdeen*, and lay an Arreftment
'upon the Land of *Glencat*; and after that
'was done there was a Meffenger fent into the
'Abbey of *Holy Rood Houfe*, to ferve an In-
'hibition upon *John Gordon* there, and then
'I had nothing more to do, but to caufe the
'Inhibition to be Regiftred in the Rolls at
'*Edenborough*, and fo to make the beft of
'my way to *London*; but it being an ill time
'of the Year to Travel by Sea, I deter-
'min'd to ftay a fhort Time longer there, to
'compofe my poor old Head, and endeavour
'to make my Peace with God, after reflecting
'and confidering well what a ten Months Work

I

'I had made, and in that little time which I
'ſtay'd there, I muſt acquaint my Readers of
'what ſtratagems *John* and his Counteſs fell
'upon in that time which they ſtay'd in the
'Abbey, when *John Gordon* and his Trolop
'went firſt in there, they was oblig'd to have
'a Servant, and it was ſaid, that they had took
'a Maid out of the Bawdy-Houſe where
'they had Lodg'd till then; but that I will not
'aſſert for Truth. But however, a Servant
'they had to buy Proviſions for them, till at
'length they provided themſelves of a hiror.
'and three Horſes, and ſlipt privately away
'to *Aberdeen*; and I was credibly inform'd
'by a Perſon of Diſtinction, who lives at *Aberdeen*,
'their buſineſs there was to break the Sale
'of *Glencat*; but *Frances Gordon*, who had
'bought the Land, and was Infeited in it,
'would not part with the Land until *John*
'*Gordon* had given back all the Money which
'the Land had coſt him; and alſo clear'd him
'of all the Arreſtments that was laid upon the
'Land, but that was ſo far out of *John Gor-*
'*don*'s Power to do, that all their wicked De-
'ſigns came to nothing; but their only aim
'was to Bilk their Creditors, who had Inhi-
'bited their Money upon the Land for their
'Security; however they Lodg'd at Skipper
'*Scot*'s Houſe, and when they went firſt there,
'Skipper *Scot* ask'd what Lady that was, and
'the Skipper was told that ſhe was a Lady of
'Quality, and a great Friend of the King's, and
'ſo he was deſir'd to ask no more Queſtions
'about

' about her; they stay'd in that House eleven
' Days, and would not want for any thing of
' Niceties, *John Gordon* had warm Sack duly
' every Morning, and his Lady had her Tea, with
' Candy-Bread, Sugar; and they had all sorts
' of Niceties to Dinner, so that in a eleven Days
' their Bill came to four Pounds odd Money
' Sterling, and when that Bill was brought to
' the Lady, she told her Landlord that she
' could not pay the Money then, but she
' had either Money or Bank Notes com-
' ing with the Post; so that in two Days
' time the Lady promis'd to pay that Bill, and
' all the rest of their Charges; but instead
' of that *John Gordon* and his sham Lady, and
' their Servant Maid, got away from Skipper
' *Scot*'s in the night Time, and they went to
' to a Merchant's House in the Town; this
' coming to the hirer's Ears, he went away
' with the Horses for fear of having them Ar-
' rested without the Saddles, which were given
' him afterwards by the Magistrates Orders,
' the want of his Hire, being judg'd loss enough
' to him; but when the Post came in, Mr. *Scot*
' went to inform himself about the Lady, and he
' found that she had neither Money nor Bank Notes
' to come, a contrary the Post-man assur'd Mr.
' *Scot* that they was Impostors, and was owing a
' great deal of Money in their old Lodgings at
' *Edenborough*, and had cheated all People that
' ever was concern'd with them, even so much
' that they were oblig'd to flee into the Abbey of

G ' *Holy*

Holy-Rood-House, to escape being Imprison'd
' for their Debts: Now this coming to the
' Magistrates Ears, they clap'd a Guard about
' the the House, where they Lodg'd, in order
' to secure them, but *John Gordon* and his fine
' Lady made their Escape out through a Win-
' dow, and were not heard of until some time
' after that it was known, that *John Gordon* and
' his Lady, with a Servant Wench, call'd at a Pub-
' lick House as they past through the *Hard-gate*
' when they made their Escape, and they spent
' a Crown in that House; and the poor Coun-
' tess offer'd to lay her Silk Plad in Pawn for the
' Money, until she came back from visiting a
' Friend in the Country, as she pretended; but
' the Lady desir'd the lend of another that was
' warmer, the Weather being then very cold;
' so the Landlady lent her best fine tarten Plad
' to the Lady, who had the Impudence to steal
' away both the Plads, and leave the Crown
' to pay, whilst the Landlady was only speaking
' with her Servant in another Room, but she
' presently sent her two Sons in search after
' them, who overtook the Lady and her Maid
' at the Bridge of *Dee*, two Miles out of *A-*
' *berdeen*, and the young Men thrash'd the poor
' Countess, and took their Mother's Plad from
' her, and made the Slut to pay the Crown
' which they had spent that Morning, and then
' the two Jilts being set at Liberty, they trudg'd
' it on their Feet until they came unto *Edenbo-*
gh again, and *John Gordon* still keeping his
' old

'old Post, run after them separately, they
being apprehensive of being pursued after
and taken back to *Alerdeen*, and it was
with good Reason, for there was several
in Search after them to take them Up, and
secure the Crew, in order to prevent their doing any further Damage to the Publick; but
there is one thing that I forgot to acquaint
my Readers of, that is, when *John Gordon*
and his Lady left Skipper *Scot*'s House, they
said they were going to take a little fresh Air
before they went to Bed, and the Lady gave
the Maid servant a strict Charge that no Person should go into her Room, in which there
was a little Trunk full of Jewels and other
valuable Things, therefore she bid the Girl
be very careful of it; but when they found
that the Lady did not return, they opened
the Trunk, and found nothing in it but an
old pair of ragged Breeches that *John Gordon* could not wear any longer; however,
the poor Girl was then eased of her great
Charge, and the Impostors got clear off to
Edenborough, where they went to their old
Quarters again in the Abbey of *Holy-Rood-
House*; but two Days before I came away
from that Place; but I had not been more then
a Month, in *London*, before I met my old
Friend *Gordon* at *Little-turn-stile*, which no
little surpriz'd me; he told me then that
he had left his Lady at *Edenborough*, he
thank'd God for it, and he hoped never to
see her again, although he had but just then
left her at his Lodgings, at the *Edeborough*
' Castle,

'Castle Ale-House by the *Hermitage* Stairs,
'where he Cohabited with her that Night;
'however I was resolv'd to know whether he
'was ever to be believ'd again or not, and
'therefore I went the next Day to the *Her-*
'*mitage Stairs*, and enquired there what Ships
'came in last, and what Passengers came from
'*Edenborough*; and they told me of several,
'but am not the rest, there was one Mr.
'J....son who had a *French* Wife, and the
'...oin-Boy went with me to their Lodg-
'ings, where I call'd for Mr. *Gordon*, and
'his Landlady told me that he was not with-
'in, but his Wife was above in her Chamber;
'I then asked the Woman whether Mr. *Gordon*
'and his Wife Cohabited together, and she
'actually told me they did all the time they
'had been in her House, but she desir'd to
'know what my reason was for asking such a
'Question, but I made her no direct Answer;
'for as I had no other business with that ly-
'ing Rogue, then to satisfy my own Curiosity,
'I said very little, but return'd back again,
'but was much griev'd to think that a Man
'like him should have spent so much time at
'his Studies to so little Purpose, and so much
'the more, that I found his only Practice was
'in the trade of Lying, in which he is no small
'Master off; now as he but two much makes
'it appear in all his Actions; but to go on, these
'two Impostors had not been long in *London*,
'before I had receiv'd a Letter from *Scotland*,
'which gave me Account of their last farewel
'to

'to *Edenborough*; the Countess before she came
'away from that Place, she being in want of
'several Necessaries, pretended to be with
'Child, and put something under her petty
'Coats, that she might appear to be so, and then
'she went to a Linnen Draper's Shop, pretending
'to buy Child-Bed Linnen, so the fine Countess
'bought two Pieces of fine white Linnen, and
'a piece of Dimety, and when she had done,
'she desired the Shop-keeper to cast up the
'Account betwixt them, and to send his Bill
'by his Servant, who were to carry the Cloth
'along with the Lady, and receive the Money
'for it, the Lady not having Money enough in
'her Pocket at that time for to pay the Bill;
'so the Gentleman not knowing then who he
'had got to deal with, made no Difficulty to
'send his Maid Servant along with the Lady,
'to carry the Cloth, in order to receive the
'Money for it; but as they were coming along
'the *Land-Market*, the Lady, whose Head was
'always at Work, turn'd her self to the Maid,
'and seemingly in a Surprize, said, Girl, what
'do you think, the Countess told the Maid that
'she had drop'd a piece of Shalloon down by
'her Master's Foot, and had forgot to take it
'up, so she desir'd the Girl to lay down the
'Cloath in a little Tobacco Shop, that were just
'at hand, and go back again to her Master for
'the piece of Shalloon, so the poor innocent
'Girl went into the Shop, laid down the Cloath
'there, and away she went to fetch the Shal-
                                        'loon,

(102)

'loon, mean time the Countess took away all the
'Cloath, and were never heard of any more by
'them, although there was People out in Search
'immediately for her by the Magistrates Order.
'But now the Countess getting so clear
'of with her Cloath, and knowing that there
'was a Ship ready to come to *England*, she
'were resolved to make the best use of her
'Time that she could, and therefore the Lady
'watch'd her opportunity to get to a Cheese-
'monger's Shop, where she had the impudence
'to buy two Cheshire Cheeses, altho' she had
'no way to pay for them, but by her Ledgerde-
'main, as it prov'd, for the Prentice-Boy being
'order'd to wait upon the Lady Home to her
'Lodgings, to carry the Cheeses, and he were
'also to receive the Money for them; but
'when they were pretty well advanced on
'their way to her Lodgings, the Lady told the
'the Boy that she had left her Fann upon
'his Master's Counter, and that she would
'give him Six-pence to lay down the Cheeses
'there, and go back and fetch the Fann; so the
'Boy very readily embraced her offer, and
'run back again to fetch the Fann, whilst the
'the Countess run away with the Cheeses, and
'then they left *Edenborough*, for they never
'was heard of any more in that Place, neither
'was it known which way they went, until I
'wrote to *Edenborough*, and acquainted my
'Friends there, that the poor Laird of *Glencat*,
'and his Lady *Joaney* were both in *London* a-
'gain, and that his Lady were now oblig'd to

Re-

'Renounce all Titles of Grandeur, and is known
'here only by the Name of Mrs. *Kempster*.

'The next News I heard of my old Friend
'*Gordon* was, that he were endeavouring to get
'a Place in the Custom-House, which indeed
'diverted me much, for I thought that was the
'fittest Place for him in the World, for Birds
'of a Feather, generally agree well together;
'but he did not succeed, and then he was en-
'deavouring to get a Reader's Place in St. *Dun-*
'*ston*'s Church; but I cannot say, but that I
'thought him as unproper a Person at that time
'to discharge a Duty of so high a Calling,
'as he was fit for the other; for God knows,
'that when the blind leads the blind, they
'must of consequence both fall into a Ditch
'together; but however, my Lord Bishop of
'*London*, to my Knowledge, had been too well
'inform'd of his Character, then to stuff a Pul-
'pit with such a Fellow as he is; but howe-
'ver, at length Monsieur *Labbey* was prefer'd
'to be Usher to Mr. *Pearce*, Master of the Ac-
'cademy-School in *Chancery-Lane*, where he
'behaved very well to all outward Appearance
'for some time, till at length he began to play
'such Tricks with his Master, that if Mr. *Pearce*
'had not turn'd him away as he did, he was
'in great Danger of loosing his School by his
'Means, and therefore I hope Mr. *Pearce* will
'at least always acknowledge that his Bread
'was owing to me then, for if I had not given
'Mr. *Pearce* the just Account of *John Gor-*
'*don*'s Character as I did, Mr. *Pearce* would
'cer-

'certainly have kept his Servant, until he had
'been Master himself; and this being Fact, Mr.
'*Pearce* acknowledg'd it to me in a short time
'thereafter, at which time he told me how
'many ways his Servant *John* was endeavour-
'ing to ruin him; but now I hope this will be
'a warning to all those that know both him
'and his Lady, but whether it may or not, I
'have now discharg'd my Duty to the World,
'and has publish'd nothing here but what I can
'answer before both God and Man; so this
'being Fact, we will now conclude, that since
'this said Mr. *Pearce*, upon the Information
'which I gave him, has turn'd this said *John*
'*Gordon* out of his Service, since which disco-
'very, I suppose, he may be more upon his
'Guard, and begin to think that he must be-
'have with great appearent Decency, of which
'he is no small Master off, as his Impudence has
'been already prov'd very great; he may per-
'haps endeavour to defend himself, under the
'notion that what I write against him, is the
'Effect of Prejudice, and Spirit of Popery;
'but I thank God that I have this reserve, I
'do not Act by Party, I proceed upon authen-
'tick Papers, which I am ready to produce, if
'he dares venture his Character thereupon; I
'shall say no more, only I pray God to give him
'more Grace, and me better Acquaintance, to
'which I humbly beg all my worthy Readers
'to join with me, and say, *Amen, Amen.*

ERRATA.
In Page 47. line 5. for Pray'd, read pay'd. In the Title Page, for Price 1 s. read 1 s. 6 d.

The Temple Rakes,
or Innocence Preserved

Anonymous

Bibliographical note:
This facsimile has been made from a copy in the Houghton Library of Harvard University (15496.315)

THE
TEMPLE RAKES,

OF

INNOCENCE Preserved;

BEING THE

ADVENTURES

OF

Miss *Arabella* R-----y.

A NARRATIVE founded on some late extraordinary MATTERS of FACT.

LONDON:

Printed for H. CARPENTER in *Fleet-street*.

[Price One Shilling.]

(1735)

THE
TEMPLE RAKES;
OR
INNOCENCE preserved &c.

IN that delightful Season, when the nimble-footed *Horæ* prepare the glorious Chariot and Horses of the Sun, ready for his mounting between Three and Four in the Morning, and Nature appears arrayed in her gayest Dress, to salute him at his first setting out on his Course, young *Belmour* rose early from his Bed, to taste the Fragrancy of the gentle Gales of *Zephyrus*, and enjoy the refreshing Pleasures of a Morning Walk. Pleasures but little experienced by *Belmour*, since his quitting the College to harbour among the Rakes of the *Temple:* With whom he generally caress'd the Bottle to such unseasonable Hours, as rendered him uncapable of rising till about Noon-time; nor, indeed, had he been stirring so early this Morning, if he could have met with any Rest in his Bed; but neither the Fatigue of his last Night's

Night's Ramble, nor the Wine he had drank, could procure him any Sleep there: As all Repose was driven from thence by the Thoughts of a beautiful Object, whose extraordinary Charms had been so much the Subject of his Contemplation the Night before, and had left such a deep Impression in his Memory, that it was not in the Power of any thing else to interfere with his Ideas, or expel the lovely Image one Moment from his Breast.

Belmour, at the Desire of *Townley,* his intimate Companion and general Partner in his Diversions, had agreed, the preceeding Evening, to take a Trip to *Vaux-hall.* These two Gentlemen had not been long in the Walks before they observed a young Lady, whose Person so much commanded the Attention of the whole Assembly, which was very numerous that Night, that it was impossible for her to escape their Notice. All the Gentlemen present were enraptured with her Youth, Beauty, fine Shape, and genteel Air, and bestowed the greatest Commendations on them; while the Ladies were not less engaged with her Charms, tho' in a different Manner; as they were endeavouring to detract from whatever appeared amiable in her to the other Sex, and to find a Fault, where Nature had scarce admitted the least Imperfection to appear. For, such is the peculiar Vanity of the Female Sex, that notwithstanding the superior Excellency of the young

young Lady's personal Perfections, yet there was not a Woman present, but imagined herself to be fully as Handsome; and every one of them was framing Objections to the Regularity, Delicacy, or Proportion of some particular Feature or Limb, wherein they severally piqued themselves with having the Advantage of her. So obstinately blind is *Envy*, and such is the Power of her baneful Intoxication, as to render the greatest Excellencies, either of Body or Mind, obnoxious and disagreeable to those that are under her Influence, by endeavouring, as in this Case, to convert real Beauties into imaginary Blemishes: But it was far otherwise with *Belmour* and his Companion.

He himself was possessed with such a good Taste, and just Discernment, that nothing excellent in Art or Nature could escape his Observation. Neither could *Townley* avoid taking Notice of this beautiful Person, whom they had met by chance two or three Times in the Walks: In a word, such was the Force of her Charms, that both these Gentlemen became perfectly enamoured with her, and resolved, in their Minds, to endeavour at obtaining some Knoweledge of who she was and where she lived.

Belmour, being of a very open Disposition, first declared his Resolution to *Townley*, not owning it as the Effect of any Passion he had conceived for the Lady, but only urging it as a Gratification of a Curiosity, which prompted him to discover who this young and beautiful Stranger was.

Townley readily agreed to second him in his Design, as he declared himself to be prompted by the same Motive; which, tho' each of them represented it to the other under the Veil of extraordinary Curiosity, was, in Effect, nothing less than the ardent Passion of Love, that her Eyes had kindled in their Bosoms, therefore they never suffered her to escape out of their Sight during the whole Evening. At the Conclusion of the Entertainment, the young Lady and her Company, which was a tall, thin, lank, elderly Gentleman, of a very yellow Complexion, and a short, fat, squab Gentlewoman, took Water in a Pair of Oars; and our two young Sparks took Boat likewise, ordering their Waterman to land them wherever the other Boat went to.

The Conversation of *Belmour* and his Companion, during the Evening, was chiefly upon the Charms of the young Lady; and in Conjectures on whom the other two Personages were, that accompanied her. These *Belmour* would have to be either her Father and Mother, or two near Relations; but *Townley*, from some Observations that he had made on the Reservedness of her Behaviour, more rightly judged otherwise; especially with regard to the Gentleman, who he remarked

marked she never spoke to, unless he first directed his Discourse to her, which he seemed to take every Opportunity of doing, tho' she generally returned it with an Air of Indifference.

The Lady and her Company landed at *York-Buildings* Stairs, from whence they walked up to the *Strand*, and crossing the Way they went into the *Lebeck's-Head*. *Belmour* and his Companion followed at a Distance, and came into the same House, just as the elderly Gentleman was at the Bar ordering a Supper for his Company that were gone up Stairs: And indeed the Gentleman had not only perceived their close Attendance on him and the Ladies, in the Walks, but also observed their Boat following his on the Water, tho' having lost Sight of them after his landing, he imagined their following him to be accidental; but, on seeing them enter the same Tavern, began to entertain some suspicious Notions of their Design.

Belmour and *Townley* called for a Room; and would fain have posted themselves in one of those which was nearest the Door, that the Lady might not escape their further Pursuit on her Departure; but those Rooms being already taken up with Company, they were obliged to content themselves with one above Stairs. *Townley*, who had often frequented this Tavern, was pretty well known to the Drawers; therefore, calling for a Bottle of Wine, he asked the Waiter that brought it, whether

whether he knew any thing of the Gentleman in the laced Coat and the two Ladies that came in a little before them? The Waiter told him that he had lighted them up Stairs, and that the Gentleman had immediately followed him down again, and befpoke a Supper at the Bar; but declared he could not recollect that he had ever seen any of the three Perfonages there before. Upon this *Townley* ordered a Fowl for himfelf and his Companion, and tipping the Drawer half a Crown, gave him a ftrict Charge to let them know when the Gentleman called for the Reckoning, and when the Company was going away. The Drawer promifed to obey their Commands; but unfortunately for *Townley* and his Companion, he was fent out with a Supper that had been befpoke there, to a Gentleman's Houfe in *York-Buildings*, at the Time when the two Ladies and the Gentleman left the Tavern; and he did not come back again till fome time after a Coach had carried the Company off.

The Drawer finding the Gentleman and the two Ladies gone at his Return, had only time to enquire which Way the Coach went; when running up Stairs, he informed *Belmour* and *Townley*, that he had been fent out when the Company had left the Houfe, but that the Coach was but juft gone away from the Door, and had drove up the *Strand*. *Townley* gave him a hearty Damn for not executing his
Commiffion

Commiffion better, by leaving Word with fome of the other Waiters to perform his Commands; and paying their Reckoning, our two Sparks fet out after the Coach. They rambled up the *Strand* till they came to *Southampton-Street*, and then turned up into *Covent-Garden*; but could not trace any Coach, that had three Perfons in it, or that had any one dreffed like the Company they were in Purfuit of.

Exceedingly vexed and chagrined at this Difappointment, they went into the *Rofe* in *Bridges-ftreet*, and called for a Bottle to alleviate their Sorrows, over which they toafted the young Lady by the Name of the Beautiful *Vaux-hall* Stranger; and after fome bitter Execrations on the poor Drawer, for neglect of Duty, each of them adjourned to his Chambers in the *Temple* to Bed. But the Beauty of the young Lady, and the Vexation at being difappointed in the Purfuit of her, ran foftrongly in the Head of *Belmour*, that, as we before related, it entirely deprived him of his Night's Reft; and made him feek for Refreshment from his excruciating Thoughts in a Morning's Walk.

Townley paffed his Time not much better than his Companion; tho' *Belmour* had not entertained the leaft Thought of the former's being any way captivated by the Lady's Charms, which he found had already made fuch a Havock in his own Heart; otherwife

he

he would never have called upon him at his Chambers, to defire his Company to take a Walk in the Park. Urging in Excufe, that it was a Shame to lie a Bed fuch a delightful Morning; for by fo doing they fhould lofe half the Pleafure which the Seafon afforded.

Belmour's coming thus early to call upon him, was no little Matter of Surprize to Townley. " Why how now, *Frank*, fays he,
" what the Devil has difturbed you fo foon :
" I fear the young Lady that we faw at the
" Gardens has not permitted you to fleep?"
" Indeed, replies *Belmour*, fhe has not given
" me much Moleftation, tho' the Vexation
" at our fruitlefs Purfuit, and the Warmnefs
" of the Night have not fuffered me to reft
" as ufual; but the Finenefs of the Morning
" feems to promife ample Amends.——Come
" *Jack*, ftir, and let us take a Walk in the
" Park together." " With all my Heart, fays
" *Townley*, perhaps we may there light upon
" fome new Frolick that may drive away
" all Thoughts of our laft Night's Mifchance;
" but fuppofing we had traced the Lady
" Home; pray *Frank*, what Expectations
" could have arifen to you from thence!"——
" Very few, indeed, anfwered *Belmour*, unlefs
" I could have found Means to get introduced
" to her Company—but what Hopes had you
" *Jack*, from the Purfuit?"—— " Why really
" fays *Townley*, as I judged her to be fome
" young Filley, juft taken into keeping, by
the

" the old Gentleman that was with her, I
" had some Thoughts, if we could have dis-
" covered where he had planted her, to have
" prevented his engrossing such a fair Purchase
" entirely to himself. For indeed *Frank*,
" she seems to deserve a much better Partner
" than what she has got.——What the Devil
" should such an old sallow-faced Hunks
" do with such a young blooming Bud of
" Beauty? Indeed, says *Belmour*, I cannot
" come into your Opinion of her being in
" keeping; for there seemed to be such an
" Air of Modesty in her Face, that perfectly
" forbid any one who observed her, to enter-
" tain the least Thought against her Virtue.
"————Pshaw! Damn it, *Frank*, re-
" plies the other, I find you don't know the
" Town yet.——Modesty! Why I have seen
" a Girl at her first entering upon the Town,
" as modest as the purest Virgin in a Nunnery.
" Well, come, says *Belmour*, you lose all
" the Pleasure of the Spring, by lying in
" Bed so long in the Morning: Up, and let us
" be walking, that we may get back again
" before the Sun comes out too hot."——
Townley was soon up and drest, when they
steered together towards the Park; where we
shall leave them, walking Arm in Arm up
the *Mall* towards *Buckingham* House, while
we give the Reader a little Information of
their Characters and Occupation; which by

C   this

this Time perhaps he may be defirous of obtaining.

Belmour, then, was a young Gentleman of Fortune, being Heir to a large Eftate; and had not long left the Univerfity of *Cambridge*, to compleat his Studies in the *Temple*: Where his Father had placed him, with a View to his attaining fuch a Knowledge of the Laws of the Land, as would be fufficient to enable him the better to manage 'that Eftate, which would fome Time or other come into his Poffeffion; and prevent his being defrauded by Attorneys, Stewards, or Bailiffs, on the one Hand, or injured by his Tenants, or Neighbours, on the other. As he had not as yet been long enough in Town to be corrupted by its Vices, fo he was naturally poffeffed of a fufficient Share of Virtue, and good Senfe, to withftand them: Tho' in Compliance with the Tafte of fome of his Companions, of which *Townley* was the chief, he fometimes gave way to fuch Levities, as his own Underftanding could not ferioufly approve of. For tho' he was polite in his Behaviour, yet he poffeffed a very fedate Turn of Mind; except when Company and the Bottle, wherein were his greateft Exceffes, induced him to be otherwife.

Townley was a young Fellow very deftitute either of virtuous or generous Principles; he at firft ftudied the Laws for the Improvement of his Fortune, which otherwife would have
been

been but very small, had not an old cross Aunt, whom by his wild Behaviour he had very much disobliged, happened to die intestate, and thereby he came into the Possession of about 200*l. per Annum*, which otherwise he could not have had the least Hopes of, if the old Lady had made a Will; but a Fever, that soon rendered her delirious, prevented it. Soon after this Gift of Fortune fell into his Hands, he relinquished his Study of the Law, tho' he kept his Chambers for the Conveniency of his Pleasures; and by giving himself up to the most sensual Indulgencies of his Appetites, he became a perfect Town Rake.

When our two young Sparks had reached the upper End of the *Mall*, *Townley* sat down on a Bench near some Cows, in order to divert himself by some Discourse with the Girls that sold Milk: The Dialogue between him and the Milk Girls would not be very entertaining, and perhaps too gross if we should repeat it. Therefore, leaving it, we shall inform the Reader, that the Pleasantness of the Morning invited them to walk further; and the Dispute was, which Way they should take. *Belmour* being for a Walk up the *Green* Park, and so into *Hyde* Park; but *Townley* who did not so much love Solitude, was more inclined to go and take a Breakfast at *Ranelagh*. To this at last *Belmour* consented, only urging that whether they returned by Land or by

Water, yet the Sun would cause them to have a very hot Journey back again.

Nothing extraordinary happened in their going through *Chelsea* Fields, till they came to the Breakfasting Room at *Ranelagh*. Where they sat down to a Pot of Tea and Bread and Butter; but they had not half finished their Breakfast before the young Lady, and the Gentlewoman who was with her the preceding Evening at *Vaux-hall*, entered the Room. They called for some Chocolate and sat down at a very small Distance from *Belmour* and his Friend; who both were too deeply engaged in contemplating the amazing Charms of this beautiful young Creature, to regard finishing their own Breakfast.

The Ladies having drank their Chocolate, went to take a Turn or two in the Gardens; whither *Belmour* and *Townley* immediately followed them; being both fully bent upon not neglecting this Opportunity, that Fortune had so favourably given them, either of getting Acquaintance with the young Lady, or finding out where they lived. And *Townley* was fully resolved to take the first Occasion that offered of accosting her; which he thought himself the more at liberty to do, as the old Gentleman, who had been in Company the Night before, was now absent.

It will be very proper before we proceed farther, to give some Account of the young Lady and her Companion; which we have

not

not as hitherto had any Opportunity of doing. Her Name was *Arabella R——y*, the youngest Daughter in Six of a *Leicestershire* Country Gentleman, of a pretty good Estate, but which he had the Misfortune to run through in his Life-Time, or to speak more properly, he had suffered it to be devoured by a large Pack of Hounds, Hunting-Horses, Huntsmen, Whippers-in, and Country Sportsmen. In reality, he had literally given so much of five Hundred a Year to the *Dogs*, that, on his Decease, which was about three Years ago, his Eldest Son found himself in Possession of no more than 50 Pounds a Year clear; and his Widow's Jointure, tho' but small, was obliged to go to the Maintainance of her self and seven Children, *viz.* one younger Son, and Six Daughters.

However, it happened somewhat lucky for *Arabella*, that a young Lady in the Neighbourhood, who was a rich Heiress, took such a prodigious liking to her, that she, being an only Child, prevailed with her Parents to let her have Miss *Arabella* home for a Companion: Where she had generally resided ever since her fourteenth Year; and had partly received the same Education as Miss *Betty* her self, for so was this young Lady called.

Arabella, now in her twentieth Year, was justly reckoned a perfect Beauty by every one that saw her; and possessed of a great deal

of

of Virtue, Modesty, and good Sense: So that had her Fortune been any ways answerable to her personal Endowments, she could not have failed of meeting with some very considerable Proffers before now; but tho' most Gentlemen admire Beauty, Virtue, and good Sense, and look upon them as very necessary Perfections in a Wife; yet, when they are put in the Ballance with Riches, they are generally outweighed by the latter; which was poor *Arabella*'s Case.

Miss *Betty*, the young Lady to whom she had been Companion, being lately married, tho' not much to her Inclination, yet by the Parents Direction, to a sordid young Country Squire, of a large Estate, who in his own Phrase, was for *maintaining no more Cats than would catch Mice*, became necessitated to part with *Arabella*. To whom, on her Return home to her Mother, she presented a Purse of twenty Guineas; with an Assurance of ever preserving the greatest Affection and Esteem for her, and of serving her as far as ever it lay in her Power.

This small Sum was soon exhausted, by the Necessities of such a numerous Family as she found at Home: When *Arabella*, by her Mother's Direction, came up to *London*, to live with an Aunt of hers, by her Mother's Side; who was the Widow of a Sea Captain, and was the same Lady that *Belmour* and
Townley

Townley had hitherto seen in Company with her.

Mrs. *Villiard*, for so we shall call this Lady, had been a very agreeable Woman in her Youth; and might then have laid some Claim to be called Beautiful, but her Perfections had been so much tainted by a Levity of Manners, and corrupt Conversation, that really she neither bore nor merited, but a very indifferent Character, long before she fell to the Captain's Lot. She was then Mistress of a small independant Fortune, yet such was her Love to Gaiety, that tho' she could not properly come under the Denomination of a Woman of the Town, yet she might be justly called a Lady of Pleasure: She gave her self up entirely to all sorts, even to an Excess. Her Amours and Love Intrigues would fill a large Volume, neither would the Captain have ventured upon her, had he not been in his Dotage.

As the Time of indulging her more sensual Desires was now over, so she resigned herself to an insatiable Avarice, which gradually increased with her Years; and it was with the View of gratifying this Appetite, that she had taken *Arabella* into the House to live with her; having heard such exceeding Commendations of her Beauty, that she did not in the least doubt of making a good Return, in the Disposal of her Person: And, for that Purpose, she had fixed her Eye on the very Gentleman

tleman who had been in Company with her and *Arabella* the preceding Evening.

This Person was an extream rich *Jew*, who tho' he was married, yet had such a Desire for *Arabella*, that he was willing to take her upon his own Hands, on almost whatever Terms the Aunt should stipulate for. Mr. *D——z*, for so was he called, had enjoyed the Pleasure of drinking Tea twice with the lovely *Arabella*, since her coming to Town, which had not been much above a Week; to whom the Aunt introduced him as one of her particular Friends, and it was at his Desire that the two Ladies went upon a Party of Pleasure with him, the Evening before to *Vaux-hall*, where *Belmour* and *Townley* first obtained a Sight of the lovely *Arabella*.

As the Aunt was left possessed of a very pretty Fortune, on the Decease of the Captain, her late Spouse, so immediately on *Arabella*'s Arrival in Town, she sent for the Mercer, the Laceman, the Mantua-maker, and Milliner, in order to provide for her future Appearance; and spared for no Cost to deck her out handsomely; well judging that the more she expends this way, the greater would be her Returns in the End. *Arabella*, herself, was at first, so prodigiously delighted with her Aunt's Profuseness and Generosity towards her, that she somewhat lamented the Misfortune of her Mother's not sending

her

her to Town sooner; little apprehending that all those fine Trappings, which her Aunt bestowed on her, were only designed to gratify her own insatiable Desires.

We left the two Ladies, followed by *Belmour* and *Townley*, in the Walks; where the latter soon found an Opportunity to enter into a Conversation with them, upon the Beauty of the Morning, and the Pleasantness of the Garden. As these two young Strangers appeared very genteel and well dressed, and the Aunt had not as yet made any direct Bargain for her Niece, with Mr. *D——z*, so she neither refrained herself, nor restrained *Arabella*, from the Gentlemen's Company; not knowing but they might, perhaps, prove to be some greater Persons, than what at present they appeared.

After some Turns in the Gardens, *Arabella* proposed to go home, which the young Gentlemen hearing very politely offered to conduct them; this was not refused, so they handed the Ladies in the Hackney Coach that was waiting for them, into which *Belmour* and *Townley* entered. The Aunt, by several Questions she put to the young Gentlemen, in their Passage to Town, soon found out that they were both *Templers*, which gave her no high Opinion of their Merits or Fortunes. However, when they asked leave to pay their Respects some other Time, to her and the young Lady, she did not think proper absolutely to refuse

refuse it, as she knew not as yet how she and Mr. D——z should agree Matters together; but only told them, that as both herself and Niece visited pretty much, they might chance to come several Times without finding either of them at Home. To this, *Belmour* made Answer, that the Pleasure of their Company, whenever they could obtain that Happiness, would more than sufficiently compensate for any Disappointments they should meet with. As for *Arabella* she joined but very little in any Discourse that passed by the Way; yet, what she said, was sufficient to shew that she had a large Share of Understanding, founded on good Sense, tho' her Sentiments were not delivered with such a Polite Delicacy of Expression, as is either natural, or affected, by such Ladies as have been cheifly bred up in this Town. The Coach at length reached Mrs. *Villiard*'s House, which was in one of the Streets near *Red-Lion* Square, where having handed the Ladies into the House, our two Gentlemen took their leaves; and getting again into their Vehicle, ordered the Coachman to set them down at the *Temple*.

Both *Belmour* and *Townley* were now more violently smitten with *Arabella* than ever; but in a different Manner. *Belmour* had conceived a violent Passion for her, which was justly founded on her Beauty and Understanding. *Townley*'s Passion had only the former Perfection for its Object; and he would

would have been well enough satisfied with the Enjoyment of the Lady's Person, even had her Understanding been upon the level with a Changeling's. He therefore looked upon her Sense rather as a great Obstacle to his Desires, than as any extraordinary Accomplishment in her Person.

Upon their Return to *Townley's* Chambers, " Well *Frank* " says he to *Belmour,* " I
" hope now your Curiosity is satisfied—She's
" a delicious Girl, and Fortune now has
" opened a Way for either of us to get at her.
" An Angel," cries *Belmour,* " but what
" do you mean by getting at her; sure no
" Man would offer to make any Pretences
" to such a beautiful young Creature, but
" what were founded on Honour and Vir-
" tue?"—"Yet suppose," replies *Townley,* "that
" with all her Accomplishments, she should
" not be worth a Groat, don't you think a Man
" would considerably injure his Fortune, by
" acting up to your Notions of Honour and
" Virtue, when he might reap the same
" Benefit, if not a greater, by proceeding
" without them?"—" Well, I confess for
" my part," says *Belmour.* " that let her For-
" tune be ever so small, yet my Conscience
" would not forgive me, for deluding such a
" lovely Creature."—" Certainly, *Frank,*"
says the other, " you have fallen so
" violently in Love with her, that you know
" not what you say; why there's no drawing

"ing Women againſt their Inclinations."—
"Well, but " replied *Belmour*, " there's
" ſuch a thing as decoying them to our In-
" clinations ; and that's much the ſame Thing,
" as both the one and the other muſt be found-
" ed on meer Villany."——"Phoo I find you
" are captious, ſays *Townley* ; but when do
" you propoſe viſiting this young Lady again,
" for methinks I long to ſee her ? "——" To-
" morrow Evening, if you will," ſays
Belmour. "With all my Heart," replied *Townley*, " I ſhall wait till ſix o'Clock for your call-
" ing upon me ; and when we ſee her again, I
" ſhall give you my further Opinion of
" her.

They now parted ; and *Belmour* ſpent the Time, which he thought long, but very indifferently ; no more did *Townley*, tho' he had the Art to diſguiſe it from his Friend, and to amuſe himſelf the mean while with ſome faſhionable Gaieties, that *Belmour* was not ſo much addicted to, eſpecially when any Thing diſturbed his Mind ; ſo that reading, and meditating upon the Idea of the charming *Arabella*, were his chief Amuſements till the appointed Hour arrived : In the mean while, let us obſerve how Matters went on at Mrs. *Villiard*'s.

Arabella had not been long at Home before her Aunt deſired her to dreſs, for ſhe had invited Mr. *D——z* to dine with them that Day. The Niece immediately ſet about executing

executing her Commands; but the Gentleman arrived some considerable Time before either the Dinner was ready, or *Arabella* was dressed. Mrs. *Villiard* introducing him into a back Parlour, after some previous Discourse, asked him how he liked her Niece? to which the *Jew* answered he was quite charmed with her; and that he was very sorry there was one grand Obstacle, which prevented his making her as happy as he could wish her to be; which was his being married. But, if she could prevail on her Niece to dispense with this, he would gratify her with a Thousand Pounds for her trouble, and settle two Hundred a Year on *Arabella* to be paid Quarterly during her Life.

The Aunt promised that she would try every Thing, possible in his Favour; but hoped, that as he must needs be very sensible of the Difficulty that she should have to get *Arabella* to comply with his Proposals, especially as she assured him that her Niece had refused several advantageous Offers in the Country; so she hoped that if she should prevail with her, he would not be against making up the Thousand Pounds, that he had promised her, to a Thousand Guineas; his being already married was not, she said, the only Obstacle that she had to encounter with, but also the Disparity of Years, between him and her *Arabella*, which she judged would be no small Matter of Impediment:

As

(30)

As her Niece could not promise to herself any of those Advantages, which young Widows expect upon the Decease of an elderly Husband. Tho' she did not doubt but the Girl's Behaviour, if she could be brought to comply, would sufficiently induce him to provide handsomely for her in his Will.—Mr. D——z replied, that he should not stand out for such a small Sum as Fifty Pounds more; but begged her to press the Affair forward, as any Delay, in this Case, might be equally prejudicial to all the Parties concerned.

Dinner was by this Time set upon the Table, to which they were all immediately summoned: afterwards Mr. D——z taking his leave of *Arabella* and her Aunt, withdrew; as the latter had assured him she would take the Opportunity that very Afternoon, of opening the Matter to her Niece. Mrs. *Villiard* was as good as her Word: For no sooner was he gone, than, after a long Harangue upon his Politeness, Generosity, and Affability, she asked her Niece, how she should like such a rich Gentleman for a Husband, to whom the other replied, she had not yet entertained any Thoughts of marrying, but, that, when she did she should endeavour to match with one that was more suitable to her Years; for that the Gentleman whom her Aunt spoke of was too much advanced in Age to put up with the Follies of a young Wife. —— Well, but Niece, says Mrs. *Villiard*,

Villiard, tho' I should not advise your tying yourself to an elderly Gentleman; yet supposing that he had such an Inclination to you as should induce him to maintain you like a Gentlewoman, and make you a handsome Provision for Life, do you think that you could not bring yourself to live happily with him, and submit a little to his Humours for such a fine Recompence: Pray what can one of your high Breeding, with no Fortune, expect better?————Oh! dear Aunt, answered *Arabella*, I don't understand what you mean by a Provision and Maintainance, but if the Gentleman is pleased to cast his Eyes upon me for a Mistress, I assure you he will be very much disappointed:————Believe me, I shall never sacrifice my Virtue either to Riches or Grandeur.————Mrs. *Villiard*, continued to argue the Point with her Niece during the best Part of the Evening; in order, as she said, to free her from the Prejudices of her Country Education. But indeed all that the old Lady could argue, had no more Effect with *Arabella*, than only to cause her to burst out in Tears; assuring her Aunt, that she was the last Woman whom she could have thought would have mentioned any such Things to her.

Mr. *D——z* came the next Morning to visit Mrs. *Villiard*; who acquainted him with the ill Success of her Negociation. They spent some Time together in consulting how
to

to bring the Affair about; and at laſt it was determined between them, that if nothing could be done by fair Means, he ſhould have recourſe to Force; as the old Lady judged that the accompliſhing his Ends this Way, would infallibly oblige her Niece to accept any Terms that he ſhould propoſe afterwards; but as a Reward for her extraordinary Service, in affording him a fair Opportunity of putting this Deſign in practice, ſhe made him engage, if he ſucceeded in his Atempt, to make an Addition of a handſome Gold Watch of thirty Guineas Price, to the former Gratuity, which he had promiſed her before. Tho' Mr. D——z could not help thinking the old Lady very exorbitant, yet the Violence of his Appetite for poſſeſſing the beauteous *Arabella*, would not permit him long to heſitate on her Aunt's Demands. He agreed to her Terms, and departed; leaving to her Conſideration, the Time and Place for perpetrating the black Scene which they had concerted.

Belmour came to *Townley*'s Chambers punctually at the Hour that had been appointed between them; from whence they ſet out on a Viſit to Mrs. *Villiard*'s, and found both the old Lady and her Niece at home. Tho as the former had made ſuch a fine Bargain with Mr. D——z, ſhe would very probably, have given Orders to her Servant for their being denied, if ſhe had had any previous Notice or Expectation of this Viſit. However, ſhe

she assumed a certain forced Air of Civility, very frequently practised in these polite Times, and desired the Gentlemen to stay and drink Tea with her and her Niece; tho' very likely she wished every Dish might scald their Throats. Tho' the Company passed the Time at the Tea-table in only indifferent Chat together, yet *Arabella*, from this further Insight into the Manners, Behaviour, and other personal Accomplishments of *Belmour*, was become as much enamoured with him as he possibly could be with her; and could very willingly have dispensed with the Company of her Aunt, and Mr. *Townley*, to be entertained with *Belmour*'s Conversation, which she rightly imagined was under some Constraint by their Presence.

Townley, tho' he had not conceived such a tender Affection for *Arabella* as *Belmour*, yet his Passion was more tinged with Jealousy than the other's; and as he was naturally inclined to that preying Disease, so the least Object could not fail of exciting it in him; neither could the affectionate Glances that were interchanged between the two Lovers over the Tea-table, escape his Observation. He also remarked, how readily *Arabella* came into *Belmour*'s Sentiments, on every Occasion that offered, for his declaring them on any Topic; and that she took every Opportunity of directing her Discourse to *Belmour*, without taking any other Notice of himself,

himself, than just what common Civility obliged her to.

This cool Behaviour of *Arabella* chagrined him not a little; and tho' neither of them had any Opportunity of declaring their Passion to her, as the Aunt kept them Company during the whole Time of their Stay, yet he immediately conceived such a strong Aversion to *Belmour*, whom he looked upon as his Rival, that he tryed all Means to shun his Company; and soon after took an Opportunity of quarrelling with him, in such a Manner, as broke of all their former Intimacy. Notwithstanding which, *Belmour* did not entertain the least Suspicion either of *Townley*'s Passion, or Jealousy, and consequently, did not imagine that he was any Obstacle between himself and *Arabella*.

Mrs. *Villiard*, who was pretty well versed in the Ways of Love, and generally observed very strictly what passed between any Persons of different Sexes, could not possibly avoid making her Remarks on the Change of Countenances, Language of the Eyes, and all other little secret Testimonies of Affection, that had passed between *Belmour* and *Arabella* at the last Visit. She knew perfectly well what a hard Thing it was to constrain any one of her own Sex, and especially such a beautiful young Person as *Arabella*, to act contrary to their Inclinations; and so many Difficulties occurred to her Imagination in putting the
Design

Design in Execution, which she and the *Jew* had concerted together, of forcing *Arabella* to submit to his Desires, that she resolved within herself, to make another Trial of what could be done by fair Persuasions.

Therefore, taking an Opportunity soon after the young Gentlemen were gone, of sounding *Arabella*'s Inclination toward them, she found that *Belmour* had excited no small Emotion in the young Lady's Heart; and she herself had collected, as we said before, from her own Observations during the late Interview, that *Belmour* was very much enamoured with *Arabella*. Whereupon the crafty Mrs. *Villiard*, pressed the Matter so home to her Niece, that the latter could not help declaring to her, that she thought Mr. *Belmour* to be the most agreeable, and civilest behaved Gentleman she had ever seen.

This unwelcome Discovery set the Aunt upon her Machinations how to circumvent such a formidable Rival, as young *Belmour* appeared to be, to the old Jew; and was in hopes that the dividing *Arabella*'s Inclinations, between *Belmour* and *Townley*, would leave some Room for her Friend, Mr. D——z, to obtain his Ends. In order to this she proceeded in the following Manner: " Indeed *Arabel-*
" *la,* " says she, " I am not at all surprised
" at the Weakness of your Judgment, when
" I consider how young and unexperienced
" you are in the Ways and Appearances of

Men;

"Men; and the short Time that you have been in this Town to obtain any Knowledge of the Manners of it. But, if I was as young and handsome as yourself, and was left to my Choice which of the two I should chuse for a Lover, I should surely give the Preference to Mr. *Townley*; he is certainly much the politer and gayer Man in his Behaviour; and, if I may judge by his Appearance, as he goes a great deal finer dressed than Mr. *Belmour*, so I apprehend him to be the best Gentleman of the two; therefore consequently the much fitter for any young Woman to fix her Hopes upon, either in the Way of Matrimony, or otherwise.———Tho' indeed, to tell you my Sentiments plainly, I must own that I cannot entertain any great Opinion of either of them; as your young *Templers* have seldom much to depend on, and generally are obliged to study the Law for the Acquisition of their Fortunes."

Indeed if *Arabella* could have been induced by the old Lady to judge of their Merit, or Fortunes, by outside Appearance, certainly *Townley* would have been the most in her Esteem: For he always went much more tawdry drest than *Belmour*, and was not of such a reserved Disposition as the latter, but rather abounded with too many pert Airs; which *Arabella's* Aunt either mistakenly or wilfully construed into Politeness. Tho', as
her

her Design was different from influencing *Arabella* with a real good Opinion of either of them, she went on thus: "But certainly, "Niece, tho' you may have ever such a strong "Inclination for either of these young Gen- "tlemen, yet, as you cannot flatter yourself, "as you have no Fortune, with the Hopes "of becoming his Wife, I should think that "the living happily upon a handsome and "comfortable Subsistance, with such a Man "as Mr. D——z, would abundantly out- "balance any Expectations that you can en- "tertain from these young Sparks; who, "when they have obtained their Ends, will, "it is very probable, leave you destitute on the "Town, to shift for yourself; as, on the "other Hand, you would, at least, have a "positive Assurance of never meeting with "such a Disaster."

Arabella paid a great deal of Attention to her Aunt's fine Harangue, and never once interrupted her till it was finished; when she replied, " Indeed Aunt, I am very much "surprised at your endeavouring to persuade "me to become Mr. D——z's Mistress, for "that is what I perceive to be the Drift of "your Discourse: But tho' I have had only "a Country Education, which you seem to "think a great Disadvantage to me; yet, "thanks to that Education, Madam, it has "so thoroughly ingrafted the Love of Virtue "in my Mind, that I would not be the

Mistress

"Miſtreſs even of the greateſt Monarch for
"half his Poſſeſſions.—— And as for the
"Suſpicion, that you throw out, of my be-
"coming ſuch to either of the two young
"Gentlemen, I aſſure you, Madàm, you do
"me a great injury in harbouring any ſuch
"Thought."——"You talk very heroical-
"ly, indeed, ſays the Aunt; certainly, Child,
"you uſed to read *Tragedies* pretty much in
"the Country, for you expreſs your ſelf
"nobly:——As for what I have urged
"to you about Mr. *D——z*, your own true
"Intereſt was the only Inducement that made
"me open my Lips about it; but good
"Councel I find is generally deſpiſed."
Here the Aunt changed the Diſcourſe and
ſoon after left the Room.

We have before obſerved, that all Intimacy
was broke off by *Townley* between him and
Belmour; and now they were both reſolved
to make their Addreſſes to *Arabella*. The
Paſſion that *Belmour* had conceived for her,
was too pure in its Nature to admit of his
entertaining the leaſt Thought of any Thing
to his Charmer's Prejudice: In a Word, he
was for obtaining her in an honourable Way,
without any Regard to the Difference that
might be between their Fortunes; as he
thought all ſuch Defects were amply ſupplied
by her perſonal Perfections. But tho' *Townley*'s Paſſion for the young Lady might be as
violent as *Belmour's*, yet it had not that Aſ-
cendancy

cendancy over his Reason, as to make him neglect what this represented to be a very necessary Qualification in a Wife, which was Money; and this he looked upon to be a most essential and necessary Ingredient in a Partner for Life. He thought that the Felicity of either of the Persons engaged could not last long without a pecuniary Support; and his Fortune was too small for him to think of encumbering it with a Wife, that should bring nothing but Beauty with her, for the Support of her self and her Offspring.

In order, therefore to obtain a Knowledge of *Arabella*'s Circumstances, he sent his Man *John*, who was used to serve his Master on several such necessary Occasions, into Mrs. *Villiard*'s Neighbourhood to gain him Intelligence. This trusty *Aid-de-Camp* executed his Commission very punctually; for applying himself to the nearest Chandler's-Shop, and for the Purchase of a little *Snuff, Tobacco,* and such like Trifles, he found Means to learn that *Arabella* had no Fortune of her own, notwithstanding the gay Appearance that she made; but was entirely dependent on her Aunt. That she came of a very good Family, but her Father dying worse than nothing, had left her, and several more Children, quite destitute in the World; and that had it not been for her Aunt's Generosity and Compassion, she must have been starving. This, and much more to the same Effect,

partly

partly true and partly false, *John* picked out of the Mistress of the Shop, who had learnt it from Mrs. *Villiard*'s Maid, who was one of her constant Customers; and with this News he hasted home to his Master.

Townley was very well pleased with the Intelligence his Servant had gained; as it gave him some Hopes of obtaining *Arabella*, without the Formalities of Marriage: Accordingly he resolved to address her upon a different Footing. For, to say the Truth, he was too much a Libertine, both in Principle and Practice, to have any Relish for Matrimony, where he could by any Means gratify his Passion or Appetite without it; altho' there had not been that grand Impediment, the Want of a Fortune, in the Way; but this, as we have said before, was such an invincible Obstacle to his entering into the State of Wedlock, even with the most beautiful Creature imaginable, that he could never find Heart enough to get over it.

Soon after this Discovery of the Condition of *Arabella*'s Circumstances, he took another Opportunity of visiting her; and, her Aunt being gone out about some Business, he had the Fortune to find her alone. He therefore took this Occasion to make love to her, with all the Rhetoric he was Master of, and would fain have persuaded her to let him make the best Use of the present happy Moment, which he said was destined for Enjoyment: But
Arabella,

Arabella, as soon as she perceived his Design, resisted all his Endeavours with that becoming Virtue and Modesty that was natural to her; 'till at length he grew so outrageous, that she was obliged to protest solemnly, she would call out for help, if he proceeded any farther. This brought him again within the Bounds of a decent Decorum, and induced him to make many Apologies for the Excess of his Passion, which he urged had deprived him of his Reason to such a Degree, that he was hardly accountable for any of his Actions; and it was this Frenzy which had occasioned that Transgression in his Behaviour towards her, which he begged her Compassion on his Distraction to pardon him for; vowing that he would take particular Care never to transgress again in the like Manner.

She returned this, and many more such fine Speeches, in as civil a Manner as his abrupt Behaviour would permit her to do; but earnestly desired of him, that if he valued either her Friendship, or Esteem, that he would never so grossly offend her again. This he promised with the most solemn Protestations to observe; and the Aunt coming Home, he was obliged to take his Leave of her for that Time, not a little chagrined at the Disappointment he had met with.

Belmour would have been before hand with *Townley* in his Visit to *Arabella*, had he not received a Letter from his Father, which

F   obliged

obliged him to go immediately about fifteen Miles out of Town, to a Gentleman's of their Acquaintance, about some Business of much Importance, where he could not avoid spending a Day or two: But, on his Return he went to see her the next Morning, whereas *Townley* had been there the Evening before. As the Aunt was just set out for the City to meet with Mr. *D——z*, in order to consult on the Method for putting their Design in Execution, so he, also, had the Opportunity of finding *Arabella* alone; and tho' he was entirely ignorant of her Fortune or Circumstances, yet he took that Occasion to declare his Passion to her; but in the most submissive and respectful Manner possible. *Arabella* said that she should not be displeased with his Addresses as long as he behaved honourably; but if he ever attempted to proceed to such Lengths as Mr. *Townley* had lately done, she should utterly hate and detest him.————
" How, Madam", says *Belmour*, " has he
" had the Audaciousness to offer any Insult
" to you?———His Blood shall answer for
" it".———She begg'd of him to assuage his Anger, and let the Matter drop, for that she believed she had cured the young Gentleman of any more such Attempts for the future. She farther told *Belmour* that he need not be under the least Uneasiness upon *Townley*'s Account; for that she had never entertained any favourable Opinion of him, and his late Be-
heaviour

haviour had rendered him, her Averſion.——
That, as for himſelf, ſhe had no other Objection but the Diſparity of their Fortunes; as
ſhe judged from the genteel Appearance he
made, that his was pretty confiderable, while
ſhe had nothing to depend on but her Aunt's
Generoſity.

She then gave him a full Account of her
Family and of the Indiſcretion of her Father,
that had reduced them to ſuch low Circumſtances. At the finiſhing of her Relation,
Belmour ſnatched her up eagerly in his Arms,
" and is this all the Objection you have againſt
" me, my dear *Arabella*", ſaid he?—" that
" ſhall ſoon be diſanulled, whenever you
" have a Mind to give me your Hand. My
" Eſtate, it is true, is not yet in my own
" Poſſeſſion, nor will it be 'till after my
" Father's Deceaſe, which I hope will not
" happen theſe many Years. But, however
" by the Generoſity of a late Uncle, I have
" enough for us both to live handſomely upon,
" without troubling him; that I am ſo cer-
" tain of his approving my Choice of a
" Woman of your Beauty, Merit, and good
" Senſe, that I ſhall not heſitate a Moment of
" acquainting him with our Nuptials, when-
" ever you will conſent to have them ſolem-
" nized, and I am ſure he will be the more
" pleaſed at your coming of ſuch a good
" Family, as I have often heard him declare,
" that a Woman of a good Family, and
" endued

"endued with good Senſe, was preferable to the fineſt Lady with a large Portion". "I am afraid, replied *Arabella*, that you flatter me infinitely, and would think me too forward if I ſhould give you my Conſent after ſuch a ſhort Courtſhip. Therefore I muſt beg a little more Time, that I may ſufficiently reflect on what I am about, leſt, by acting too heedleſs, I ſhould plunge both you and myſelf into irretrievable Misfortunes."——*Belmour*, then deſired the Favour of her Company to *Ranelagh* Gardens that Evening, which as ſhe could not find in her Heart to refuſe him, a Coach was ſoon called to the Door, and they proceeded on their Way thither.

Some Readers may perhaps think that Miſs *Arabella* was rather too condeſcending to her Lover, for a young Lady of ſuch Modeſty and Virtue, as we have characteriſed her to be: But when they reflect that ſhe began to get a full Inſight of her Aunt's Intention, to diſpoſe of her by way of Sale, to the beſt Purchaſer that ſhe could light of, whether upon honourable Terms or diſhonourable, they will no longer be ſurprized at *Arabella's* embracing the firſt Opportunity of getting out of her Clutches; eſpecially, when ſhe met with ſuch an advantageous Proffer as the preſent.

Our two Lovers were by this Time got to *Ranelagh*, and had taken ſome few Turns in the

(45)

the Gardens, and just seated themselves in the *Rotunda*, when in came *Townley*, and some more young Rakes, who, at his Instigation, would have intruded themselves into *Arabella*'s Company; and he had the Insolence to tell *Belmour*, that he thought he had as much Right to it as himself; tho' he had so meanly deprived him of her Favour, by some sinister Practices.———*Belmour* replied, that he scorned his Words; and told him withal, that the present Place was not proper to decide the Controversy in; but that he should take another Opportunity of doing it. These last Words he whispered in his Ear, so that they were not distinguished by *Arabella*; who being unused to the Ways of the Town, had not the least Apprehension of any farther Consequences attending their Rencounter.

Belmour walked off with the Lady, and re-entered their Coach; being apprehensive of meeting with some foul Play from *Townley* and his Companions, if he continued there much longer. He conducted *Arabella* safe Home, and from thence retired to his Chambers, where calling his Servant he dispatched him with the following short Epistle to *Townley*.

SIR,

SIR,

*I*F you are really a Gentleman, which does not much appear from your rude Behaviour, both to the Lady and myself last Night, I shall expect that you will meet me at Five, To-morrow Morning, behind Mountague-House; where you will be sure to find,

F. Belmour.

P. S. *The enclosed Ribband will shew you the Length of the Sword I shall use.*

Townley did not return from *Ranelagh* Gardens, till an Hour and a Half after the above was left at his Chambers. As he had never experienced *Belmour*'s Courage before, lo he had not entertained any great Idea of it, takeing him; as he had come so lately from the University, to be more of a Scholar than a Swordsman. He was conscious of having given the Affront, but knew of no way to recompence it, but either by complying with *Belmour*'s Request, or openly asking his Pardon. The latter he could by no Means bring his Spirit to truckle to, however fully convinced that himself had been the Agressor, and had committed an Error in so doing. Therefore he stept out to an adjacent Sword-Cutler's, and, having matched *Belmour*'s Length, returned again to his Chambers, and gave his Man strict Orders to call him by Four o'Clock the next Morning.

His

His Servant performed his Commands very punctually; and *Townley* reached the Fields a little before *Five*, where he found *Belmour* ready to meet him. Few Words were exchanged between them before they both drew, when after some Passes *Townley* received a slight Wound in the Sword Arm, and was almost immediately disarmed. He was now obliged to beg his Life of *Belmour*, which was granted upon Condition that he should ask *Arabella* Pardon for the Affront he had given her the Night before, by endeavouring to force into her Company, and that he should delay the doing of it no longer than that very Afternoon. This Offer he very readily embraced; so walking down to *Bloomsbury-*Square together, they took Coach, and drove to a Surgeon's near the *Temple*, where *Townley* had his Wound dressed, and *Belmour* departed to his Chambers.

While these Transactions happened, Mrs. *Villiard*, finding her former Endeavours to corrupt *Arabella* unsuccessful, had been consulting with the *Jew* in what Manner they should compass their Designs; and it was agreed upon between them, that they should be put in Execution that very Afternoon; when she was to dispatch the Maid on an Errand, to the farther End of the Town, and nobody was to be in the House when Mr. *D*—*z* came but herself and *Arabella*.—— This was done accordingly, and about three o'Clock he came to Mrs. *Villiard's*, who

shewing

shewing him up to her Niece, left them together in a back Room, while she went down Stairs under the Pretence of making some Coffee.

After some few Compliments, and a little introductory Discourse, the Gentleman got up from his Chair, and walking for some small Time about the Room, he suddenly took hold of *Arabella*, and lifting her up from her Seat, carried her in his Arms to a Couch, that was at one End of the Chamber. The young Lady struggled as much a possibly she could, but he being too strong for her had got her down, just at the Time when *Belmour* knocked at the Door. The Aunt, who was below in the Kitchen, did not answer either to his first or second Rap, well knowing what a Hindrance he would be to her Benefactor above Stairs; and was in hopes by her delaying to go to the Door, that *Belmour* would imagine they were all gone out, and so go away again: But he, finding Nobody answer, continued knocking louder and louder till the Aunt was obliged to go to the Door, least any of the Neighbours should inform him that she was at Home.

Tho' *Belmour* had knocked so hard, yet neither the *Jew* nor *Arabella* heard him; they being too eagerly engaged, the one in the Pursuit of his Prey, and the other in the Defence of her Chastity, to have any Regard or Attention to any thing else. Poor *Arabella* was almost spent and breathless with the
Struggle,

Struggle, when her Aunt opened the Street-Door to *Belmour*, so that she was now obliged to have recourse to her Out-cries as her last Resource. These soon reached the Ears of *Belmour*, even before he had entered the Parlour, and on his asking Mrs. *Villiard* what was the Occasion of those Shrieks that he heard, she very coolly replied, that it was only the Maid playing with some Workmen, that were in the Garret.——Then Madam, says he, I am afraid they play too rudely with her, for the Girl cries out dreadfully——he had no sooner uttered these Words, but the Noise redoubling, he presently recollected it to be his beloved *Arabella*'s Voice, tho' he had never heard it at such a high Pitch before. He immediately springs out of the Parlour, and flying up Stairs rushed into the Room, from whence the Sound came; where he found the poor young Lady on the Couch, with her Cap and Handkerchief torn off, her Nose all bloody, her Mouth in a foam, and the yellow-faced *Jew*, with his Wig off, at top of her, keeping her down by his Weight, and endeavouring to force her own Handkerchief into her Mouth, to prevent her crying out. For, notwithstanding all his Endeavours, he had as yet obtained no farther Advantage over her than what we have here mentioned, *Arabella* being pretty strong for her Size; though had not *Belmour* come in at the Instant, he might perhaps have perpetrated his

G Villainy,

Villainy, as thro' the Fright and Fatigue of the Scuffle she was almost fainting.

It is well that *Belmour* had not then his Sword on, or he would have stabbed the Villain to the Heart; but seizing hold of his Collar, he dragged him off from the Couch, and instantly knocked him down upon the Floor, with a Cane he had in his Hand. The *Jew*'s Head now bled as plentifully as *Arabella*'s Nose had done before; and as she had very well mauled his Face with her Nails, he cut a most rueful Figure. On his recovering himself he endeavoured to get at his Sword, which hung up in a Corner of the Room, till then unperceived by *Belmour*; but *Belmour* was too nimble for him, and, seizing hold of it, drew immediately, swearing that if he did not directly quit the Room, he would run him thorough. The *Jew* finding himself under a Necessity of obeying *Belmour*'s Commands, hastened down Stairs as well as he could; where the good old Gentlewoman of the House met him, and, conducting him into the Parlour, got him some Water and Brandy to wash his Head and Face with, as also a Plaister for the broken Place in the former.

Belmour, having raised up *Arabella*, applied himself to the Stair-head; where he stood roaring so loud for the Maid to bring up some Water, that Mrs. *Villiard* was obliged to tell him, tho' in flat Contradiction

diction to herself, that the Maid was not at Home. Upon this he ran down into the Kitchen, and brought her some up in a Bason, wherewith she was very much refreshed. When going down again into the Parlour, where sat the old Lady and the *Jew*, with a large Bottle of Cordial Waters before them, he snatched up that and the Glass, carrying it up Srairs to the young Lady's Assistance.

This unexpected Scene immediately gave *Belmour* a thorough Insight into what sort of a Person *Arabella*'s Aunt was; and as his own Eye-sight had convinced him of the Villainy of the Affair that had been in Agitation, so it appeared the blacker, when *Arabella* informed him of the Proposals that her Aunt had made her on the Part of Mr. *D——z*, with her absolute Refusal to comply with them. And it plainly appeared to them both, by the Maid's being sent out of the Way at this Juncture, the Aunt's not regarding *Arabella*'s loud Out-cries, and the abominable Falsity that she would have passed them over with to *Belmour*, at his entering into the House, that she had resolved upon sacrificing her Niece's Virtue to the *Jew*'s Lust.

This Scuffle was hardly ended, when somebody knocked pretty smartly at the Door; and who should it be but *Townley*, who was come to perform his Promise that *Belmour* had exacted from him in the Morning. Upon hearing his Voice below in the Passage, *Bel-*

mour immediately called him up Stairs, and acquainted him with the whole Proceeding. Tho' *Townley*, as we have before obſerved, was none of the moſt virtuous of Mortals, yet he was exceedingly aſtoniſhed at this Adventure. He then offered his Submiſſion to *Arabella* which ſhe as generouſly refuſed; declaring that if ſhe had conceived the leaſt Thoughts of the Conſequence, that had happened between him and *Belmour*, ſhe would have taken ſome Method to prevent it: And deſired withal that the inadvertent Behaviour of Mr. *Townley* to her, at *Ranelagh*, for ſhe now believed him to be heartily ſorry, might occaſion no future Breach of Friendſhip between them. *Belmour* replied, that after what had happened, he ſhould think no more of it. He then deſired *Townley* to be ſo good as to ſtep down Stairs and get ſomebody to call him a Coach, and that he would aſſiſt him in conducting the Lady ſafe out of the Houſe. This he readily complied with, and ſteping into the Street called a Porter, whom he immediately ſent for a Coach, which ſoon came to the Door.

Belmour then handed *Arabella* down Stairs, and they and *Townley* entered into the Parlour, to take leave of her Aunt and the old Gentleman. *Belmour* told the former that her baſe Actions, toward ſuch a fine young Creature, evidently ſhewed that ſhe did not deſerve to have the Care of her any longer;

longer; and therefore he should take her out of her Power. Upon this the Aunt began to storm, rave, and swear like a Fury, telling him it should be at his Peril if he took her Niece out of the House without her Leave; that she knew him to be a lewd, debauched Fellow, who had ruined a great many young Girls before, and had now a mind to do the same by her Niece. *Belmour* replied that he scorned her Words; when turning to Mr. D—z, the *Jew*, who sat mute, he gave him several very hearty Curses, for an old lecherous Villain, and told him he deserved a much worse Punishment than what he had received from his Hands. The other made no Reply, so he and *Townley* opened the Street-Door, and put *Arabella* into the Coach, the Aunt all the while raving at and abusing them.

The two Gentlemen getting into it drove away from the Door, leaving the Aunt and the *Jew* to settle Matters together, and carried *Arabella* to a Tavern at some Distance; where they drank a Glass of Wine together for Refreshment, and entered into a Consultation how to dispose of her, so as to prevent her Aunt's finding her out. When at length it was concluded upon, that she should go, for the present, to a Gentlewoman that was a near Relation of *Belmour*'s, and whose Husband, being Captain of a trading Ship, was gone a Voyage to the *Baltic*. This she readily

agreed

agreed to; and they presently conducted her thither.

Townley, having already suffered so much in his Pursuit of *Arabella*, and giving over all Hopes of Success from any future Attempt, entirely laid aside all Thoughts of obtaining her. And *Belmour* now urged his Addresses so strongly, that after his late honourable and generous Behaviour, it was impossible for her to refuse him. Neither indeed had she any Reluctance, but only a Fear that he might injure himself in his Father's Esteem, by marrying a Woman with no Fortune. He pressed her so strongly, with firm Assurances to the contrary, that in about a Fortnight's Time she agreed to give him her Hand, and soon after their Marriage they set out together for his Father's Seat; he having beforehand apprized him of the true Character of *Arabella*. As *Belmour*'s Father was no ways a worldly Man, so he came the readier into an Approbation of his Son's Choice, whom he was doatingly fond of, he therefore received the new married Couple with the greatest Pleasure and Satisfaction; and *Arabella*'s intellectual Perfection soon gained her his Love and Esteem, as much, or rather more, than if she had brought *Belmour* the largest Fortune.

F I N I S.